Emergency

AFRICAN/AMERICAN LIBRARY

GENERAL EDITOR *Charles R. Larson*

A continuing series of works of literary excellence by black writers in the United States, Africa and the Caribbean.

THE BEAUTYFUL ONES ARE NOT YET BORN, *by Ayi Kwei Armah*
Introduction by Ama Ata Aidoo

THE HOUSE BEHIND THE CEDARS, *by Charles W. Chesnutt*
Introduction by Darwin Turner

NOT WITHOUT LAUGHTER, *by Langston Hughes*
Introduction by Arna Bontemps

AMBIGUOUS ADVENTURE, *by Cheikh Hamidou Kane*
Introduction by Wilfred Cartey

dem, by William Melvin Kelley
Introduction by Willie Abrahams

WEEP NOT, CHILD, *by James Ngugi*
Introduction by Martin Tucker

HARLEM GALLERY, *by Melvin B. Tolson*
Introduction by Karl Shapiro

BLOOD ON THE FORGE, *by William Attaway*
Introduction by Edward Margolies

SPORT OF THE GODS, *by Paul Lawrence Dunbar*
Introduction by Charles Nilon

IN THE CASTLE OF MY SKIN, *by George Lamming*
Introduction by Richard Wright

AFRICAN SHORT STORIES, *by Charles R. Larson*, ed.
Introduction by Charles R. Larson

BOY!, *by Ferdinand Oyono*
Introduction by Edris Makward

EMERGENCY, *by Richard Rive*
Introduction by Ezekiel Mphahlele

THE INTERPRETERS, *by Wole Soyinka*
Introduction by Leslie Lacy

THE BLACKER THE BERRY . . . , *by Wallace Thurman*
Introduction by Therman B. O'Daniel

EMERGENCY

A novel by
Richard Rive

With an introduction by
EZEKIEL MPHALELE

COLLIER BOOKS
COLLIER-MACMILLAN, LTD.,
LONDON

ACKNOWLEDGMENT

Special thanks to *Jackie Hoogendyk*
for her considerable assistance

for JAN RABIE *and* MARJORIE WALLACE

Contents

Introduction

They did not know the police were in a foul mood, that they would shoot, and shoot to kill. The followers of the Pan-Africanist Congress were simply going to meet and move about without their passes. Then the police would arrest them. The people would refuse bail, defence, and fines. And on that black Monday, March 21, 1960, when they congregated in front of the police station at Sharpeville (Transvaal Province) to declare their nonviolent intentions, the police did the unexpected. They opened fire, killing 69, wounding 180. Nine hundred miles south, at Langa, Cape Town, Africans went on strike. Over the troubled period between March 21 and April 19, eighty-three blacks and Coloureds (people of mixed descent) were killed. Saracen tanks patrolled these and several other areas in a country that was expressing its horror and indignation.

It has always been like this in South Africa. Some "men of reason" will tell you it is not a police state—not yet. And yet meetings have always been dispersed by violent methods—shooting, baton charging. After this, power demonstrations by the government; then provocation by the police, always itching for action; then rioting and still more shooting. So on the cycle goes.

Martin Luther King, waiting to lead the march, is gunned down by some white man who thinks he has a cause to advance. Gandhi is gunned down by an incensed Mahasaba devotee. Robert Kennedy is gunned down by an incensed Arab boy. John F. Kennedy is killed by some crazy who-knows-what. Freedom fighter Eduardo Mondlane of Mozambique is flattened by a bomb that explodes in his hands. The law may only indirectly connive at such killings. But in South Africa, it is seldom the incensed individual who shoots down a black man. The law itself, in more than nine out of ten cases, takes a heavy toll on black life. The police torture you to death and then certify "death from natural causes" or "death from suicide." If the law does not organize murder, it sanctions it, implicitly or explicitly. After this, the case is closed. There is no more to be said.

Your National Guards, your state police in Alabama or Mississippi, or Georgia, in Illinois or California may kill. But your press, your public will scream murder and the Federal judiciary will listen and probe and probe. The South African judiciary is corrupt. The international body of jurists has discovered as much. For example, no sooner was it discovered that the Sharpeville police had used bullets that explode in the body (whatever the difference *that* made) than the state rushed a Bill through parliament placing the police out of reach of indemnity suits expected from the next-of-kin of the victims. More recently, a defence counsel wanted to recall as evidence the words of a black prisoner who had been murdered in his cell by the officials and strung up so that it looked like suicide. The counsel was representing the widow of another man who had been murdered by the police and strung up on a belt for a similar reason. The government thereupon banned the dead man whose words were so vital. The banning order was made to operate retrospectively. As no banned person can be quoted orally or in print, the dead man's words were frozen.

You are born in a ghetto. You are black. At the age of sixteen, you must carry a pass. This is a small book with many entries. From that time onward, you shall be known by a number. The pass does not only identify you, it marks you out implicitly as black. One entry permits you to live in an urban or rural area; another to seek work and be employed; another to leave such an area; yet another permits you to enter still another area. Every month your employer signs the passbook to show that you are still in his employment. He must sign it when you resign or he discharges you so that at any time the police will know if you ought to be where they find you. It is a common thing for Africans to be led in batches to the police stations for failing to produce their passes. They are fined on the spot by the police. If they do not have ready cash, they are packed off on waiting trucks to serve their "sentence" on white people's potato and maize farms. Their people will never know where they are until they are released. Those who die on the farm are buried secretly in the bush. Again, as so often, the law has sanc-

tioned shanghaing and murder. By means of the pass
system, the ruling whites can supply cheap labour for the
farms and for urban industry where needed, and can shut
off the supply where it is deemed enough. As the International Labour Organization has established time and again,
the pass regulations legalize forced labour.

When the Pan-Africanist Congress called the Sharpeville meeting to compel the police to arrest them for
breaking the pass law, they were singling out only one
from the spate of apartheid laws as a symbol of the
black man's burden, of his hatred of white supremacy. It
was hoped that the campaign would snowball and throw
the country into a state of confusion. The same method
had been used in 1952 by the African National Congress
(from which the Pan-African Congress broke in 1959)
during the country-wide Defiance Campaign—a programme
of civil disobedience conceived in the spirit of Gandhi's
Satyagraha. It had failed: the state had prosecuted the
leaders and charged them with attempting to overthrow
the government by means of violence (well aware that
constitutional channels are not available for the black
man), not simply with breaking apartheid laws. This was
intended to terrorize the masses. It halted the campaign.
Gandhi's tactics do not work against sustained savagery. If
you throw yourself on the ground, the machine flattens
you. Custodians of civilization? *White* civilization—yes.
You can feel its muscle in South Africa, in the American
Negro ghettoes. You can smell its gunpowder, you can
hear it grate on tarmac in ferocious menacing caterpillar
motion, ready to reply to voices of dissent.

The main cause of the Pan-Africanists' split with the
ANC was the PAC's insistence on blacks going it alone
even while declaring the ultimate goal of a nonracial society, as against the ANC's alliance with Indians, Coloureds, and radical whites (not "liberals"). The differences
are now academic, as both organizations have been banned
in South Africa. The leaders—black, white, Indian, and
Coloured, people like Nelson Mandela, Walter Sisulu,
Braam Fischer, Kathrada (all of the Congress Alliance)—
are locked up on Robben Island, serving life imprisonment.
Of the Pan-Africanist leaders, Robert Sobukwe has now
been released after nine years on the island. But he now
lives under house arrest. Several from both organizations

are serving terms of up to twenty years. Since Sharpeville, both have dedicated themselves to the overthrow of white rule by the only means revolution dictates.

Such is the background of Richard Rive's *Emergency.* We see here a few individuals whose lives are woven into the fabric of events covering three days. We are taken back and forth in time, anticipate events and take glimpses of the protagonist's childhood and that of his playmates in the District Six ghetto. Made to feel guilty about the death of his mother, Andrew Dreyer leaves home to live with his elder sister, a woman almost devoid of a will of her own, brutalized by a besotted husband. Unwanted by his brother-in-law, Andrew nevertheless finds their sub-urban home a most welcome escape from District Six. He never wants to return to ghetto life again.

Mostly coloured people live in District Six. They are trapped here, living as they do in houses that are disin-tegrating, in squalid tenements vividly described by an-other Coloured novelist from Cape Town, Alex La Guma. As in New York's Harlem, only a few people can work themselves up economically and move out of the ghetto into middle-class areas like Walmer Estate in Rive's novel. The Jongas, the Amaais, and their like will never, as Andrew does, survive District Six. Poverty and lack of schooling will lead them to worse things, which in turn will fetter them in greater poverty, in darkness, and des-pair. Those who go to high school and places of higher learning have at least a fighting chance. But to do what? There's the rub. There is a chance to become a doctor, a teacher, a nurse, a lawyer, a secretary, but little else.

Coloureds used to be treated as an appendage of the white man. They could even live among whites in the Cape Peninsula, where they are most concentrated. Since 1948, when the Afrikaners, the descendants of the Boers, took over the government, they have continually told the Coloured people that they should not regard themselves as an appendage of the whites, but as a race apart. They, like the Africans and the Indians are *non*whites. But they can consider themselves "more advanced" than the blacks —even if only a *little* more. They will therefore not be assigned to areas like Bantustans, the so-called homelands of the blacks that are scattered over the country. But they will live in separate townships, and it won't matter if these are near the town or city—white man's territory. Some learned Afrikaner even worked out a theory of "biological states" for the Coloureds as distinct from separate geographical areas. He argued that you do not have to belong to a geographical area to become a member of a state. It is this doubletalk that has victimized the two million Coloureds of South Africa for centuries. And they are still on no-man's-land. Gradually some of them have come to feel that their identity perhaps lies with the oppressed majority—the blacks.

It is now generally agreed (except among the Afrikaners) that not less than seventy-five per cent of whites in South Africa have Coloured blood—Hottentot, Bushman, Negro, Malay, and so on. But it was an implicit appreciation of this theory that drove the Afrikaners to introduce its population registration measures. People who are suspected of "playing white" are called before the Reclassification Board to defend themselves. The onus is on the subjects to prove that they are white.

A person shall be classified as White if his natural parents have both been so classified; he will be classified as Coloured if both his parents have been so classified, or if one of his parents is classified as White and the other as Coloured or African, he will be classified as an African if both his parents have been so classified (and, presumably, if one parent is Coloured and the other African). Descent then, will in future be the determining factor in determining race. His habits, education, and speech and deportment in general shall be taken into account. The person must be generally accepted as white in the place where he ordinarily resides, is employed, mixes socially with other members of the public, and in his association with the members of his family and other persons with whom he lives. In the absence of proof that any person is generally accepted as a white person or an African, it will be assumed that he is generally accepted as a Coloured person, except where such person is in appearance obviously a member of an aboriginal race or tribe of Africa. The law is retrospective to 1950.

If a man is declared Coloured and his wife is not, or vice versa, they must be separated by the terms of the Immorality Act. This law forbids intermarriage or any other intimate relations between white and nonwhite, and it is retrospective. In such cases, the children have to be subjected to the board's arbitration and may also be separated from their parents. After reclassification, Coloured children have to leave white schools, the father has to leave his employment, church, residential area, and so forth. Africans have to leave Coloured institutions. The law does not "elevate" a person from his Coloured status. It can lower the status of a white man or leave it as it was before the investigation. Abe Hanslo could not, after having been accepted generally in his neighbourhood as Coloured, successfully claim to be white, even though he looks it so convincingly that the station clerk won't serve him while he is in a nonwhite line.

Coloured people are normally better paid than Negroes in the same jobs; their schools are better equipped; more is spent on every child in school than on a black child; they do not carry passes. But, like blacks and Indians, they do not enjoy direct representation in parliament. Like the Negroes and the Indians, they have a separate university college. Also, the doors of English-language universities that used to admit races other than white are now closed to all nonwhites. While blacks have their own separate elementary and high schools, Coloureds and Indians can go to the same schools. They can own property in the urban areas, while Africans must always be municipal tenants. The inhabitants of Langa, a municipal "location" of Cape Town, are all black. Every such "location" in the towns and cities is administered by the City Council through a white superintendent who runs his office in the location. In times of upheaval, Coloureds, Indians, and whites are prohibited to enter a location or a black rural reservation. Whites are not admitted at *any* time without special written permission.

Just as the Coloured People's Congress would act in sympathy with the African National Congress, Justin Bailey, himself Coloured, is among those who would demonstrate publicly in sympathy with the PAC, even though the Coloureds are not affected by the pass laws. And so we see Justin become involved in the Langa demonstration against the Sharpeville massacre. It does not come naturally because of the relative traditional positions of Africans and Coloureds in the eyes of the white man's law. What came to be referred to as the Congress

Alliance, otherwise the Congress Movement, existed in the
form of a joint planning council of the ANC, the Coloured
People's Congress, the Indian Congress, the Congress of
Democrats (made up of radical whites). It was formalized
in 1955, before the PAC broke away. Then the African
organization felt a freedom charter was needed for South
Africa. The oppressed and their white sympathizers needed
to get together to draw up such a charter. It would be
both an expression of the broad principles they conceived
for the kind of society South Africa should construct and
an implicit affirmation of the fact that such a society is
only possible if there is a complete overhaul of the constitution in which white supremacy is entrenched—in other
words, if there is a revolution.

The Freedom Charter asserted: no government can
justly claim authority unless it is based on the will of
the people; the people, black and white, should govern
on the basis of non-racialism, equality of opportunity, and
standing in the statutory bodies; the wealth of the country and its land shall be shared by all who work for it—
equality before the law; there should be work and
security for all in the domains of labour, housing, health,
etc., and the right to collective bargaining; the doors of
learning to be open to all. The Charter was adopted by
the Congress of the People, a meeting of thousands of
blacks, Coloureds, Indians, and whites. Now that the
ANC in exile is a body consisting of people from the
various races as full individual members, and now that it
is committed to revolution, the accent is on the majority,
or black rule rather than on unqualified equality. The
white man who wants in must earn his position; he must
take his chances.

Abe Hanslo represents the highly intellectual Coloured
and Negro people who belonged to the Non-European
Unity Movement. This was a federal union of blacks,
Coloureds, Indians, and radical whites. It claimed a genuine
spirit of unity—"principled unity"—which was to cut
across racial barriers, as distinct from the PAC, with its
blacks-only stand, or the Congress Alliance, of which each
component part was still an autonomous entity. Where
Justin Bailey would say that mass demonstrations and all
their accompanying slogans and symbols were a way of
organizing people and educating them about politics, Abe

Hanslo would say this was adventurism that had nothing to do with political education. Abe would say that people should be educated by means of study groups and such. Justin would say again that one never knew whether or not people were enlightened and mature unless occasions that needed overt protest could be exploited.

Abe agrees with neither the PAC line, which is to him racialist because of its orientation, nor with the ANC's which he also regards as racialist, because its cooperation with other racial groups implies a basic recognition that they are different groups. He insists on the role of ideas in political education, on the grand idea of "our common humanity," which must replace the sense of multiracialism. He has contempt for black nationalism because he does not see the South African conflict as a racial one but rather as a class conflict. As far as he is concerned, whites need to be liberated just as much as the blacks who feel the brunt of actual oppression. It is against the intellectual sterility, the nonpolitics of people like Abe and the Unity Movement, that Justin rails: "Principles be damned! You talk of principles while people are starving, gaoled and banished. You talk about humanity in high-faluting academic terms while the dead of Sharpeville are crying for revenge. Does the other side bother about humanity and principles?"

And so the half-truths fly about on the back of polemical debate: one strategy is crisis-oriented, the other refuses to be born. You didn't know the police would be waiting there with guns at the ready, so you went ahead. You knew the Sten guns would be waiting, so you didn't go— you never will because the guns will always be there. Rive is well aware of the half-truths. And he is not categorical about anything. When Andrew eventually decides not to run away like Abe, he opts for Justin's way. And yet it is not a decision to identify totally with Justin's ideas. He is still cautious about them.

All this is part of the orchestration in the novel—the orchestration of a brutal situation. And no less brutal is the interplay of shades of colour among the Coloured people. Andrew is darker than the rest of his family, so he is a man apart: he is discriminated against by his own people. The portrayal of Andrew's character strikes an autobiographical note. Amid the violence, the blood,

Andrew must make decisions. They are not epoch-making decisions either.

The novelist in the South African setting has to handle material that has become by now a huge cliché: violence, its aftermath, and the responses it elicits. In this, he travels a path that has many pitfalls. He can depict a situation so immense and characters so tiny that we fail to extract a meaning out of the work; he can create symbols and "poetic" characters so that reality eludes us; he can be melodramatic; he can be too documentary. Richard Rive has avoided these pitfalls. He has chosen to pack the action and the politics into [233] pages representing a span of three days. His prose maintains its tension and its pressurized drive throughout. And the reader is pleasantly struck by the novelist's economy of diction and structure.

University of Zambia,   Ezekiel Mphahlele
Lusaka
Zambia.

Each new morn
New widows howl; new orphans cry: new
  sorrows
Strike heaven on the face, that it resounds
As if it felt with Scotland, and yell'd out
Like syllable of dolour.

Shakespeare

So long as people are being ill-governed, suffer
from hunger, criminals will never disappear. It
is extremely unkind to punish those who, being
sufferers from hunger, are compelled to violate
laws.

Kenko Hoshi

Prologue

The main action of this novel is played out in and around Cape Town between the 28th and the 30th of March 1960. The short summary of events which follows gives the background to this action. The summary starts with the Pan African Congress's announcement of its campaign against the Pass Laws which was to start on March 21st: the novel ends on the day a state of emergency is declared after the conscience of the world had been shaken by the shootings at Sharpeville and Langa. Since to my knowledge there is no recorded history of this important and dramatic period in South African history, I have had to rely on my own compilation gleaned from newspapers of the time. Under the circumstances it is as accurate as possible. Although events after March 30th proved as momentous, they fall outside the scope of the novel. I have used the declaration of a state of emergency in order to focus attention on the development of particular characters and not as an end in itself.

RICHARD RIVE

Cape Town
London
Eimbeckhausen, Germany
1963

Preface

On Friday, 18th March 1960, Mangaliso Robert Sobukwe, Junior Language Assistant at the University of Witwatersrand and President of the Pan African Congress, held a press conference in Johannesburg. Speaking steadily, he outlined the Anti-Pass Campaign of his movement. It was to be a sustained, disciplined, non-violent campaign against the Pass Laws, starting on Monday, March 21st. As long as the Campaign was on, no one would go to work. Africans would leave their reference books at home and surrender themselves at selected police stations under their local Pan-Africanist leaders, saying, "We do not have passes. We will not carry passes again. Millions of our people are arrested under the Pass Laws, so you had better arrest us all now." The Campaign would last until their demands were met.

The P.A.C. had invited the African National Congress —from whom they had originally broken away—and the Liberal Party to "create history by taking part in the Campaign." They also addressed a letter to the Commissioner of Police announcing the Campaign and requesting assistance in maintaining non-violence. A leaflet was produced. "If one man is arrested for not having a pass, you will stop there and then and tell the police you do not have passes either. Demand that they arrest you all. Go to gaol under the slogan 'no bail, no defence, no fines'. In the first phase of the struggle you must see to it that all men go to gaol."

Monday dawned, and everywhere people were on the alert to see whether the P.A.C. leaders would leave their reference books behind and court arrest and to assess the support the Campaign had mustered. At 6 a.m. Sobukwe with other leaders including Ndziba, Ngendane, Nyoase and sixty followers marched to Orlando Police Station, and announced that they had left their passes behind. They were later arrested and by evening were securely locked in the police cells.

At Bophelong Location in the Transvaal, men did not

go to work. Crowds at the police station were ordered to disperse and this ended in a full-scale baton and rifle-butt charge. Tear gas bombs were thrown. When the crowd dispersed a nineteen-year-old youth was left dead on the road. Three armoured cars rolled into Bophelong and four bombers roared overhead. There was a general strike at Vereeniging, and Iscor was forced to suspend operations. Evaton did not go to work. In Port Elizabeth Saracens patrolled New Brighton.

The open space in front of the police station at Sharpeville resembled a battleground. Sixty-nine people including eight women and ten children were killed. One hundred and eighty were wounded, including thirty-one women and nineteen children. Ambulance-loads deluged Vereeniging Hospital and some patients had to be treated on the grass. The people claimed that the police had shot at them from behind a wire fence. The police justified themselves by claiming that they had been stoned and fired upon. Three policemen were slightly injured. Women covered their heads with their arms as they walked over dead relatives. As the news spread, tension built up and Saracens rolled in.

At 6 a.m. a thousand miles away at Nyanga, near Cape Town, demonstrators marched the three miles to Phillippi Police Station. Spokesmen for the crowd stated their purpose: they had left home without reference books and wanted to be arrested. Demonstrators had their names taken and were warned to appear at Wynberg Magistrates' Court on the following Tuesday. There were no immediate arrests.

At the nearby location of Langa, no workers presented themselves for arrest, but thousands gathered early in the morning at the Bachelors' Flats and at 6 p.m. 6,000 people responded to a P.A.C. call for a meeting. The meeting had been banned under the Riotous Assemblies Act. The police launched a baton attack and fired into the crowd. Three Africans were killed and the people hit back. Police were stoned and buildings fired. The Labour Bureau, administrative offices, Library, Market Hall and schools were gutted. As the flames danced, Saracen armoured cars patrolled and occasional bursts of firing were heard. Army units were called in to help the police.

The same evening, the A.N.C. issued a statement expressing severe shock at police violence. The statement also condemned the ill-organized, ill-defined action of the P.A.C. which, it said, could cause harm and reduce the struggle's effectiveness. The A.N.C. felt it could not call on or encourage people to participate in the Campaign.

Throughout the week, which was punctuated with arson, sporadic bursts of shooting and arrests, Africans stayed at home. In Port Elizabeth the police, with Saracens, broke up road-blocks and dispersed groups of Africans wherever they were found. At Walmer Location over a hundred Africans danced and sang around a bonfire as reference books were burnt to ashes. The world press focused its attention on South Africa and protests poured in.

On Thursday, March 24th, there were nation-wide raids on political suspects whether connected with the P.A.C. Campaign or not. Police bearing warrants under the Criminal Law Amendment Act or the Riotous Assemblies Act sought links with the Pan-Africanists. The Minister of Justice dramatically banned all public meetings of all races in twenty-three magisterial districts.

The following day the Minister of Justice gave notice to introduce a bill to empower the Governor-General, with a view to the safety of the public and the maintenance of order, to declare the A.N.C. and P.A.C. and certain other organizations to be unlawful organizations by proclamation in the *Gazette*.

Two thousand Africans massed outside Caledon Square Police Station in Cape Town in a peaceful demonstration. They dispersed quietly after being told by their leader, the student Philip Kgosana, that the police could not arrest them as there was not sufficient room in the cells. Police leave was cancelled throughout the Union and all men told to stand by. A hundred and one African men appeared in the Cape Town Magistrates' Court on charges of failing to produce reference books when called on to do so. In Paarl a bag containing hundreds of reference books was dumped on the ground behind the Magistrates' Court and defiantly lit. Four Africans were detained, two of them women, when the Location school was burnt down.

At noon on Saturday, police throughout the country were officially instructed that no more African men or women were to be arrested for not carrying reference books until further notice. Ex-chief Lutuli burnt his pass in Johannesburg. The A.N.C. called on its members to follow the example of the leader and burn theirs.

On Monday, March 28th, 57,000 of the Cape Peninsula's Africans stayed at home in answer to a call by both Congresses for a day of mourning for the dead of Sharpeville and Langa. Thousands of Coloured workers did not report for work or left their jobs early. Nearly all non-white schools in the Northern Municipalities closed before lunch on the insistence of panicking parents and children. Cape Town docks came to a virtual standstill. Coal deliveries were hit to such an extent that only essential services could be supplied. There was a complete stay-away of Coloured and African workers at the abattoirs. Building projects and milk deliveries were seriously affected.

In Durban an African was killed and several were injured in hand-to-hand fights with the police at Clermont near Pinetown. At Worcester five churches, a school clinic, administrative offices and the houses of African policemen were burnt down in the "Country of Hope" Location. At Stellenbosch, also in the Cape Province, an attempt was made to burn down the administrative offices of Kayamandi Location.

At Langa 50,000 people of all races massed for the funerals of the three shooting victims. At the graveside the coffins were borne high on the shoulders of a phalanx of silent, grim-faced Africans. In Cape Town itself six separate attempts were made to set buildings on fire in and on the fringes of District Six. In Longmarket Street petrol was thrown on cars and ignited. Three Coloured men were arrested in the crowd that had assembled on the Grand Parade.

Throughout the Union tension was mounting as passes were being defiantly lit and Africans demanding arrest.

Part One

Monday, 28th March 1960

By 5:30 p.m. a crowd of well over a thousand people, mainly Coloured, has gathered near the fruit-stalls on the Grand Parade in Cape Town. Police warn that the Meetings Ban is being violated and ask the crowd to disperse. The crowd refuses to do so and baton charges are unleashed. When the police leave, the crowd reassembles on the Parade and on both sides of Darling Street. Buses and passing cars are stoned. The police reappear armed with rifles and wearing steel helmets. Tear-gas bombs are thrown as the crowd scatters.

1

Andrew Dreyer ran across the Parade, then darted between the fruit-stalls, making for the station. He changed his mind and slipped breathlessly into the men's urinal at the corner. He panted heavily, trying to catch his breath, a tight ball stretching across his chest. His tie almost choked him and his legs felt like iron weights. Hell, what a day, what a bloody day. He wondered whether the police had followed him. He now realized how foolish it had been to run into the urinal. There was no escape. Trapped like a bloody rat. Andrew heard footsteps coming down and looked around hunted. He caught a glimpse of himself in the mirror. Hair dishevelled, his brown, handsome face distorted, nostrils pulsating. Christ, was a situation. He relaxed when he saw that it was only a young man leading an old Moslem who appeared shocked and shivering, mumbling unintelligibly between his toothless gums. The younger man tried his best to calm the elder, mopping his brow with an expensive silk handkerchief. More people now crowded into the urinal, including three women. Frightened, garrulous, hysterical, boastful. Discussing the baton charge in high-pitched voices. Andrew wondered about the hawker he had seen just before the rout. At first the vendor had been clowning in his dirty-white coat, humouring the crowd, offering fruit to the police. The next moment he had abandoned his cart and was running down Corporation Street, stumbling with the batons on top of him. Fruit scattering. He managed to regain his balance, blood streaming from his head and all over his coat, and ran on, leaving one shoe behind him. Strange how one always thought about irrelevant things at such a time. Andrew wondered how the hawker would get home with a bleeding head and only one shoe.

What a bloody day. He had left his Inter-Schools Sports meeting, slipped away early, and had gone with Abe to attend the funeral of the shooting victims at Langa. There had been no sentries at the Location entrance, no permits to fill in, only the charred remains of the booth, and grim-faced Africans who stared suspiciously at the two Coloured men. After the funeral they had come through to Cape Town together in Abe's car, but had somehow lost contact after that. They had missed the first two baton charges, and had found only the excited crowd. But he was right in the third one. He tried to dispel it from his mind, eradicate it, but the impression was too vivid. The curt order to disperse. The look on the face of the police officer. The sudden electricity in the atmosphere. The bizarre antics of the hawkers. Bananas Baas! Six for a bob! Have a banana Baas! And before he knew what had happened people around him were running, struggling, shouting hysterically. A woman stumbled and fell. A newspaper-boy ran holding his bleeding head. Andrew found himself darting between the stalls, dodging the police and the crowd, till he reached the urinal.

The place now became uncomfortable with people jammed against the lavatory doors, sitting on the wash-basins, standing on the steps. A notice was fixed to the wall. Please stand close in. It was stuffy and moist with the smell of sweat, stale breath and urine. A woman laughed in a high-pitched girlish giggle, and was promptly silenced by those immediately around her. He felt he had to get out even at the risk of police batons. Get home to Grassy Park or to Ruth's flat. Get the hell out of this place. What if the police came and found them trapped like rats in a sewer, or was it like rats in a urinal? His body itched all over and he felt sweat trickling down his back. He had to get out. Andrew struggled his way up the steps and cautiously peeped from the entrance. He could faintly detect the acrid smell of tear gas still lingering in the air. How long had he been below? Twenty minutes? Or maybe twenty-five? The Grand Parade was completely deserted, not a policeman in sight. Papers scattered everywhere, shoes here and there, a child's dummy, broken bottles.

"It's all right!" he shouted down, "It's O.K. you can come out!" He buttoned his jacket, adjusted his tie, and quickly crossed the road to the station.

2

The station swarmed with people. Police stood around grimly staring at the crowd, hands resting on their revolver-holsters. The atmosphere was tense and hostile. Andrew walked to the non-European ticket box and bought a single to Plumstead. From there he would have to catch a bus to Grassy Park, and those buses were never on time. Then home at last, wash, eat, and go to Ruth's. He wondered what had happened to Abe, whether he had escaped the baton charge and made his own way back to the car. Oh well, he would have to phone Abe. Crowds milled around on the platform, loudly discussing the police, the charges, the Langa funeral, the stay-at-home. Andrew heard the voices around him but was not attentive. All he wanted to do was to get home. He wondered whether he shouldn't go to Ruth at once. No, better to see her later when he was in a more settled frame of mind. As the train pulled into the platform, the crowd surged forward and some were forced back by a young white constable. There were angry murmurs and threats. The policeman unbuttoned his revolver-holster, staring nervously at the crowd. For God's sake, thought Andrew, for God's sake, not again.

He managed to squeeze through the door and settled down next to the window. Next to him sat a garrulous woman who was busy giving a graphic description of the events on the Grand Parade. Apparently she had lost a carrier of groceries and she held the Government responsible. She vaguely reminded Andrew of Mrs. Carollissen. The same bony, peasant face; the flat sing-song voice. His landlady was O.K. Not bad. She could have been a lot worse, in spite of her upper-class ideas, "respectable Coloured" as she referred to herself.

"Mr. D."—she called him Mr. D., which annoyed him— "Mr. D., do you really read all those books in your room? Surely not all of them?" She always spoke English with a strong Afrikaans accent. "They must cost you a lot of money. But we Coloured people must be prepared to pay for our learning if we want to get anywhere."

What a bloody woman. She had been Millie Arries in
her maiden days, Millicent Arries, but had had the astute-
ness and good fortune to marry a socially more acceptable
surname; and as Mrs. Millicent Carollissen she presided
over her husband, a negative, vague person, five children
and Andrew. He smiled cynically when he thought of her.
Over-dressed, over-bearing, over-powdered, she was a pillar
of the local Dutch Reformed Mission Church. She had
forced her husband to become an elder in the congrega-
tion, much to his discomfort and her prestige. Her lounge
was highly polished, with huge, vulgar pieces of furniture
she had inherited from her mother, and the walls were
decorated with enlarged photographs of *her* ancestors, not
his, in oppressive black frames. In the passage hung two
reproductions, one of Christ holding his bleeding heart
and another of Queen Elizabeth II. Mrs. Carollissen
dominated her husband and four sons, and lavished attention on her only daughter Charmaine, who was learning
to play the piano to Andrew's complete annoyance. He
knew that his landlady resented his presence, but needed
his social standing as a High School teacher and the money
he paid in board and lodging. He also realized that as
soon as Eldred qualified he would be asked to leave. One
teacher in the household was quite sufficient for academic
and social purposes. And then of course he wasn't quite
sure how she felt about his political activities. It seemed
that she knew what was going on, but never commented.
He hoped she was dependable in a crisis. It seemed so.

Take the morning of the 24th. When was it again?
Five days ago. Sunday, Saturday, Friday, Thursday. Friday
or Thursday? Yes, Thursday. The day he had last seen
Ruth and told her about the raid. One had to be careful
about white girls, but Ruth was different. Yes, it was
Thursday morning at five o'clock. Must have been Thursday when Mrs. Carollissen had tapped lightly on his door.

"Mr. D.?"

He rolled over, annoyed, and re-adjusted his pillow.

"Mr. D.? Are you awake?"

What the hell. He fumbled for the bed-switch and
blinked his eyes in the sudden light.

"Are you awake, Mr. D.?"

"Yes, what's the matter?"

He glanced at the alarum. Ten past five.

"Detectives are here to see you."

He was wide-awake in a moment. What the devil did they want at that early hour? Oh damn. It might be the political branch. There were books on his shelves. Pamphlets in his satchel. He should have been more cautious. Minutes of political meetings.

"Where are they now?"

"In the lounge. They want you at once!"

"Tell them to bloody-well wait!" he said, latching his door. He struggled into his dressing-gown, searching for his slippers while his eyes ran along the book titles. *Modern Mexican Painters. Inside Africa. Northwest Passage.* Volume II of *Analytical Calculus.* Oh to hell with it. There was nothing he could do. What did they want at that blooming hour? He unlatched the door to find a frightened Mrs. Carollissen in the passage.

"It's all right," he whispered, "don't worry. Just go to bed. By the way, get my satchel into your bedroom, just in case."

He was surprised at her meek acceptance, but there was no time to be surprised now. She nodded assent as he walked into the lounge. Two plain-clothes detectives, one white, the other Coloured, stood at the french door. He recognized the Coloured detective as September.

"I'm Detective-Sergeant Bligenhout, Special Political Branch."

"Yeah?" he said indifferently.

"May we ask you a few questions?"

"At this God-forgotten hour?"

"Yes."

"Well, have a seat," he said, indicating the couch with affected nonchalance.

"Let me see. You are Dreyer. Andrew Dreyer?" the detective asked, referring to a list and searching in his pocket for a notebook and pencil. September stood guard at the door.

"Yes?"

"You stay here?"

"I board here."

"You are a teacher, not so?"

"Yes."

"At Steenberg High School," September snapped. It was the first time he had spoken. Andrew looked at him contemptuously.

"I notice your spies are well informed."

"We're not asking for that."

"Go on."

"Are you a member of P.A.C.?"

"Don't be ridiculous!"

"Are you a member of P.A.C.?"

"The Pan African Congress only accepts Africans as members. The State has classified me as a Coloured man, whatever that may be."

"Are you a member of P.A.C.?"

"No!"

"A.N.C.?"

"No!"

"Any left-wing organizations?"

"Ottery Road Table Tennis Club and Steenberg High School Cultural Society."

"May I warn you that this is serious?"

"How am I to know what you understand by left-wing?"

"Don't your friends tell you? You are very popular in certain circles."

"Really?"

"As you say, our spies are very well informed. You are a teacher. Who pays your salary?"

"I work for it!"

"I would like to search your room."

"Go ahead."

Andrew felt that he had already said too much. He had been warned to say nothing. Keep control. He ushered them into his bed-sitting room. Bligenhout ran his fingers along the rows of books.

"Nothing here?"

Andrew kept silent. The detective reached for a pile of unmarked school essays. Andrew noticed with relief that his satchel had been removed.

"Those are class compositions on 'The Problems of Modern Youth and Extra-Mural Activities at School.' "

"You seem to have more than sufficient extra-mural activities. May I see your school-bag?"

"What?"

"Your satchel. What do you carry your books in?"

"I left it in my cupboard at school. You may phone my Principal."

"That won't be necessary. Thank you. We'll be seeing you. Regards to Ruth Talbot."

They left. Hell, did they know about Ruth as well? That was unpleasant. He would have to phone her. No, that was dangerous. See her somehow. Arrange a meeting in a private place. The University library perhaps. He shivered and felt a headache coming on.

"Mr. D.?"

"Yes?"

"Was it serious?"

"No, it's O.K."

"I'll make you some coffee. Your satchel's in the bathroom."

"Thank you very much."

He was far from sleepy, and threw himself on the bed, staring at the light.

That was Thursday. He had seen Ruth that same evening and warned her to be careful. They were being watched. Yes, Mrs. Carollissen could be trusted, but for how long?

Kenilworth . . . Wynberg . . . Wittebome. It might be wise to leave home and school for a short time. School wouldn't be difficult. He could phone De Jager and get a doctor's certificate somewhere. More raids, were expected, there might be detentions this time, and he wasn't going to get caught so easily. Not by Bligenhout or September or the whole damn lot of them. What a bloody mess, he thought, as the train pulled into Plumstead.

3

Andrew bought a *Cape Argus* outside the station and glanced up at the sky flecked with black and grey. The bus should come at 8:10. He looked at his watch. Half an hour to wait. In any case what could one do but wait patiently. There was not the slightest guarantee that it would arrive on time. One just waited and waited while the queue grew longer and longer. The people around him seemed excited about the day's events. Quite a few had come from Cape Town and were giving eye-witness accounts of the baton charge. Others spoke about the absenteeism at their work. The stay-at-home had obviously been successful. Their conversations were a mixture of fear, confidence, worry, anxiety, relief, insecurity, boastfulness, fierce racial pride, and indifference. As the minutes dragged on the bus failed to appear, and the mood of the queue changed from jazzy and beat to a slow, melancholy blues. Voices became hushed. Abandoned laughter changed to resigned whispers and then to a brooding silence. A slight drizzle set in, and Andrew wished to God that the bus would come soon. Buses on a Coloured route were always late. Never on time. What with late buses, baton charges, mass funerals, dawn raids, Mrs. Carollissen and Ruth. Well, if it was any consolation, Ruth was pleasant to think about. Good-looking, with a puckish nose and black hair. If only she wouldn't put that funny stuff on her eyes. Mascara or something. But then, she was a drama student.

It was rather amusing the way he had first met Ruth. Through Braam de Vries. Yes, it was the night Braam had invited him to supper. Braam was a type. An Afrikaner from some forgotten dorp in the Orange Free State, he had come to University in the Cape and, after graduating with an Honours degree, had become ultra-liberal and ostentatiously Bohemian. He wrote bad poetry and even worse political tirades. He embraced the Movement with a bear-hug, and was the self-styled leader of its lumpenproletariat. He carefully ruffled his hair, seldom washed, and wore khaki shorts under a duffle-coat so that street workers whistled at him. His clothes were meticulously torn. He was disappointed at not having been banned by the Government as a Communist and felt personally insulted when not arrested during the treason raids.

Andrew had come from his first evening lecture at six to find Braam waiting for him on the steps of the University. He was in a hurry as he had an Accounts lecture within ten minutes. Braam sported a heavy blond beard and wore the now fashionable crucified look.

"Care to come for supper?"

"I still have another lecture."

"What time do you finish?"

"At seven."

"I'll see you then."

"It'll be difficult to come for supper. I'm seeing Abe tonight."

"Who?"

"Abe Hanslo. You must know him. I think we met when our graduation results came out. You might also have seen him with Justin."

"The teacher?"

"Yes, he teaches with me."

"Ask him around as well."

"I'll try. See you outside the Library."

"O.K."

Abe seemed reluctant but had finally agreed after some persuasion.

"He's crazy, you know."

"Not so bad, really."

"Well, over-enthusiastic then. Such whites wear me out. You know the type I mean. You don't know where you are with them. When they greet a black man they shove out their hands a little too soon."

"I'm sure Braam is sincere."

"I'm sure he is. It is a form of compensation I suppose. Romantic white University graduate leads inflamed black masses. The Byron touch. Where the devil does he stay?"

"Bree Street somewhere. Do come along."

"All right, if you insist. See you after lectures."

"I said we'd meet him outside the Library."

"See you there."

At seven o'clock they found Braam deep in conversation with an attractive white girl.

"Oh this is Ruth Talbot. Meet two so-called Coloured friends of mine. Andrew Dreyer and . . . I forget the name."

"Abraham Hanslo."

"That's right, Abraham Hanslo."

She nodded a shy greeting. Andrew took in her slim figure and neat ankles.

"Well, have we transport?" Braam asked.

"Abe has a car."

"Good. May we cadge a lift to my place?"

"Sure," said Abe indifferently. "I'm parked outside the Arts block."

The journey to Bree Street was uneventful until they

stopped in the centre of Town to allow Braam to buy bread. Andrew felt that he had to say something to Ruth.

"You're a friend of Braam's?"

"Well, in a way."

"You know him a long time?"

"No. As a matter of fact I only just met him ten minutes ago for the first time. I was sitting in the Library and he came up and invited me to supper. So I came. It's as simple as that."

"Oh."

There was an uncomfortable pause. Andrew found her upturned nose attractive. There was something coquettish about her, impish. Maybe he was wrong but he wanted to know more about her. He kept an embarrassed silence.

"Are you at University?" she asked, hesitantly.

"Yes. I actually teach, but I attend evening classes. Trying an extra degree."

"For what?"

"B. Comm."

"Oh. I'm at Drama School."

"Full time?"

"Yes."

Braam reappeared, shivering with indignation.

"The bloody Fascist swine. I came in after a so-called African. The bastard wanted to serve me first, so I objected. Then he wouldn't give me half a loaf till I threatened to sock him."

"Hope you didn't," said Abe, surveying Braam's slight frame.

"Had the cheek to tell me that only Kaffirs bought half-loaves. Then I let him have it!"

"Did you throw in the Freedom Charter and the Bill of Rights?"

"The works. I really told him where to get off!"

He was still quivering when they reached a dilapidated double-storeyed building. A bar, frequented by dock-labourers, occupied the whole ground floor.

"This is where I stay."

"Oh?"

"Upstairs I mean."

"That's better."

"You first, Ruth."

The group stood puzzled and uncertain.

"Where?" she asked, searching for the door.

"Oh, the entrance is round the corner. I lost the key a week after I moved in. We'll have to use the drain-pipe, I'm afraid."

After shinning up the pole and climbing through the window, to the amusement of passers-by, they found that Braam's room was in chaos. Everything was dumped in the middle of the floor. Clothes, books, records, a spirit-burner, sleeping-bag, potatoes, wine bottles, knives and forks, a record-player, food.

"I mean to clear this mess some time," he said apologetically. Ruth offered to help him cook and followed him into the kitchen. Abe cleared a space on the floor and gingerly sat down.

"Is this the rebellion of modern youth?"

"Seems like it. He's not really so young you know."

"Save me from such. Isn't it dangerous to have these people in the Movement? They're the ones who always get caught."

"I dare say they are a bit indiscreet. It's symptomatic of our type of organization that we attract all types. We can't afford to discriminate against anyone who shares our ideas."

Abe picked up some books and periodicals from the floor after moving two billy-cans out of the way. Tolstoy's *Confession, Vindiciae contra Tyrannos, China Reconstructs, Dialectical Materialism, Salvador Dali.*

"I wonder if he ever reads these."

"I presume he does. I don't altogether think he's a fool. Merely an inverted projection of an aggressive personality."

"Hell!"

"I hope that's right."

"I sincerely hope so. I like the dame. Ever seen her before?"

"No, but I have an idea this is not the last time I'll see her."

"Ever heard of the Immorality Act?"

"So what?"

Braam returned with a bottle of wine. He deftly knocked the cork into the bottle with his thumb.

"Have some. Careful of the cork. There are some glasses on the floor. I must apologize, gentlemen, but there is only enough grub for one. Still, I'm sure you won't mind sharing. There's plenty of gravy and bread. Anyone like toast?"

"If it's not too much bother."

"Not at all. I'll switch on the electric iron. Can't afford a toaster."

"Go ahead."

They sipped the wine slowly, becoming more and more uncomfortable. Abe found the studied untidiness and pseudo-Bohemianism repellent. Finally, Ruth entered, bearing two enamel plates. Braam followed with the pot.

"Let our guests have the plates, Ruth. You can have the pot, I'll take the lid. There are spoons near *The Life of Toulouse-Lautrec*."

Andrew surveyed his unappetizing meat swilling in gravy, and picked it up delicately.

"Horse meat," Braam said shortly.

"Oh?" Andrew said.

"You like horsemeat? A bit sweet, but I like the taste. And it's a damn sight cheaper. Have a potato."

"Have you removed the saddle?"

"Go ahead and eat it. It won't bite back."

Andrew tested his gingerly. Abe refused.

"I'm sorry if you don't like it. Have some toast and wine."

Abe suggested that they go to a restaurant and Andrew heartily agreed. He was hungry by now. They all shinned down the pole and drove off to Khayyams. Andrew felt he had to see Ruth again. He managed to speak to her alone and made a date for the following Saturday.

Since then the situation had developed a lot further.

Andrew surveyed the queue and tried once more to concentrate on his newspaper. Yes, Ruth was all right. He hoped that she would be in. He wasn't expected, but it was imperative to make plans for the following week. He might not see her again for a long time. Have a bath, eat, and then take the bus to Rondebosch. If only he had transport. A car like Abe's. He mustn't forget to phone Abe. Tell him of his safe arrival. Leave a message with his mother if he wasn't home yet. If only the damn bus would come.

The drizzle stopped, and Andrew again opened his damp newspaper. It was useless to try to concentrate on anything until he was settled in the bus. He glanced at the headlines. Peninsula's Native Walk-Out is 95% Effective. Mourning Day Hits City Services. Crowds Mass for Funeral at Langa. Natives Burn Passes on Rand. Hell, they're scared, damn scared. What if the bus didn't come? Drivers striking in sympathy with stay-at-home? It would mean walking three miles, past the Klip Cemetery and Bartlett's Wood Yard to 1st Avenue. And then the door would be locked with Mrs. Carollissen asleep, which would mean waking her. And he knew what that meant.

4

Andrew glanced up to see a double-decker swerving round the corner. The mood of the queue alerted and freshened. His watch said 8:35. Nearly half an hour late. Half a blooming hour. The orderliness dissolved as the bus screeched to a stop. People fought and scrambled for seats and Andrew allowed the momentum of the crowd to carry him forward until he stumbled against the step. With a quick, angry pull he hoisted himself on and lurched towards an empty downstairs seat. Barbarians, he thought, as he tried to straighten himself out and open his torn newspaper.

5

He tried to read but the bus was far too crowded. Stuffy inside with the windows dulled and clouded. He wiped the pane with his sleeve and tried to peer out. The drizzle had stopped by now and the sky was clearing again. The bus passed knots of people grouped around stops, while others were walking the three miles to Klip and Busy-Corner. He missed the Africans in their greatcoats and heavy boots, tramping to their shanties at Cooks Bush. The call for a stay-at-home seemed to have been highly successful. At Southfield some people alighted and the congestion in the bus eased. At the Victoria Road Mosque more people got off. Andrew was now able to relax, and he reopened his newspaper. He felt even better

at the prospect of a hot bath, eating, and afterwards going
to Rondebosch. Maybe a chat with Eldred while dressing.
To order a bath in the Carollissen household required a
minor operation, to get it, a major one. After Mrs. Carollissen had grudgingly agreed, the paraffin tin would have to be
filled with water by one of the children, most probably
Paul, and a fire would have to be lit outside. When the
water was lukewarm it would have to be carried through the
kitchen to the bathroom. Since it would be damp outside,
Mrs. Carollissen would have to be asked to relight her
stove. And after all the fuss he would most probably find
that she had locked away the soap and towels in her
bedroom.

"I say."

A yellow, rat-faced youth of about nineteen, dressed in
hospital-blue jeans and a maroon jersey, sidled up to
Andrew.

"Give us a cigarette, pal."

He felt in no mood for company and continued reading,
realizing that the youngster was bent on trouble. He
smelt of stale breath and wine.

"I'm speaking to you, damn it all. Think you're God
Almighty?"

Andrew preferred to ignore him. To react in any way
was to admit recognition.

"Give us a bloody cigarette!"

It would be quite easy to put down his newspaper, turn
calmly, and knock the guts out of the youth. He felt
severely tempted to do so, but decided to remain cool. No
exhibitionism. People would stand and stare at the unusual sight of a High School teacher in a bus fight. He
turned over a page in the newspaper.

"Wait till the bloody Kaffirs get you select Coloureds!"

"Yeah," Andrew replied wearily.

"For my part, they can kill the bloody lot of you. All
the f—— whites and you upper-class Coloureds."

"Yeah."

"What the hell, you think you better than us?"

"Go and jump in a lake."

"You still talk a bloody lot? Wait till we get you
uppity Coloureds. Your day will come."

He appealed to the rest of the bus. People giggled.

"That goes for all teachers and bloody stiffies. Wait till the Kaffirs are on top. Then we'll give you all hell."

Andrew was by now distinctly uninterested. Not disgusted, just impassive. He tried to concentrate on the editorial. The youth continued to stare hostilely at him for a long time, hoping to evoke some response, but Andrew refused to be baited. The youngster got up in disgust, mumbling threats as he lurched towards the platform.

Andrew swore softly under his breath. What a political lee-way to make up. He felt somehow that he could understand the youth's raw and primitive reaction. He identified clean collars and the ability to read newspapers in a bus, respectability, with *herrenvolk* status. Part of the *élite*. Whites and upper-class Coloureds. How Mrs. Carollissen would have loved it. People who had electricity in their homes, refrigerators, and cars, white-collar workers, people who had breakfast in the mornings and had never suffered the cold, seeping damp of Cooks Bush and Windermere, where one fought, drank and fornicated to forget. Maybe the youth had something there. Against whites in general and those who spoke academically of oppression in well-modulated voices. Maybe he had something in his own, crude way. Still there was no justification for interfering with others. Becoming drunk and aggressive. Andrew now felt like smoking, but decided against doing so lest he attract the attention of the youth.

The bus turned into Lake Road and he realized with relief that the next stop would be his. He would have to phone Abe to find out what had happened. He wondered whether Ruth would be home. The bus suddenly pulled up with a jerk, catapulting him into the next seat. He got up confused and recovered his newspaper from the floor. There was some commotion on the platform. Passengers straining their necks to see. Andrew stood up. It was the youth in blue jeans. Yellow-faced with a foam-flecked mouth, he was lunging at the conductor with a knife while the latter was trying to ward him off by lashing with his money-belt. Coins were scattering in all directions. A middle-aged woman got up to remonstrate and the youth lunged at her, grazing her arm. She screamed as blood soaked through her sleeve. Andrew felt the anger rising in him. It might be better to walk the remaining stop in case he lost control of himself. He felt he had had far too much for one day. The funeral, the baton charge, trapped in a urinal, and now this. O Gertrude, Gertrude. When sorrows come they come not single spies but in battalions. Hamlet in a Grassy Park bus. How completely out of place. Shakespeare at this juncture. Getting off would mean passing the two lunging figures. Risking a knife-wound or a blow from the money-belt. He forced his way down the aisle, struggling through the frightened spectators.

"Excuse me, please," he said pale, and shivering.

The conductor automatically stood aside and Andrew grimly walked past the youth who was breathing heavily and watching his opponent with glassy eyes.

Once in the street, he breathed the cold, stinging air. He felt dizzy. A crowd had collected, laughing and whooping as they pursued the scattering silver and coppers. The driver sat in his seat, immobile and ashen beneath his brown skin, afraid to intervene. Andrew hesitated, not knowing quite what to do.

"Hi, Mr. Dreyer! Were you in the bus?" It was Eldred Carollissen.

"Christ, yes!"

"That boy's sure reckless!"

"The swine tried to interfere with me."

"So?"

"I don't quite know. Next thing I knew he was trying to stab the conductor."

"Anybody hurt?"

"A woman."

"What happened?"

Andrew wanted to get home.

"What happened?" Eldred persisted.

"Come, let's get the hell out of here. I'll tell you on the way."

"All right," Eldred agreed. He was a healthy, bronzed solidly-built Matriculation student at Steenberg High—in Andrew's class in fact. He wore a grey pullover and khaki shorts and sandals. At sixteen he worshipped his teacher, and Andrew in turn found him the only approachable member of the Carollissen household. Eldred was always apologizing for the rest of the family.

"Come on, let's move."

They started walking down Lake Road. The asphalt was black and mirror-wet with damp, yellow pools of light under the lamp-posts. Eldred was still busy plying Andrew with questions about the incident when they heard the bus behind them. Andrew signalled and as it slowed down they both jumped on.

The bus was empty, except for the conductor, who was nursing an ugly wound in his shoulder, and the woman whimpering in a corner seat.

"Did the police come?" Andrew asked the conductor.

"We're going there now."

"Why didn't you phone the cops?"

"They're too busy beating up Natives to bother about us."

"You get the guy?"

"No, he ran away."

"Know his name?"

"No, but they say he lives in 7th Avenue."

"The bastard!" Andrew said vehemently. "Well, you can quote me as a witness. He tried to interfere with me as well."

He wrote his name and address on the back of an old envelope he found in his pocket and then rang the bell as the bus approached his stop.

"Sorry about the trouble," he shouted as Eldred and he alighted.

"Don't forget, Andrew Dreyer's the name."

"O.K.," said the conductor as the bus picked up speed and careered along Lake Road.

"Damn," said Eldred, "I almost forgot to tell you!"

"What?"

"Two detectives were at home for you."

"When?"

"This afternoon. About three o'clock. Ma said they were sitting in their car waiting. They may still be there. I came round the back way."

"What they want?"

"They spoke to Ma. They wanted to see you."

"Hell."

"Ma feels that it's best if you don't come home tonight. They asked her all sorts of things about you."

"I see."

"Have you any cash? She sent a pound note in case you need money."

"It's all right, I have enough."

"I can bring your satchel to school tomorrow."

"O.K., Eldred. If you have to contact me, phone Mr. Hanslo. He'll know where I am. Don't tell a soul."

"Right."

"So long, then."

"Good luck. Hope to see you tomorrow."

Andrew walked quickly past his stop along Lake Road.

6

At nine o'clock in the evening the street was deserted. Houses and trees stood silhouetted against the night with weak blobs of light from shop-windows and under lamp-posts. Andrew was uncertain about his next move. Go to Ruth's flat or go back? The Special Branch call might be merely routine. Merely to ask questions. No, that was unlikely. They wouldn't spend all their time sitting in a car if it was merely for that. Not at this period. He really felt tired now, physically and mentally exhausted. Go to Ruth's or phone Abe? Might as well get buses and go to Ruth's flat. Yeah, get buses. Hell, that meant another hour's travelling to Rondebosch. A bus to Wynberg, another to Mowbray, then a walk of about half a mile. In addition he felt hungry and dirty. Not very hungry but extremely sweaty and itchy. It might well be better to get to Rondebosch. Man on the run, like a cheap American thriller. At the flat he could get a shower and something to eat. Then he could sort things out.

No bus was in sight and Andrew knew that it would take at least half an hour before the next one came—that was barring stabbings. He decided to walk the mile or so to the Mosque Terminus at the Key. It would calm him down and give him time to think, put him in a better frame of mind. He heard a car hooting behind him and instinctively quickened his pace. The car roared past and Andrew relaxed although his heart was palpitating. It was useless getting jumpy but he was like that; as Mrs. Heidemann used to say, "Andrew is so over-sensitive. He really belongs to the gentry." Yeah, Mrs. Heidemann was a type. Overwhelming in affection and always smelling of stale sweat and alcohol. At least more human than Annette and Aunt Ella. Hell, that was a long time ago. Long time ago. He started humming. De little black bull went down de meadow, long time ago. There was something warm and vibrant about his childhood in District Six, slum as it was. District Number Six as they used to say. Crazy, crazy as a two-pound note, with a background music of laughter and guitars.

The apricot-warm day when he had first made his way down Caledon Street to Primary School. Not quite seven and glossy-eyed with excitement. Past Bernstein's Bottle-Store and Langman's shop and other children walking down both sides of the street with bare feet scrubbed raw and red, all going to St. Marks. The boys played games during the first lunch-break, but he was too self-conscious to join in. He stared with wide, black eyes at the teachers and the classrooms and the Biblical pictures on the wall and the miniature tables and chairs and the neat pile of worn readers in the cupboard. See me, Mother, can you see me? And life was beautiful and golden-brown on those apricot days when he was seven.

And then the gang, the Jungles they called themselves. Jonga, Broertjie, Amaai and himself had plotted for days to make a Dracula costume. Cloak and mask and fangs. The Vampire Man. And then they had dressed Broertjie up after much argument and painted his face. He was supposed to throw open the door and impress the rival gang sitting on Mrs. Heidemann's stoep, but he only succeeded in giving Aunt Ella a start, who complained about it to his mother after she had had brandy to soothe her nerves.

And James, he was afraid of his elder brother; James had beaten him for breaking one of the dining-room chairs. James was very fair, a play-white, always cold and aloof. It was Easter and he had balanced the chair on its hind legs while admiring his chocolate egg. It was beautiful, was the egg, wrapped in red, white and blue tinsel. And then he had toppled over and busted the back of the chair. He had cried and Miriam had helped him to eat the egg, in sympathy.

And the slightly acid smell of the brown water in Hanover Street Swimming Baths. The wet, concrete pavings and the quiet unruffled stillness of the deep end of the pool. Jonga had pushed him into the water and then dived in after him. He had gone home alone, frightened and resentful, balling his fists in anger.

And singing in the Inter-Schools Ash-Shield Competition. In this Hour of Softened Splendour and Sleep Gentle Babe and Old Father Thames and Slaap my Kindjie Slaap Sag. Oh yes, and De Little Black Bull. And one wore a white shirt and navy blue shorts and a red tie. And he had walked down Darling Street to the City Hall with two girls from St. Paul's and they had argued and argued about the merits of their respective schools.

And the ripe warmth of Christmas morning, dressed in a grey suit from Waynicks and far too tight patent-leather shoes. And stopping at Langman's to buy an ice-cream cone before going to wish Aunt Ella happy Christmas.

And the excitement of going to Kalk Bay on Boxing Day. The packing and guitars and primus stoves and blankets and left-overs from Christmas. Mrs. Heidemann already drunk, handing out pocket-money to all and sundry, including the white train conductor.

Then the long drowsy winter days with the rain beating down on the balcony. And the landing smelling damp and mouldy, and old tin-tubs and enamel basins carefully placed in all rooms to catch the water dripping through.

And taking a bus round the Hanover Street route just for fun with Jonga and Broertjie and Honger. Past Castle Bridge and down Wale Street to Bree Street Terminus. Then through Central Town to Windsor Street, near to where Annette and Miriam stayed, and then back into Hanover Street.

And the fuss and the bother and the dirt and the rubble and the gaiety and sadness of District Six in his early years. Till his mother died. Then came Walmer Estate and Grassy Park and of course Mrs. Carollissen.

What a woman. It was considerate of her to have sent Eldred with money. Extremely solicitous. A paradox of a woman who locked away the family toothpaste in her bedroom, but sent a pound when he was in trouble. He wondered how she had reacted to the detectives the second time. A policeman at Mrs. Carollissen's home. Andrew realized that he would soon have to get out and find another boarding place. The scandal of having detectives all over her home. Well, Mrs. Carollissen could work it out for herself.

He reached the Key and decided to wait for a bus. The day's events seemed far in the distance. The Sports Meeting. He wondered how his school had fared. Strange that Eldred hadn't mentioned anything, but then the boy never really had any chance to speak about it. And the funeral at Langa, packed to capacity. He liked the singing at the graveside. How did Abe put it again? Natural indigenous harmony. And then the baton charge and the hawker losing his shoe. Ruth might not be home, he should have phoned. But it would make no difference, he couldn't return to 1st Avenue. Well, then, wait outside her flat till she came. And that swine at the bus. The bastard. Wanting a blooming cigarette and then stabbing the conductor. Hope they catch him. Where did he live again? 6th or 7th Avenue? In any case it didn't really matter.

He leaned against a lamp-post and then realized that he must have left his *Argus* behind in the bus. Never mind, he could buy another. Pawp! He heard a car hooting behind him. His chest tightened. Hell, he had almost forgotten the Special Branch. Pawp! Pawp! He looked up carefully.

"Christ, Abe!"

The Volkswagen pulled up.

"Hop in!"

"Sure!"

He felt unnaturally overjoyed and relieved, as if meeting a long-lost companion. Abe opened the door for him and then drove on until he pulled up under the trees in Victoria Road.

"Hell, I'm glad to see you. Cigarette?"

"No, thanks," Abe said.

"What on earth happened to you?"

"You mean on the Grand Parade?"

"Yeah."

"I ran like hell."

"Where to?"

"I made for the car. I thought you would do the same.

Police were beating people all around me. They seemed to have left me alone. Suppose they thought I was white."

Abe had a freckled skin, green eyes and a shock of fair hair.

"That always exposes one to play-white tendencies."

"Oh, go to hell!" said Abe slightly annoyed. "So there I was between the devil and the deep blue sea. They were stoning cars. The Volkswagen got off with a few scratches. I saw some lousy things. Nevertheless I had to get back to Walmer Estate via De Waal Drive. District Six was too risky. I just popped in at home and came through to find you. Luckily I spotted you at the bus stop."

"You could have phoned."

"I did, but Mrs. Carollissen seemed incoherent. How did you get home?"

"I took a train."

"Why didn't you run for the car?"

"There wasn't time for that. I headed for the Gents' Toilet at the station corner and had a long crap till it was all over. Then I took a train and bus home."

"Did you spot Braam on the Parade?"

"No, was he there?"

"Yes. He and Justin. They had enormous placards saying, 'Let our leaders go!'"

"Is Braam trying to play black now?"

"Suppose so."

Then after a pause.

"I haven't been home yet, Abe."

"Well, let me run you down."

Abe proceeded to switch on the engine.

"No, hang on. Switch off."

Abe obeyed him.

"I think they're after me. The Special Branch I mean. I was warned by Eldred that two gentlemen were waiting outside in their car. It might very well have been Bligenhout and September. I think they're after my blood, you know, after the last raid. They also know about Ruth."

"Hell. How did you find that out?"

"Didn't I tell you? They mentioned her just as they were leaving."

"That's dangerous."

"Well, we can all look forward to more raids and

arrests, and worst of all they might declare a state of emergency."

"A most inviting prospect."

"Then the State would be in complete control. I think it might be very healthy for me to get out of circulation for a time. I was just on my way to Ruth's flat."

"Come to my place."

"I have to see her. In any case I think you're suspect as well."

"I suppose so. What are you doing about School?"

"Yeah, what am I doing about School? Tell the Principal I'm ill. Very ill in bed. Say anything. I think De Jager knows, so he'll understand. I'll work it out afterwards and try and get a doctor's certificate."

"O.K."

"Also tell him I apologize for not staying till the end of the Sports Meeting. No, he'd better not know that. You might also get it in the neck. Teachers are not supposed to play truant."

"I don't think he need know that. We left early for University lectures. That should suffice. We left early for lectures."

"All right, use your inventive genius. I won't be at school for a few days so you might have to take my class for literature."

"If things come to the worst I might also have to do a bunk. So, get you to Ruth's? It's on my way home."

"Yes. And thanks for coming all the way to Grassy Park."

"Pleasure's all mine as the prostitute said."

Abe started the car and they headed for Rondebosch. Andrew liked Abe, had known him since they hat been at High School together. At first they had not got on well because he had been self-conscious about his District Six background, slum child, and his dark complexion. Abe to him had represented the hallmark of Walmer Estate quality. Fair, good-looking, a sharp brain, and affluent background. It was only in the Matric class that they had become friends, when he had gone to live with Miriam in Nile Street. Then the two had gone to University together and now they taught at the same school. Strange that Abe had always been so politically inclined, what with his comfortable background. He could easily have crossed the line and played white. But if anything, Abe was more embittered than he was. Worked harder, read any political material avidly. They had been, and still were, good friends. Abe, Justin and himself. He wondered about Justin's teaming up with Braam. What an unholy alliance.

"You know, Abe, in spite of all these dynamic events I keep thinking of trivial things."

"Such as?"

"Well, I saw a man losing his shoe during the baton charge. I keep worrying whether he'll ever find it. And then I'm suffering terribly from childhood reminiscences."

"How deliciously sickly and sentimental."

"I suppose it's escapism. It's rather silly, but I got an Easter egg when I was eight and I busted a chair."

"With the Easter egg?"

"No, man. Oh, I give up. Then I was thinking of Justin."

"Well, he's in the thick of this, placard and all."

"Do you know whether he's been raided?"

"He would be most offended if he weren't."

"Like Braam?"

"Like Braam."

They reached Rondebosch Fountain and turned down the main road till they pulled up near a huge block of flats. Andrew got out.

"Well, thanks a lot, Abe. If I really need you I'll phone."

"Sure, pal."

"I'll either be here or at my sister's place in Nile Street."

"Good."

"And extend my apologies to our dear Principal with bated breath and whispering humbleness."

"Say this, 'Fair Sir, you spit on me on Wednesday last. You spurned me such a day, another time you called me dog.' "

"All right, Shylock. See you soon."

"Good night, sweet Prince. Phone you tomorrow."

"Good. Thumbs up."

"Afrika! Or rather Izwe Lethu! It's more fashionable."

Abe chuckled as he pulled away. Andrew felt much better. The conversation had really proved a tonic. He hummed De Little Black Bull as he mounted the stairway to Ruth's flat.

7

On Monday, March 28th, Mrs. Nhlapo of Steenberg felt terribly depressed because she had no black to wear for the funeral at Langa.

Matabele Ben, the last white man to have known Lobengula, died at Plumstead at the age of ninety-eight.

Braam De Vries was convinced that he could compose an epic on Sharpeville and Langa, preferably in free verse.

Wilberforce Nxeli, Municipal Constable at Nyanga East, decided to move out after residents had threatened him for the second time.

Miriam Peters decided she must see *The Nun's Story* at the Kismet as she had always been an Audrey Hepburn fan.

Mrs. John Frazer was terribly disappointed that the Eoan Group had cancelled their performance of *La Bohême* as she found Coloured people so musical.

James Dreyer was confident that no one would recognize him as Coloured as he sipped brandy and soda at the Toledo.

A nurse from Holland who had been injured by rioters on Vanguard Drive decided to return home to the Continent.

Mrs. Frazer decided to hear Elsie Hall and Michael Doré at the National Gallery instead.

At the Castle, *Son et Lumière* had its 113th performance in aid of Red Cross Funds.

Ruth Talbot hoped that Andrew would stay out of trouble. She was so afraid for him.

Danny Appolis swore under his breath when he read that *Jack the Ripper* was playing at a white cinema, and as a consolation went to see *Monster on the Campus* at the Orpheum.

Justin Bailey realized the risk involved in canvassing Coloured workers in Woodstock to support the stay-at-home strike.

Joe's Milk Bar in Kenilworth wanted a European or slightly Coloured assistant to start work immediately. References essential.

Eldred Carollissen determined to do better in the 220 yards final after he had just managed to qualify in the heats.

Coloureds who had accommodation problems could phone Pops at 713204.

Mrs. Millicent Carollissen came home with sore feet after searching all morning to find a royal-blue jumper for Charmaine.

The first thing she had to do was to get her shoes off and soak her feet in hot water. It was the corn on the little toe. Must get Minnie to put some plaster on it. First soak her feet and then worry about lunch for Charmaine, Paul and Jeremy. She hoped that Eldred and Vincent were all right, what with all the trouble about. They were probably enjoying themselves at Goodwood. She would have gone to the Sports Meeting herself, but Charmaine had to have a jumper for the following day. Well, she would have to be satisfied with sky-blue. Most probably Eldred and Vincent would come home together at about six. Funny how the two differed. One would never say they were brothers. Vincent might be two years younger and only in Junior Certificate, but he was far more reliable than Eldred. Always did his homework and was more than ready to oblige. He was fair, took after her own people and could go far one day if he used his colour and common-sense correctly. Now Eldred. She didn't quite know how to take the boy. Not because he was dark, well not quite dark really, light-brown like his father. Always sulking, obstinate, neglecting his work. Far too often in Mr. D.'s room reading those thick books. All about politics. She wasn't going to tolerate that any longer. No, Mr. D. would have to leave if he was going to influence her children. Already Eldred was refusing to go to Sunday School. She would have to speak to Mr. D. about finding alternative accommodation. Can't have detectives all over the place like last Thursday. She couldn't sleep that night. She wearily opened the door and slumped down in the nearest armchair she could find.

"Charmaine!"

She wondered whether the children had come home yet. Charmaine and Jeremy always arrived first from Preparatory School.

"Charmaine!"

"She's not home yet."

"That you, Minnie?"

"Yes, Mrs. Carollissen."

That was all right. At least Minnie was in. The maid could run hot water into the basin and she could rest her feet. Not that Minnie was really a maid. More a companion and help who came in four times a week to do the floors and washing.

"Minnie?"

"Yes?"

The latter appeared from the yard wringing her wet hands.

"What you doing now?"

"Washing underclothes for tomorrow."

"Oh my poor feet. You know I spent the whole of this morning looking for a royal-blue jumper for that child. They just haven't got any, so I had to buy sky-blue instead. Anybody home yet?"

"Yes. Paul was sent home early from school. I sent him to the Klip for more Rinso."

"All right. Run some water into the basin for me, then make us some coffee while I soak my feet. Also bring the corn plaster."

"Yes, Mrs. Carollissen."

A bit annoying that Minnie never called her madam. She heard the water running into the basin. They only called white people madam, though Coloured people treated them just as well. Mrs. Carollissen removed her high heels and stockings and walked heavily to the bathroom.

"You know, Minnie, there are no natives to be seen in Town."

"Really, Mrs. Carollissen?"

"No. None in Town or on the bus. Did the milkman come this morning?"

"No."

"What an absolute nuisance. No milk, no newspaper boys. No nothing. I hope Mr. D. doesn't get into any more difficulties. All those Natives on strike and simply looking for trouble. I wonder if the boys will be all right."

After she had soaked and treated her feet, Mrs. Carollissen started preparing lunch. Make something light for the three. They can all have a heavy meal in the evening.

Eldred and Vincent would be hungry after the Sports. Pity she could not be at Goodwood. Yes, Mr. D. would have to leave. Wonder what time he would be home, unless he went to Miss Talbot first. She liked Ruth, but the whole set-up was dangerous. Extremely dangerous. What with a white girl and a Coloured man. They could be gaoled for six months under the Immorality Act. She didn't mind Ruth or any white people visiting her. For that matter she liked it, but it was a different business altogether when they came as girl-friends to her boarders. What if the police found out? It just wasn't fair to her. She had already spoken to Mr. Carollissen about it, but that man just shrugged it off. Like that, just shrugged it off. Police all over her place.

Shortly after Paul returned, Charmaine and Jeremy came home. She was literally worn out by the time she had fed the children and had broken the news to Charmaine about the sky-blue jumper. The child just wouldn't understand. Mrs. Carollissen retired to her bedroom for a short nap, instructing Minnie not to wake her for an hour. She was just dozing off when she heard loud knocking at the front door. She heard Minnie shuffling along the passage and the knob turning. Then voices she could not identify.

"Mrs. Carollissen?" Minnie whispered through her key-hole. Although annoyed at being disturbed she was curious to find out who had called.

"Yes?"

"It's two men for Mr. Dreyer."

"Tell them Mr. D.'s not here. He's gone to a Sports Meeting. He'll only be home about six."

"I told them, but they want to speak to you."

"Who are they?" she asked with misgivings.

"I don't know. A white man and a Coloured man."

"Show them into the lounge. I'm coming."

She rose stiffly and searched for her slippers. She ran a brush over her hair and straightened her dress.

They were the same two detectives who had called for Mr. D. on Thursday. She recognized the white one by his ginger moustache.

"You are the lady of the house?" he said, recognizing her.

"Yes?"

"I'm Detective-Sergeant Bligenhout."

"Yes? Have a seat. Is anything wrong?"

"No, nothing serious."

"Please sit down. Minnie, warm up the coffee."

"Thanks."

"You are Mrs. . . . ?"

"Carollissen."

"Yes. Well, Mrs. Carollissen, we understand you have someone staying here. Andrew Dreyer."

"Yes. He's my boarder."

"Teacher at Steenberg High?"

"Yes."

"We've come here before to see him."

"I think I remember."

"We would like to ask you a few questions."

Mrs. Carollissen tensed. In a peculiar way she enjoyed the experience, but at the same time she was determined that they wouldn't get any information out of her.

"He has friends who visit him?"

"I suppose so."

"Who are they?"

"I don't know. Usually members of his school staff."

"Any whites?"

"Not that I know of."

"Quite sure?"

"Quite sure."

"What about his girl-friend?"

"Who?"

"His girl-friend."

"To my knowledge he has never had one."

"Sure of that?"

"Well, if he has, then you know more than I do."

"Does he belong to any organizations?"

"How should I know?"

"Doesn't he often go to meetings?"

"I don't know his business. He is often home in the evenings."

"This is serious, Mrs. Carollissen. We're trying to keep him out of trouble."

"I'm sure you are."

"We don't like his company. You know, the people whom come here. White agitators and Communists."

"I don't allow any agitators or Communists in my house."

"When will he be home?"

"He's gone to an Inter-Schools Sports Meeting at Goodwood. He might be home late, as he'll most probably go to. . . ."

"To where, Mrs. Carollissen?"

"To . . . to his sister's place."

"Where's that?"

"I don't know. Walmer Estate somewhere I think."

"We'd like to have a look at his room."

"He keeps his door locked and takes the key with him." Mrs. Carollissen hoped that Mr. D.'s door was not standing ajar.

"Then how do you get into his room?"

"What for?"

"To clean it!"

"He does it himself."

"And you have a maid?"

"Minnie's not a maid. She does my floors and washing."

"Mrs. Carollissen, it might be better if you helped us."

"I have nothing more to say, gentlemen."

"I warn you this is serious."

"Thank you. I must see to my food. Good afternoon."

She bustled out of the room leaving the two detectives sitting. After a time they left, banging the door behind them, and sat outside in their car for a long time. Mrs. Carollissen was glad that Minnie had not brought the coffee. She now felt a peculiar loyalty towards Andrew, although she was still convinced that he must go. She said as much to Mr. Carollissen when he came home at five. The detectives were still sitting in their car waiting, and she was on edge lest Andrew should come. Shortly after Eldred and Vincent arrived, they drove off. It would be best to warn Mr. D. not to come home. They might return at any moment. She could definitely not keep him as a boarder any longer. Eldred was growing up and needed a room for himself. It was far too dangerous with detectives sitting in cars outside one's home.

"Eldred!"

The boy never listened when one spoke.

"Yes, what do you want?"

"Did Mr. D. mention what time he was coming home?"

"No. I never saw him this afternoon at all."

"Wasn't he at the Sports Meeting?"

"I only saw him in the morning."

"Well, the same two detectives were here for him who came here before. After supper go to the bus stop, go round the back way and when you see him, warn him not to come home. I'm certain they'll be back tonight. Here, take this pound note and give it to him in case he has no money."

"O.K."

"Did you hear me?"

"Yes, I heard you."

She fumbled in her apron pocket and gave Eldred the money.

"Warn him not to come home."

"All right, I heard you."

Mrs. Carollissen was glad she hadn't given the detectives coffee.

8

Andrew arrived in the brightly-lit, but now empty, foyer of Milner Court and briskly mounted the staircase to the second floor. He felt much better after his talk with Abe. Rejuvenated to a certain extent. Abe always made one feel good. Really a nice guy. Andrew hummed De Little Black Bull to himself. A real dependable guy. One felt fresh after speaking to him. De Little Black Bull went down the meadow. At the same time it was advisable to be cautious of the other white tenants. Coloured men just didn't visit unmarried white girls at ten in the evening. De little black bull went down de meadow. Long time ago. He reached her flat, 19, and was disappointed when he found it in darkness. He brightened up, however, when he found a note pinned to the door. "Dear Andy"—he wondered why she always called him Andy—"see my letter box in the foyer." He tore off the note, then crumpled it in his pocket. In her box he found an envelope addressed to him.

"Andy,

I've been visited by two members of the Political Branch

who asked me a lot of personal questions. I waited until 9 and then decided to try and find you in Grassy Park. This note is in case we miss each other. Enclosed please find the key. Let yourself in and wait.

RUTH."

So the bastards had already been to her. What the hell was all the fuss about? His gaiety was suddenly dampened, and he was back in the world of police-raids, interrogations, baton charges and gaolings.

He let himself into her flat when he saw that nobody was watching, and switched on the light. Her bed-sitting room was tastefully furnished, with Sekotos and Van Gogh reproductions on the wall. Her books ran the length of one side. Dr. Du Bois, Paton, Maupassant, Gorky, Steinbeck, Howard Fast. The record player was situated next to a comfortable couch, almost smothered with coloured pillows. The room led through french doors to a balcony giving a view of the University and the mountain. A kitchen and blue-tiled bathroom made up the rest.

He decided firstly to freshen up and have a shower. He felt a pleasant warmth creeping over him as water poured down his neck and over his tired body. He raised his head and allowed the stream to splash in his face. He wondered what they could have asked Ruth. They really were hot on his trail. First Grassy Park, then here. What the devil for? Having the wrong friends? The wrong ideas? Being in love with a white girl? A security risk? A progenitor of the P.A.C. Campaign? Whom the Gods wish to destroy they first make mad. He dried himself vigorously, and then felt extremely hungry. Even ravenously so. He hadn't eaten all day. Unskillfully he cut the bread, warmed the coffee and heated the pan to fry eggs. He decided to have two, no three. He found some tomatoes in the refrigerator and sliced them up, then settled down to his meal. A Congress notice, faded and brown, was pinned behind the door, calling for a boycott of Nationalist-controlled products. The list of goods not to be bought followed.

He felt much better after he had eaten and, fresh and contented, he went back to the main room to wait for Ruth. Through the door he could see the lights of the University set against the black mass of Table Mountain. He could make out Jameson Hall and the Residences, little dots of lights against the mountain. Andrew poured himself a brandy and mixed it with soda. There was an unread *Argus* on the couch, but he felt in no mood to read. Music. That was it. Her record cabinet was at the side of the player. Smetana. He knew the work backwards. *Moldau* from *Má Vlast*. My country. Patriotic music, the stirring of national consciousness. A firm favourite of his. He opened wide the french doors and a slight breeze smelling of pine blew in. He put the record in position, started the player, and switched off all the lights. Then he settled back comfortably on the couch with his brandy. He had always played it at Abe's place. He had read somewhere that Smetana, like Liszt, had shown that music might be brought in touch with the intellectual movement of the time, and had enabled it to play its part in the fight for progressive ideas which could give a better, freer impulse to the life of Europe. How erudite and learned. Yes, sir, as Abe would say, what we need in this country is the development of all indigenous cultures for the furtherance of a truly South African art form. Solo flutes described the River Moldau as it started from its source high up in the forests of the Sumava. Yes, he knew every part of it, recognized every instrument, every note. Hell, waiting for the strings to take up the motif in the middle of pass-burnings and rioting, while on the run from the Special Branch. Fiddling while Rome burnt. The swelling of the mood indicating rustic revelry. Country folk dancing and singing at a rural wedding. The green banks of the Moldau strewn with the dead of Sharpeville and Langa. And waiting in a flat for a white girl he loved passionately and sensuously. Then with Ruth through Prague to Vyšehrad where the river broadens into wide, majestic stream. Flooding like the crowd at the Langa funeral. Black faces stretched from bank to bank. Dignified but dangerous under the unruffled stillness. Like the water at the deepend of Hanover Street Swimming Baths. And then the increase in vigour and tempo as the Moldau shoots over the St. John's Rapids. A sudden eruption. Startling and ominous, like a crowd suddenly turning dangerous. Defiantly burning their passes. Uncontrollable like the south-easter whipping around Tennant Street corner. Or his mother's temper. Controlled anger for which he could not be held responsible. Which could bring death thirteen years before on a windy day. Long time ago, long time ago. De little black

bull went down de meadow, long time ago. With the
smell of sweat and wine and decaying vegetables in his
nostrils. District Six. *Má Vlast*. My country. Based on national stories and a grand, spacious, heroic theme which
runs through the music. The brandy needed more soda.
Why the hell wasn't Ruth back yet? Wonder what Mrs.
Carollissen would tell her? The music becomes enriched
harmonically and melodically and passes into a long coda,
and is carried forward to a last view of the distant river
as it sweeps unrelentingly forward to the sea. Down to
de sea. Long, long time ago. When de little black bull
went down de meadow, long time ago.

9

        The south-easter could sometimes be worse
than the rain. When it really blew, it whipped around the
corner of Tennant Street, chasing old newspapers, empty
cigarette packets, cardboardboxes and pieces of horse-dung
before its crazy fury. On a mad March day in 1947 it had
almost spent itself, yielding before winds blowing in from
Table Bay, with heavy clouds rolling over Signal Hill. But
it still retained some of its old vigour and it howled as
Andrew turned the corner into Caledon Street, backing
against it. He knew his mother would be angry. She was
like that lately. Thin and frail, she was a picture of fallen
respectability, completely out of place in District Six. She
had asked him to take a message to Aunt Ella at Castle
Bridge and he had protested because of the wind. She
had looked at him in her peculiar way, and grabbed her
overcoat, frayed at the sleeves, and gone herself in the
howling wind. She was like that. A short while after she
had left, he had regretted his refusal and had run after
her. He must have missed her and didn't dare enquire at
Aunt Ella's. It was best to go home and face her cold
hostility.
    They occupied three dingy rooms on the first floor of
a double-storeyed tenement flat at 302. It was always
referred to as 302. One first entered a landing which smelt
damp and musty and echoed eerily when the wind blew
through it. Flats 1 and 2 were on the first level. Then up a

pitch-dark staircase till one fumbled for the knob at No. 3 and entered a shabby bed-sitting room grandiloquently called the dining-room. This was dominated by a huge four-poster bed with brass railings, an old-fashioned horsehair couch with chairs to match, and a side-board cluttered with Victorian bric-à-brac. A cheap but highly-polished table was squeezed between the bed and the sideboard. A bedroom led off this, occupied by James and Peter-boy. Here another four-poster bed was situated in the centre, with an ancient tallboy leaning against the wall, adorned with a pink and white basin and picture. Two broken french doors led to an unsafe, wooden balcony. One had to go back to the upstairs landing to reach the Boys' Room which Andrew, Danny and Philip occupied. It contained two beds and a chest of drawers and had the musty smell of stale air and perspiration.

Andrew intensely disliked the place and as intensely disliked having to share a bed with anyone. Both his sisters were married and had emigrated from the filth of District Six to the pseudosophistication and pretentiousness of Walmer Estate. Andrew was the youngest of the family, sensitive and introspective. He wanted to get out of the slum away from the dingy landings and rickety staircases that were District Six. He felt extremely self-conscious about his surroundings, would never bring his schoolfriends home and seldom went out himself. He would usually lock himself in the stuffy Boys' Room and pore over library copies of Dickens, Sir Walter Scott and Hardy, which he devoured voraciously.

His brothers, other than Daniel the second youngest, for the most part ignored him because they could not understand his strange reticence. He had always been afraid of James, the eldest, who had assumed the function of head of the family on the death of their father. James was very fair like his mother, went to white cinemas and bars, had been a gunner in an artillery regiment during the war, and only his responsibility towards the family still kept him in District Six. He in turn despised Andrew, whose dark skin he found an embarrassment. Peter-boy, the second eldest, was rat-like in appearance, mean and moody, seldom working but always with plenty of ready money. Philip, Andrew seldom saw. He wore stylish clothes, smoked expensive cigarettes, and had had a job as a

European messenger till his address gave him away. He
had aspirations to leave home as soon as he could escape
James's grip, and frequented the cheaper white milk-bars
of Woodstock and Lower Salt River.

Andrew got on well with Daniel. He was quiet and an
introvert, something like himself, without the bitterness
and resentment. Daniel was good-looking, soft-spoken and
understanding. A regular church-goer, he had very little in
common with the rest of the family other than his mother
and Andrew. They often spoke, Danny and he, in the
quiet hours of the morning while they lay next to each
other. His brother was appreciative and honest in his
opinions. He liked Danny best of all.

Andrew didn't quite understand his mother. She tried
desperately to maintain a standard within the framework
of their shabby confines. She allowed only English to be
spoken in her home, not the bastardized Afrikaans used
in their surroundings. Andrew was warned to stay away
from his only acquaintances in the District. *Skollie*-types
like Broertjie, Amaai, Honger and Tana. He had always
worn shoes and socks to school, not only at High School,
but since his Primary days at St. Marks. Broertjie and
Amaai went to school with uncombed hair and dirty,
swollen feet.

As he battled against the wind, Andrew spotted Amaai,
Jonga and Broertjie in the doorway of the Brigade Hall.
He joined them silently. Amaai was his age, sixteen years,
dark and sombre. Broertjie, his brother, was a year younger
and dirtier. Yellow in complexion, he had a shock of
black, untamed hair. Jonga was the natural leader of the
three. A pickpocket, he had already escaped twice from
reformatory. He was one of Mrs. Heidemann's many children from as many men. Amaai and Broertjie worshipped
Jonga's easy ways and ready cash.

"Going to the Star tonight?" Andrew asked in Afrikaans,
referring to the local cinema.

"Sure," said Amaai looking hopefully at Jonga.

"You haven't any bloody cash," said Broertjie.

"Says who?"

"Me."

"How the hell you know?"

"Where you gonna get it from?"

"My bloody business!"

"What's showing?" Andrew asked, to stop the brothers' quarrel.

"Sabu."

"In what?"

"*Elephant Boy*."

"Jeeeesus. See im in *'e Drum?*"

"Sure."

"Dat boy's sure good!"

"Bloody good!"

"Bloody bloody good!"

Jonga fished about in the wide pockets of his trousers.

"Go an' buy a packet fish an' chips," he ordered Broertjie.

"O.K. Where's 'e cash?"

"Here. An' a packet Mimosa Ten."

"O.K."

Broertjie smacked Amaai across the backside and raced down the street with the wind. The remaining trio stood quietly observing the deserted street.

"Going to rain bloody hard," Amaai said.

"How you know?" Jonga asked.

"I just know," he replied, trying to appear wise.

"Yeah," said Andrew, "there are heavy clouds over Signal Hill."

"You see! He's a bloody clever guy. He learn it all in school, hey?"

"Yeah," said Andrew indifferently.

"Don' you ever go to Bioscope?" Jonga asked him.

"No."

"Why not?"

"I don't really like it," Andrew lied. His family couldn't afford to sit in the stalls at the local cinema, and it was sacrilege to occupy the cheap, wooden seats downstairs, where Jonga, Amaai and Broertjie usually sat.

"Don' you ever go?"

"No."

"Hell."

"He ain't got no time," Amaai generously explained, "he's too busy reading thick books."

"You're a bloody clever guy, hey?" Jonga agreed. "What standard you now?"

"Matric."

"What's that?"

"Standard ten."

"Hell, that's smart. Goin' to be a doctor?"

"No."

"Teacher?"

"No."

"Lawyer?"

"No."

"What 'e hell you gonna be?"

"Don't know yet."

"What you study at school?"

"All sorts of things."

"Like what?"

Andrew loved being drawn out. It gave him a feeling of superiority playing hard to get.

"Don't bother."

"Like what?" Jonga insisted.

"Oh, Science, Mathematics and Latin."

"Can you talk Latin?"

"No."

"Then what 'e hell you study it for?"

"We translate."

"What's that?"

"Change it into English."

"C'mon speak some Latin."

"Drop it."

"Aw, c'mon."

"Forget it."

"Hell, I want to learn French."

"I want to talk American like Charles Starret," said Jonga, nasalizing his words. Broertjie ran up holding the oily parcel of fish and chips. Jonga unwrapped the newspaper covering and made two parcels. He took the major share and shoved aside the remainder.

"Grab, fellows!"

Broertjie dived. Amaai grabbed his ankles and they rolled over on the pavement, fish and chips spluttering from their clenched palms. Andrew watched in disgust while Jonga kicked Broertjie viciously in the ribs.

"Get up, you rude bastards. Must you behave like that before a guy in Standard 10?"

Andrew watched impassively, a slightly contemptuous sneer around his mouth. Broertjie and Amaai got to their feet, panting heavily and stuffing the remains of the fish

and chips into their mouths, spluttering and coughing.
Jonga offered Andrew some of his.

"Have some fish. The rude bastards!"

"No thanks."

"C'mon, have some."

"No!"

"You see. It's because you black swines have no bloody
manners," he said, addressing Amaai and Broertjie.

"It's not because of that," said Andrew.

Broertjie licked the greasy newspaper, then suddenly
looked in horror at Amaai.

"Jeeesus, you dirty!"

"What the hell is wrong?"

"Sis, you rotten!"

"What you mean?"

"You broke a wind!"

"You lie!"

"Can't you guys smell?"

"You lie, you bastard!"

Broertjie shoved the oily newspaper with scraps and
all into Amaai's face. Andrew felt nauseated. He still had
his mother to face. He wondered whether she had already
returned and whether she would tell James. Why should
she behave so peculiarly? Ask him once and then go
herself? He would certainly have run to Aunt Ella's if
she had waited a little.

"So long, chaps!"

"Where you going?"

"Home."

"Why so soon?"

"Have to."

"O.K. Don't go read Latin, hey, it make you mad!"

"Yeah."

"See you."

He battled his way up the street and turned in at
302. A drunk sat slobbering on the cement steps. He raced
furiously up the dark stairway and stopped abruptly on
the upper landing. Something was wrong. The dining-
room door stood wide open. Very, very unusual. Inside he
found a hum of activity. His mother lay immobile on the
bed and Jonga's mother, Mrs. Heidemann, and Aunt Ella
were fussing over her. He dreaded asking what was wrong,

knowing that Aunt Ella had always disliked him for some unaccountable reason. She now turned around angrily.

"Where you think you come from?"

He resented the question and felt like telling her to mind her own bloody business.

"Where you come from?"

He kept silent, reddening under his dark skin.

"Why must you allow your own mother to go out in the wind?" She received no answers to her questions.

"Where's James and Peter-boy?"

"I don't know," he replied for the first time.

"You better go out and find them. Go as fast as possible. Your mother's had a stroke."

10

Andrew had locked himself in the Boys' Room, and stood staring through the cracked french windows at nothing in particular. The south-easter had given way to raw gusts of cold, in-blowing winds, and mists swirled over Kloof Nek and Signal Hill. Ominous clouds chased across the sky from Table Bay. The street-lamps lighted up, glowing feebly in the early twilight. He couldn't remember how long he had stood there. Two hours. Maybe three.

A thin, pale rind of a moon swam between a rift in the clouds. Andrew stared moodily at it. Its appearance was icy and dispassionate, evoking no feeling or emotion. They must have fetched a doctor by now, as well as James and Peter-boy. Maybe his sisters were there as well, Miriam and Annette, with their husbands. All the way from the comforts of Walmer Estate, braving the wind, the slums and the indignity. He continually heard strange footsteps up and down the stairs and on the landings, and hushed voices filtered through from the dining-room. Would they blame him? Could he blame himself? He felt limp with fear and anxiety. He could make out the lights flickering on the lower slopes of Lion's Head and the dark outline of the City Hall and the Old Mutual. He could hear the wind chasing tin-cans up Caledon Street and whistling in the lower landing. He thought he heard the sound of crying. He jerked upright, attentive and all ears. If only they would leave him alone and not enter the Boys' Room. The crying became more pronounced and he nervously twitched his fingers, listening intently. What would James do to him if Aunt Ella told everything? Someone was fumbling at the doorknob.

"Andrew?" he heard his name whispered through the keyhole. He recognized Mrs. Heidemann's voice.

"Andrew?"

He stood tense and expectant.

"Andrew, open the door."

He started to pant.

"Open up, Andrew," she said knocking feebly.

He stood undecided for a moment, then turned the key and quickly resumed his former position. What the hell did the woman want?

"Andrew?"

He could feel her behind him.

"Andrew, listen to me!"

"Yeah."

"Your mother is dying."

He said nothing but could feel the saliva thickening in his mouth.

"Your mother's dying, my boy."

"Yeah."

"Don' you realize it?"

"Go away!"

She came up against him and put her arms around his neck pressing her cheek against his. He was overwhelmed by the smell of stale breath and perspiration.

"Andrew, dear."

He stared straight ahead of him with loathing.

"Poor boy."

"Go to hell!"

She dropped her arms, shocked.

"Andrew!"

"I said get the hell out of here!" He pushed her viciously and she stumbled, screaming, over the bed. He ignored her and walked quickly down the stairs into the street. A fine drizzle struck him full in the face, stinging his cheeks. He turned up the collar of his coat and walked towards Castle Bridge.

11

He passed Langman's shop which was brightly-lit and looked warm and cosy inside. Amaai was standing at the counter arguing with the young Indian shop assistant. Andrew walked quickly, hoping that he would not be spotted.

"Andrew! I say, Andrew!"

He stopped.

"Where you going?"

"Out."

"Where to?"

He was in no mood for company and wanted to get rid of Amaai as soon as possible.

"Where to?"

"Oh, just somewhere."

"In 'e blooming rain?"

"Yeah," he shrugged his shoulders.

"Can I come with you?"

"No."

"Aw, c'mon."

"No!"

"Broertjie went with Jonga to the Star."

"Why didn't you go?"

"Got no cash."

He sensed that Amaai wasn't merely interested in holding a friendly conversation.

"I hear your Ma's sick."

"Yeah."

"What happened to her?"

Andrew realized that Amaai was fishing for information he already had.

"I don't know."

He moved off abruptly. So everybody knew. Every bloody soul in District Six. Every Coloured busybody. He crossed the road to Castle Bridge to avoid Aunt Ella's house. It didn't matter much because the place was all in darkness and the curtains drawn. He continued without any fixed destination, past the corner pharmacy and the Castle, till he was surprised to find himself on the Grand

Parade. The square was almost deserted, with pools of standing water from the rain which he made no attempt to avoid. Opposite, the City Hall clock chimed 8 p.m. The fruit and ice-cream stalls were doing very little trade. A small group of Apostolics stood under a street-lamp near the public toilet, braving the drizzle. There were two weather-beaten men with guitars, the elder with his eyes tightly shut as he strummed and sang in a high-pitched voice. A middle-aged housewife and a small boy holding a pile of hymn-books made up the rest.

Empty garbage cans were scattered around and the colossal superstructure of the Post Office loomed overhead. Andrew, though contemptuous, felt part of this spiritual entity, overwhelmed by the concrete jungle of girders and asphalt, whose normal background was the revving of engines, the wailing of sirens and the sharp staccato of pneumatic drills. Things were unnaturally quiet now without the crowds and the cars and the fruit-hawkers and the flower-sellers and the taxis and the buses.

But for the insignificant group under the street-lamp. He joined them because he sadistically despised their irrational and rustic faith pitted against the slickness of urban sophistication. The little boy offered him a damp hymn-book which he refused. He wondered when he dared go home. Could he ever face his mother again? Guilt burnt inside him, ate and consumed him. Could he ever look her in the face after this? Suppose she died? He had only Mrs. Heidemann's word for it. The drunken bitch. But suppose his mother died? How would he ever live through that? She had always been strange in her attitude towards him. Sometimes gay and maternal and then suddenly cold and impulsive. He wondered whether it had anything to do with colour. She was fair, like James and Annette, whereas he was dark, the darkest in the family. Sometimes when they walked together in the street, he had a feeling that she was ashamed of him, even in District Six. She often called him piccanin, but there was a coldness when she said it. Something neutral. And then at times she acted impulsively, like going to Castle Bridge in the wind. What would James do once he knew? He had always been afraid of James. Everyone in the family was afraid of James. He remembered the time Peter-boy came home and said he had been dismissed from work for stealing cosmetics. James had grabbed him by the throat and throttled him. Peter-boy had struggled helplessly, turning blue, with spume bubbling from his mouth, and only the combined efforts of Danny, Philip and himself had prised James loose. His mother had watched without showing any reaction.

Andrew was vaguely aware of the pathetic group around him braving the skin-soaking drizzle. Two white women hurried through the rain for the bus-shelters. A drunk joined the prayer-circle, noisily chewing peanuts.

There was the time when his mother was washing-up in the scullery after supper and asked him to dry. He was engrossed in *Far from the Madding Crowd*. He had just discovered Hardy's Wessex and his mind was far away, deeply involved in the intricacies of sheep-farming and the rivalry of Gabriel Oak and Boldwood for the fair hand of Bathsheba.

"Andrew, I'm speaking."

"O.K."

"Are you going to dry up?"

"Yeah." He went on reading. He was just back at the Sheep Fair in Green-Hill when the first plate crashed to the floor. He looked up confused. She smashed another plate.

"No, Ma!"

A saucer crashed to the kitchen floor.

"Please!"

She coldly and methodically dashed all the crockery to the ground while he watched helplessly. There was nothing he could do when she acted like that.

The singing on the Grand Parade had drawn to its dreary conclusion and the younger of the two men was preaching in Afrikaans. The little boy shivered in the drizzle and clutched his hymn-books more tightly.

Then there was the time when she embarrassed him before a crowd. They were playing Charlie Chaplin shorts in the Brigade Hall. The place was crowded and a small group who could not get in was watching through an open window.

"Andrew!"

She stood on the outskirts of the group. He had a vantage point sitting on the window-sill.

"Andrew. Do you know it's already past eleven?" He felt his embarrassment mounting.

"If you don't come home at once I'll fetch James!"

The crowd tittered.

"Are you coming now!"

Then someone in the crowd commented.

"He's so black and you still want to speak English!"

The crowd roared with laughter. He edged his way out shamefacedly and slunk home crushed and humiliated. She sometimes did things like that. But there were times when she forgot their poverty and ignored the letters of demand she could not meet and shielded him from James and Peter-boy. They would sit in the kitchen, laughing and chatting like two old friends. She tried desperately to maintain a standard of shabby gentility, but the odds were heavily loaded against her. He only hoped to God she would be all right. He knew for a fact Mrs. Heidemann was lying. Must be lying, the dirty slut of a busybody. He couldn't imagine his mother dead. It just wasn't possible.

It was getting colder with dark mists swirling down from Table Mountain. The tiny group stood dwarfed by the buildings and the elements. The little boy's knuckles showed white where he clutched the hymn-books. The group stood with bowed heads for the last prayer.

The drunk stumbled noisily to the urinal.

Onse Vader . . .

He shut his eyes and folded his hands tightly.

Wat in die hemel is . . .

He hoped to God she would be all right, hoped with every nerve and fibre of his body.

Laat U naam geheilig word. Laat U koninkryk kom . . .

The rain stung his face and drops of water rolled uncomfortably under his collar.

Laat U wil geskied soos in die hemel, so ook op die aarde . . .

It wasn't his fault. James must understand that it wasn't his fault.

Gee ons vandag ons daaglikse brood . . .

She must live so that he could explain to her that he hadn't meant it. Never meant her to go in the wind.

En vergewe ons ons skulde, soos ons ook ons skuldenaars vergewe . . .

And forgive us our trespasses, as we forgive them that
trespass against us.

> *En lei ons nie in versoeking nie, maar verlos ons
> van die bose . . .*

But deliver us from evil.

> *Want aan U behoort die koninkryk . . .*

Mrs. Heidemann was a lying bitch, his mother wouldn't
die like that on him.

> *En die krag en die heerlikheid . . .*

If only he could be certain that she was all right. He
clenched his hands till the veins stood out.

> *Tot in die ewigheid . . .*

For ever and ever.

> Amen.

12

Outside the station Andrew caught a Hanover
Street bus home. It was almost deserted inside, which was
extremely unusual. He checked his money and found that
he could just manage his bus fare. It was senseless walking
home in the rain. Already he was soaking wet with his
socks squelching uncomfortably in his shoes. He stopped
with a jerk on the platform when he spotted James and
Annette in deep conversation in the front row. Mercifully
they had their backs to him. He hurriedly ran upstairs and
fell panting into the first seat. They couldn't have spotted
him, but nevertheless it had been a close shave. Did
James already know? Had Annette gone to fetch him at
the white pub in town? Where did the two come from?
The doctor? The hospital? He found himself involuntarily
shivering. His sister Miriam was all right, he got on well
with her, but Annette was different. She was fair and
rat-like in appearance like Peter-boy. She had found herself
pregnant at nineteen and had been forced to marry a man
she despised. Now she lived in Walmer Estate, materially
and socially well above her former level in District Six.
Her eldest son, Mervyn, was two years younger than
Andrew, but still struggling through Primary School. He
knew that Annette was jealous of his success at school.
He seldom visited her face-brick house in Walmer Estate

except at Christmas time, and she in turn seldom came to District Six. James and she had never got on together, so it must be serious if she was with him now.

The bus passed Castle Bridge and then tortuously manoeuvred its way up Hanover Street. It must be serious if they were together. Annette seldom bothered about any of them. At Tennant Street he saw the two alighting. Andrew was uncertain about his own movements and, jumping off at the Star Bioscope, stood in the foyer, half-noticing the garish posters advertising Sabu in *Elephant Boy*. He couldn't remain there all evening. Should he wait for Jonga and Broertjie to come out of the cinema or would it be best to go home and face the music? He nervously turned up Clifton Hill and walked in the direction of 302.

13

Andrew quietly tiptoed up the stairs. The dining-room door still stood open and he saw people sitting on the couch and chairs. He passed quickly so that he did not recognize anyone. Most probably Mrs. Heidemann and Aunt Ella would still be there. Daniel, Peter-boy, Philip, Miriam and Annette. And James. He only hoped that no one had heard him. All he wanted to do was to slip quietly into the Boys' Room and creep into bed. He hoped that no one would be there. He turned the knob softly and squeezed through the doorway. There was a slight creak.

Philip's bed was empty, but a bundle indicated where Danny was lying covered from head to foot in blankets. Andrew removed his wet jacket. He could see in the dark because of a slight ray of light which filtered through from the street lamp. He decided against lighting the candle and sat exhausted on his bed. He gently shook the sleeping figure.

"Danny," he whispered.

"Yes, Andrew?"

"Are you awake?"

"I've not been sleeping."

"Is it serious?"

"You mean Ma?"

"Yeah."

"Yes, it's serious."

"How's she now?"

"It's all over."

"What do you mean?"

"She's dead."

He wished he could react. Cry, scream, do anything. But he remained silent, showing no emotion. Danny lay facing the wall without moving.

"Why did you do it?"

"What?"

"They're blaming you."

"But I did nothing."

"Aunt Ella told everything."

"But it's true, I did nothing."

"You smacked Mrs. Heidemann."

"That's not true."

"She was hysterical."

"Is James home?"

"Yes, in the dining-room I think."

"And Ma?"

"They've taken her to the morgue."

"You must believe me, I did nothing, Danny."

"She asked you to go to Castle Bridge."

"I went."

"Afterwards."

"But I meant to go."

"It's too late now."

Andrew sat without moving. Danny lay facing the wall, refusing to turn around. He had to convince someone of his innocence. He felt limp and frightened, afraid to realize the enormity of the situation. A hard ball tightened in his stomach. The injustice of the false report about Mrs. Heidemann weighed heavily upon him.

"I didn't smack her," he protested feebly. "It's true, Danny."

There was no response.

"I didn't smack her."

He heard James's voice outside on the landing.

"Daniel, is Andrew back yet?"

He started shivering and his mouth suddenly felt full of saliva. He heard the door-knob turning and a match being struck. A flame glowed in his brother's cupped hand as he searched for the candle. The wick flickered feebly then sprang to life. James stared down at him.

"Where the hell have you been?"

"Out."

"Out where?"

"I went to the Grand Parade."

"While your mother was dying?"

There was no answer he could think of. All he knew was that he hadn't smacked Mrs. Heidemann.

"While your mother was dying?"

Andrew stared, as if hypnotized, at the candle.

"Why didn't you go out for Ma?"

"I went."

"Stop your lying, you black bastard!"

"But I went."

"Then why did Ma have to go?"

He had no reply to this. He swallowed saliva uncomfortably and the ball in his stomach tightened even more.

"Why didn't you go?"

Andrew didn't dare look up. James grabbed him by his shirt collar and hauled him to his feet.

"Why didn't you go, you black bastard?"

He couldn't avoid the flat hand as it slapped heavily across his face. His cheek stung.

"Why did you smack Mrs. Heidemann?"

"True as God, I didn't."

"You lying again, you black swine?"

He tried to turn his face away, but James put force behind the next blow.

"I didn't, James!"

His brother smacked again, this time harder and drawing blood. Danny sat up wide-eyed, not daring to interfere.

"You black bastard!"

A fist crashed into Andrew's face. He fell against the bed-rail, feebly trying to defend himself.

"I didn't smack her," he still protested.

"Stop your bloody lying!" James pulled him up from the bed. "You're not only a lying bastard, but a murderer as well!"

He felt sick and bilious with the nauseating taste of warm blood.

"You're a bloody murderer. You killed your own mother!"

Andrew now shivered uncontrollably, sick with pain, fear and helplessness. Suddenly he lashed out with his fists, getting James squarely on the chest. He hit furiously, screaming and clawing while striking out. He felt himself being torn away, people milling around him, faces, voices and more faces. Somebody poured brandy into his mouth. It burnt his raw and bleeding gums and he tried to struggle, but strong arms pinned him down and forced him to lie flat on the bed. He turned his face away and cried convulsively.

14

Broertjie lay back in the sun on Mrs. Heidemann's stoep listlessly watching the people outside 302. It was a warm Thursday afternoon, three days after the wind and the rains, and the cement was comfortably hot. Amaai and Jonga sat on either side of him, all three basking and fairly indifferent to the world around them. The hearse had not yet arrived, but three saloon cars, shiny and black, stood parked outside the Brigade Hall. Mourners continually fussed in and out of the tenement entrance; women in sober black and men in dark suits and ties stood whispering in solemn groups. The sun streamed down on the lazy trio, half-watching the proceedings. Jonga stared dispassionately at a fly buzzing around his scruffy toes.

"When I die, I don' wanna be buried in no blooming grave," he commented philosophically to no one in particular.

"Why not?" Amaai asked.

"Who wants to rot in 'e ground?"

"Then what do you want?"

"I wanna be burnt."

"That cost a lotta money."

"I don't care a damn."

"They can sell your body to 'e University."

"What they do with it there?"

"Cut it up."

"Why?"

"They study yer insides."

"Hell, it's a sin."

"What?"

"Fer white people to study yer insides."

"Why they do it?"

"They fin' out about diseases."

"They pay you?"

"Sure. You get cash."

"They can't pay you if yer dead."

"Then who the hell gets the money?"

"Oh, yer ma or someone."

The fly left Jonga to land on Broertjie's knee. Deftly he caught it in his cupped hand and then squashed it against the cement with his thumbnail.

"I wonder what Andrew's gonna do now."

"Yeah, I wonder."

"They say he ran away."

"Why?"

"His brother beat him up."

"I know. He smacked my ma," Jonga said.

"What you gonna do about it?"

"F—— him up when I get him."

"He's a nice guy!"

"He smacked my ma."

"He's O.K."

"Who the hell he think he is 'cause he's educated?"

"He's O.K. He's a clever guy."

"What the hell does that matter."

They watched the local parish priest weaving his way down the street. He wore his cassock which he carefully prevented from getting soiled on the pavement. Under his arm he clutched a gilt-edged Bible and prayer-book. Amaai eyed him suspiciously.

"I don' like priests."

"I don't like that one," Jonga said knowingly.

"I hear things about him."

"Like what?"

"Real bad things."

"Yeah?"

"Honger and Tana told me."

"I don' believe it."

"It's true."

"Like hell."

"True as Gawd!"

"You got proof?"

"Ask Honger and Tana."

"Tana's a liar."

"So's your ma and pa."

"Leave my ma and pa out of it."

"Aw, drop dead!"

Those outside followed the priest up the stairs. Annette arrived, dressed fashionably in a skin-tight black dress, sniffing at a bottle of smelling-salts and supported by her husband and son Mervyn. James appeared on the balcony for a brief moment, looked searchingly down and then disappeared back into the Boys' Room. Amaai reverted to the subject of Andrew.

"They say he wouldn't go out for his ma."

"Yeah, the same afternoon he was with us."

"So she went out in the wind and got a stroke."

"So he smacked your ma?"

"Who?"

"Andrew."

"Yeah, he smacked my ma."

"You see what comes of education?"

"Matric and Latin and that sorta thing. He's too bloody clever."

"I wonder if she gotta stroke because of him?"

"Sure."

"Can people die from a stroke?"

"Sure. They can die from anything."

"What about Honger's ma?"

"What about her?"

"She drank a Bubbly Cola so she died."

"And his mother drank a Bubbly so she died."

"Den she fried!"

"An' she cried!"

"On her side!"

"So his mother drank a Bubbly an' she died!"

They rolled over on the warm cement, clutching one another and shrieking with laughter.

"Jeesus, you're a poet."

"Must send it to the *Argus!*"

"So his mother drank a Bubbly an' she died!"

They sat up exhausted with laughing. Broertjie choked, which produced further peals of laughter. Funeral-goers stared at them shocked and horrified.

"Hey, shurrup!" said Jonga, trying to keep a straight face. "Haven't you respect for a bloody funeral?"

"Yeah, we better shurrup."

"Behave your bloody selves!"

They tried to control their laughter. Broertjie looked at Amaai, biting his lips.

"So his mother drank a Bubbly an' she died!"

They rolled over again on the stoep and laughed against the cement pavings.

"Hey, cut it out," Jonga warned. "Here comes Andrew's brother."

James was dressed in a black suit. He was freshly, but badly, shaven, his neck bristly. The boys suspected that he was coming to reprimand them. They watched him making his way through the crowd in the doorway and crossing the street to the stoep.

"He can't bloodywell stop us," Broertjie said, on the defensive. "I can laugh when I like."

"Let's tell him to go to hell, the damn play-white," Amaai added with pseudo-bravado.

"They say he's blooming tough."

James came up to where they were sitting, paused for a brief moment, then cleared his throat. It was obviously an effort for him to condescend to speak to the youngsters.

"You are Andrew's friends?" he asked.

"Whose?"

"My brother, Andrew's."

"Sure."

"Sure, yes, we know him."

"Do you know where he is now?"

"No."

"He disappeared three nights ago."

"Hell!"

"He's not back yet."

"So?"

"The funeral's in an hour's time."

"An' you want us to find him?"

"Yes. Here's half a crown. Try and find him."

He turned self-consciously and walked back across the street. Broertjie and Amaai stared at the half-crown in Jonga's hand.

"Hell!"

"Christ alive!"

"Where do you think he can be?"

"In Bioscope maybe!"

"No!"

"Maybe he wen' to the Library!"

"No!"

"Or the Swimming Baths!"

"No!"

"Mus' we go an' search for him?"

"Where the devil will we find him?"

"He can go to hell for my part, he slapped my ma."

"On her side!"

"Den she cried!"

"An' she lied!"

"So his mother drank a Bubbly an' she died!"

15

It was late the same evening, three days after he had left home, that Andrew slowly walked up Hanover Street to Miriam's place in Nile Street. He was hungry and dirty and suffering acutely from lack of sleep. A yellow Van Gogh moon hung over Table Bay and the night air was ominous and electric. He wondered what his sister would say. Miriam was easier to get on with than Annette. She was almost as dark as himself, quiet and detached. He had never really known her. She had married a bus driver when Andrew was eight and had then gone to stay in Walmer Estate, seldom visiting District Six.

He remembered her wedding day clearly. She had washed him in a tin bath over the lavatory, before preparing herself. He had sat next to his mother in a hired car, stiff and uncomfortable in a new navy-blue suit and patent-leather shoes, his hair sleek with coconut-oil. And then the wedding at St. Mark's and the photographs at Kirstenbosch and then to the reception at the Fidelity Hall. They had played the Wedding March from Mendelssohn's *Mid-*

summer Night's Dream Overture and he had shyly been introduced to a flower-girl whom he had discovered had the same Godmother as himself. He wondered what Miriam would say. Would she be angry because he had not attended the funeral? Would she believe that he had murdered his mother?

He passed Sheppard Street and noticed as he approached Zonnebloem how the houses became less mean and grimy. They were now pleasant and solidly-built with neat lawns and gardens and electricity and bathrooms. . . . He turned down Nile Street and stopped outside Miriam's gate. A light was burning in the lounge and he hesitated, uncertain what her reaction would be to his sudden appearance. He had been to her place only twice since her marriage, twice within the last eight years. He envied people living in Walmer Estate. Their comfort and sophistication. Upper-class Coloureds with electric stoves, refrigerators and venetian blinds on their windows. As soon as a family established itself, it moved to Walmer Estate and made a definite point of forgetting the past.

He walked hesitantly up the garden path and rang the bell. No one answered. He wondered whether her husband, Kenneth, would be home. Should he leave at once before anyone answered? But where else could he go? Back to James? He rang again and thought he detected a movement behind the door. Miriam whispered through the keyhole.

"Who's there?"

"Me. Andrew."

There was a pause, then she fumbled with the key and opened the door.

"Come in."

She ushered him along a narrow passage into her kitchen.

"Have you eaten yet?"

"No."

"Well, let's see what there is. Wash your face and hands in the bathroom. There should be a clean towel."

She fussed around the kitchen, heating coffee, cutting bread and frying bacon and eggs. Miriam was slightly built, with her mother's good looks which she still retained at thirty. Although Andrew had hardly eaten since he left home, he had not really given a thought to food. Now, however, he felt ravenous. Miriam proceeded to lay the table.

"I'm sorry, there's only bacon and eggs."

"That's fine, thanks."

"I only cook for Kenneth and myself, and we've eaten already."

"Where's Kenneth now?" he asked.

"He works night-shift on the buses. He's a driver now, but you wouldn't know that because you haven't been to see us."

He accepted the mild rebuke in silence. He knew he was guilty of anti-social behaviour, but then she seldom, if ever, came to Caledon Street. He sensed that she was deliberately avoiding the happenings of the last few days. She must have known all about it and missed him at the funeral.

"All right, Andrew, your food is ready."

She left to fetch her knitting. He ate quickly, not daring to look up when she reappeared. He concentrated on his plate to try and avoid her eyes. When he had finished he dropped his knife and fork nervously.

"Had enough?"

"Yes, thanks."

"There's some cheese and bread."

"No, thanks."

"Marmalade?"

"No, thanks. I've had enough."

"Sure?"

"Quite sure."

"Let me give you some coffee."

After she had poured two cups, she sat back. There was an uncomfortable silence. Miriam picked up her knitting and clicked busily at a jersey for Kenneth, her eyes fixed on a pattern in the *Ladies Home Journal*. Andrew felt he had to say something, had to speak, explain himself.

"Miriam."

"Yes?"

"Do you believe I killed Ma?"

"No."

A feeling of relief slowly came over him.

"She asked me to go to Aunt Ella."

"Yes?"

"And I didn't go because of the wind."

"That was wrong."

"But I went afterwards."

"I know."

"And when I came home, I found Ma was dying."

"She had had a stroke."

"Miriam, was I the cause of it?"

He looked at her intensely, his lips quivering.

"No, you were not."

"Am I a murderer?"

"No."

"James said so."

"James is wrong."

"But he said I killed Ma."

"You mustn't blame him, he was beside himself."

"And I didn't smack Mrs. Heidemann."

"I'm sure you didn't."

"I pushed her because she tried to put her arms around me."

Miriam smiled wryly which added to his confusion.

"I mean she tried to comfort me. I mean . . . Miriam, you know what I mean."

"All right, Andrew, I know."

"So I pushed her."

There was a pause punctuated by the clicking of knitting-needles. He knew what Miriam's next question would be and dreaded it.

"Why were you not at the funeral today?"

There was another silence. The needles clicked busily. He pulled himself together with an effort.

"I was afraid, Miriam."

"Of whom?"

"Of James and Peter-boy. And Annette and Philip and Danny. And you."

"You need not have feared me."

"But most of all I was afraid of Ma."

She looked at him strangely and then concentrated on the pattern in the magazine. Her fingers continued busily.

"I think I understand."

"After James hit me, I walked to the Foreshore and then along the National Road. Night and day. I walked and walked till I decided to come to you."

"Three days?"

"Yes."

"You missed school."

"I realize that."

"Are you going back?"

"I don't know. I don't think so."

He paused, struggling with the next statement.

"Miriam, I'm afraid to go back to James."

"What else can you do?"

"May I stay with you?"

"I can't really say. I must speak to Kenneth and James about it. We haven't over-much room here."

"I have nowhere else to go."

"I must first discuss it with Kenneth."

He felt weak, helpless and insecure. He hated Caledon Street and 302. He was afraid of James. To go back to those rooms filled with the memory of his mother? To the dirt and squalor of slum life? District Six? And Jonga and Broertjie and Amaai? Drunk Mrs. Heidemann and Aunt Ella?

"Please, Miriam, I would like to stay with you."

"I will have to speak to Kenneth."

She poured more coffee for the two of them and they sipped it in silence. When they had finished she got up in a business-like manner.

"Well, I'll make your bed in the spare room. I think you'll need some rest. Have a bath first. The tap with the red dot is the hot water."

For a long time he lay awake, wide-eyed and alert. Would James throw him out and wash his hands of him completely? Mother-killer. He flinched involuntarily as he thought of it. A car pulled up. Andrew knew it must be Kenneth. He heard footsteps crunching up the path and the key turning in the lock. He remembered his brother-in-law as always having been aloof and somewhat distant. A pale, sickly-white skin and dull, expressionless, green eyes. He wondered what Kenneth would say. Would he be annoyed because Andrew had not attenneed the funeral?

After a long silence he heard voices filtering through from their bedroom. They were obviously discussing him, and Miriam seemed to be dominating the conversation. He strained his ears to hear more clearly, but the sounds were indistinct and unintelligible. Finally he fell into a deep sleep, exhausted physically and mentally.

He was still half asleep, when he heard Miriam drawing the curtains apart. For a moment he did not know where he was, then everything came back to him in a flood.

"Up you get, it's seven o'clock."

"I'm sorry, Miriam."

"You must be in time for school."

He tried to protest. He had no clean clothes, his books were still in Caledon Street, he wasn't even sure whether he had a home.

"Come on, lazy-bones. Get cleaned up while I get breakfast ready. Then you go home first—remind me to give you the bus fare—and change your clothes and get your books. James will be at work, so you're safe. When Kenneth wakes up he'll fetch the rest of your things."

"Miriam."

"It's all right. I'll look after you. Now, out of bed!"

He almost wept as he went to the bathroom. To belong somewhere again. Live in Walmer Estate away from James and Peter-boy. And Broertjie and Amaai. He would miss Danny. And Ma. But the sun filtered brightly through the bathroom window.

16

It was while Ruth was having a shower that the two detectives had called. In fact she was thinking of Andrew, hoping he wouldn't do anything foolish. She knew that he had been raided quite a few times, and the situation was becoming even more tense. Sometimes, especially lately, his attitude had been strange. He was deep in thought for long periods, never spoke and played endless records. He also smoked far too much. If her parents should know about the two of them. Hell, Thank God they were far away in the Transvaal. The last letter from her father had been a hastily scrawled note about Sharpeville, how he went about armed and how he had taught her mother to shoot. The natives were becoming more arrogant. Look after yourself, my dear, and trust no non-

European. They are all alike, all of them. And she was ready to give up everything for a Coloured man. Everything, even her parents. But they had never really understood her. She had never really understood herself. Maybe it was best that she had come to Cape Town to study Drama and get away from the stifling atmosphere of her hometown. They had treated her well, she really had no complaints, an only child, daughter of James B. Talbot, stockbroker, who was prepared to give her all she wanted, even his consent to her coming to a University in the Cape, though with fears and misgivings. She turned on more hot water and allowed the shower to play over her shoulders and neat breasts. If only Andrew would come. She liked to watch him while he listened to records. The way he combed his hair, his full lips and square chin, and the arch of his neck. The door-bell rang. That must be Andrew. She dried herself hastily, leaving the shower running.

"Coming, dear!"

It rang again.

"Don't be so impatient!" she answered lightly.

Ruth slipped into a dressing-gown and slippers and ran a towel quickly over her black hair. She tripped happily to the door, intending to surprise him by suddenly jerking it open. She smiled pleasantly as she pulled hard, then her face fell.

"You Miss Ruth Talbot?"

"Yes?" she said as she surveyed the two men.

"We want to speak to you."

"What about?"

"I'm a Detective-Sergeant of the Political Branch."

"Oh?" she said limply, suddenly feeling faint and dizzy. She stood stupidly barring the doorway, not quite knowing what to do.

"We would like to come in."

"Why, certainly."

She stood aside and the detectives entered, their eyes searching the room. She was very conscious of the fact that she was only wearing her dressing-gown.

"Excuse me!"

"Where you going?"

"To dress."

"All right," the detective said suspiciously.

She came back straightening her skirt and tossed her wet hair behind her shoulder.

"You are a University student, Miss Talbot?"

"Yes?"

"Not originally from Cape Town?"

"No, I'm from Transvaal."

"Vereeniging?"

"Yes."

"That's very far away."

"So?"

"We are here to protect you."

"Do I need protection?"

"We think so. These are troubled times. Do your parents know?"

"Know what?"

"About Andrew Dreyer."

She felt limp again and knew that her face was giving her away. Control. That was important. She must control herself. She did not know how much they knew. The other detective was going through her books.

"What about Mr. Dreyer?"

"You know him?"

"I have seen him at University."

"You are, let us put it this way, rather intimate friends?"

"I have spoken to him once or twice on the campus."

"Nothing more between you?"

"I don't know what you're driving at."

"You are more than intimate friends?"

"I object to your question."

"That won't help you, Miss Talbot. I'm sure you have heard of the Immorality Act."

"I suppose I have."

"Six months in gaol is no joke."

"If you have nothing more to say, I beg you to leave."

"We are at the moment busy contacting your parents."

"Oh!" she said, feeling her world collapsing.

"Where is he now?"

"Who?"

"Andrew Dreyer."

"How should I know?"

"Are you quite sure?"

She remained silent until she suddenly realized that Andrew might be coming at any minute.

"Yes. I'm sure. Please go!"

Her ears listened for the slightest crunch on the step. The other detective disappeared into her kitchen.

"You know that your boy-friend is a trouble-maker."

"That's none of my business."

"That he has contact with the P.A.C. and Congress."

"So?"

"Are you prepared to identify yourself with people who break the law? Rabble-rousers? Communist sympathizers?"

"Why are you telling me all this?"

"Because we want to help you."

"Please leave me alone. I have nothing more to say."

"All right, Miss Talbot. You are apparently not prepared to co-operate with us. It's not healthy for you."

"Please go!"

They left, and she was terrified in case they met Andrew on their way down. She peeped through the French windows and saw them getting into their car and pulling away. Then she buried her face in the pillows on the couch and cried quietly. The shower continued to run.

Oh God! She had better warn Andy. Phone him up. No, that would be risky. There were rumours that lines were being tapped. Better go to Grassy Park. She rubbed her hair with a towel, trying to dry it. Then she put on her duffle-coat. Where the devil were her car keys? The damn shower was still running. So they knew everything. How much did they know? Her parents in Vereeniging. Well, Andy must be warned. She hastily scribbled a note and put it into an envelope with a spare key. She pinned instructions on her door. Then she ran down the steps and dropped the envelope into the letter-box. At the car park, she looked around to see whether it was quite safe. She had been too confused to notice what kind of car the Special Branch had used. Suppose they followed her? She unlocked the door of her Austin and slipped in. She drove steadily, watching her rear mirror in case she was being followed. It must be Andy they were trying to get at. They had been gunning for him a long time. Strange that he had not yet been dismissed from school, but he always claimed that it was merely a matter of time. She could have phoned Abe, now she came to think of it, and told him to contact Andy. No, that would take too much time. She turned down deserted Klip Road into Lake Road and parked outside Mrs. Carollissen's house.

Eldred answered the doorbell. She liked the boy. Handsome and intelligent and always smiling. Andy had once said that he was the only likeable member of the Carolissen household.

"Hallo, Eldred, how were the Sports today?"

"Fine, thanks."

"You do well?"

"Passably."

"Mr. Dreyer at home?"

"No, he's not in."

Her face fell. Where could she find him if he didn't come to the flat?

"He hasn't arrived yet?"

"Well, he has, but he left again."

"Have you any idea where he's gone to?"

"Well, not really."

"Eldred!" she heard Mrs. Carollissen's voice. "Who's at the door?"

"It's Miss Talbot."

Mrs. Carollissen bustled down the passage.

"Oh. Step inside." There was a cold ring in her voice. Ruth entered the lounge and sat down. She could feel her damp hair sticking clammily to her neck.

"Good evening, Mrs. Carollissen. I thought I might find Andy in."

"I'm sorry, he's not here."

"Oh dear. It's important that I see him as soon as possible."

"I would prefer it if you never saw him again."

"I'm sorry if I have in any way offended you. I will stay away from here if you prefer it."

"I run a decent house."

"I hope you haven't found my appearance objectionable."

"No. I only don't want any trouble."

"Why? Is Andy in trouble?"

"There were detectives here for him."

"They came to my flat as well. That is why I came to try and warn him."

"Well, I cannot allow that sort of thing here."

Eldred appeared in the doorway and stood listening.

"But Andy hasn't done anything wrong."

"It's against the law for the two of you to be together."

"But we love each other, Mrs. Carollissen."

"I didn't make the law."

"Can't you see he's the only person I really care for?"

"He's a Coloured man."

"Should that make a difference?"

"Look. I have a husband and five children and I cannot allow detectives all over the place. I have to protect my home. I will not expose myself to scandal. My husband has a good job and is an elder in the Church. All my children are still at school."

"You're talking rubbish, Mother," Eldred cut in angrily.

"Who's asking your opinion? Go to your room!"

"But you're being silly!"

"Go to your room at once! I'll see your father about you."

Eldred bit his lip and walked out of the front door, banging it behind him.

"Rude devil. Is that what they teach them at Steenberg High? No, Miss Talbot, there's nothing I can do about Mr. D. I've spoken to my husband about it and he agrees. Mr. D. must leave."

"But where can he go?"

"He's single and a teacher. He earns a good salary and should be able to find a place somewhere. I believe he has a sister staying in Walmer Estate."

"But surely he has done nothing wrong?"

"I cannot allow detectives around my place."

"Do you see anything immoral in our loving each other?"

"It's against the law."

"Weren't you in love yourself once?"

"I have children to protect."

"Mrs. Carollissen, you must try and help us. Or rather try and help Andy."

"When he comes back here he will have to leave. Vincent and Paul will pack his things in the meantime. I can't ask Eldred to do anything."

"What if he ends up in gaol?"

"It's his own affair. He's a grown-up man. I cannot allow that sort of thing to go on in my home."

Ruth realized the uselessness of pursuing the argument any further.

"Where can I find Andy now?"

"I haven't the slightest idea. I sent Eldred to warn him not to come home tonight."

"So he won't be back?"

"I hope not."

"Well then, thank you very much, Mrs. Carollissen. Good night."

"Good night."

Mrs. Carollissen shut the door firmly behind her. Eldred stood waiting at the Austin.

"That bloody woman," he said heatedly. "She's just plain bloody stupid!"

"She's afraid, Eldred. Everyone is these days."

"Mr. Dreyer said that if anybody wanted him, they should phone Abe, I mean Mr. Hanslo."

"Thanks a lot. I'll do that when I get home."

"Best of luck."

"And to you, Eldred. Don't be too hard on your mother."

"That blooming woman!"

She climbed into her car and reversed into Lake Road.

17

The record had long stopped playing when Andrew got up to refill his glass. The day's events seemed far away, and he now felt more settled and comfortable. Life with Miriam and Kenneth had followed its own quiet and even tempo. The garden was a profusion of dahlias, zinnias, phlox and snapdragons. White, mauve, orange and brilliant red. Andrew fitted in well and Nile Street suited him. The subject of his mother was never mentioned. James he had seen once, and once only, the evening following his arrival at Miriam's, when his sister, Kenneth and James had held a long conference in the kitchen. He had sat in the spare room with palpitating heart, while his future was being decided for him. Miriam's raised voice had filtered through, she seemed to do most of the talking, and James had finally left in a temper, banging the door behind him. Miriam never told him about the discussion, and Kenneth he seldom saw, except on Sundays. Andrew kept to himself, studied hard and read voraciously, trying all the time to appear as inconspicuous as possible. He never for one moment missed Caledon Street and Jonga and Broertjie and Amaai. Sometimes he thought wistfully of Danny, and he heard from Miriam that Peter-boy had left home.

Every weekday morning he met Abe Hanslo and Justin Bailey, two of his classmates, at College Street corner, and together they would walk along Constitution Street, past the high-stoeped houses where whites lived cheek-by-jowl with Coloureds, past dingy, mean Indian shops, till they turned off near Constitution Street Flats.

Abe was a bit of a dreamer, excellent at languages, with a flair for expressing himself well. He was fanatical about politics. Fair, with freckles around the nose, and green eyes and a mop of fair hair. Justin, on the other hand, was an extrovert. He discussed everything and argued heatedly, and was on friendly terms with all his schoolmasters, whom he referred to privately with great relish by their Christian names. These two were a contrast to Jonga, Broertjie and Amaai. Andrew was determined to blot out the memory of the slums, the dirt, the poverty. He remembered the feeling of shame and humiliation he had experienced when Miriam had told him that Justin and Abe had come to pay their respects in Caledon Street after his mother had died. He was glad he had not been home. He wondered how they had reacted. Had they realized before that he lived in a slum?

For a short time afterwards he had avoided Abe and Justin, but they showed no difference in their attitude towards him. He decided to seal his District Six background forever in the limbo of the past.

In the mornings on their way to school, his two friends usually discussed school life, sports and politics. Mostly politics. Andrew seldom joined in the conversation. He suffered from acute self-consciousness tinged with a strong feeling of inferiority.

"You know," Justin would begin. "I'm sorry I was born Coloured."

"Oh, rubbish!" Abe would cut him short.

"I mean because of all it means in South Africa."

"What on earth is that?"

"Well, you know. Whites only, Non-Europeans Keep Out, all the humiliation."

"One only becomes Coloured when one thinks of oneself as Coloured."

"Do I?"

"Yes, if you think in terms of Coloured, white, African and so on."

"But there are different races. There is a difference."

"It's artificial."

"Then what the hell are you?"

"I'm South African."

"Coloured South African?"

"There is no such animal as a Coloured South African or a European South African. There are only South Africans."

Andrew listened admiringly to the discussion. The generalities, truisms, semantics. What a difference between these youths and Jonga and Broertjie. Abe, he discovered, read widely, Cedric Dover, Howard Fast, Dostoyevsky, Thomas Paine. He was an executive member of the Modern Youth Association, a radical students' organization, and usually returned from discussions and lectures with what Justin referred to as half-digested scraps of political theory. Justin usually started the argument from something he had heard or read. He had a genius for not being original.

"You know Chinese are accepted as Europeans in South Africa?"

"I have always considered China and Europe as two distinctly different places."

"Chinese are allowed to sit in the reserved seats on trains and are allowed in white cinemas."

"What a crazy situation."

"While we are kept out."

"Segregation works only one way in this country. Against Coloureds, Africans and Indians."

"So you do use those terms. I thought you were ostentatiously South African."

"I use racial terms only as a matter of convenience."

"And you have the nerve to call me a racialist?"

"I have said before that race barriers are artificial."

"Do you want to attend a white cinema?"

"I just want to attend cinemas."

"White cinemas?"

"Any cinemas."

"You go to a segregated Coloured High School?"

"I have no alternative."

"Therefore you accept segregation."

"No!"

"You attend white sports meetings?"

"No. Do you?"

"Sometimes."

"Why?"

"I can learn something from them."

"From your segregated seat on the grandstand?"

"Why not?"

"Are you prepared to learn at the expense of your principles?"

"Isn't that what you are doing at a Coloured school?"

"That's different."

The argument would continue in the Quadrangle till the bell rang for the first period. Andrew admired Abe for his tenacity in argument. He always silently disagreed with Justin, although he knew the latter was often right. There was something about Justin which rubbed him up the wrong way. Like Herby Solomons. He was a play-white, was Herb, and lived in the European area above Mountain Road. He sat at a rear desk and seldom spoke to anyone other than Abe. Justin told Andrew in confidence that all Herby's friends were play-whites whom he had convinced that he was a student at Cape Town High. For that reason he walked all the way to Oranjezicht every afternoon when school closed, and took a bus from the white Institution. Andrew and Justin ignored him openly.

They would usually stroll home at a leisurely pace, Justin and Abe arguing all the way. Miriam would be waiting and prepare his lunch in her quiet, efficient way.

Time passed and November came rich and warm, which meant the start of Matriculation examinations. Hard work and furious cramming. Latin hexameters, the Extension of Pythagoras, the importance of the supernatural in *Macbeth*, atomic weights. He found no difficulty in adapting himself to his new surroundings. What a difference between this and Caledon Street. Even the air smelt cleaner, and

from his window he could see the broad sweep of Table
Bay with Robben Island in the distance.

Abe had often invited him to visit him at home, but
he had always declined out of self-consciousness. One
evening, taking a break from studying, he walked up towards De Waal Drive to Abe's home, and after long
hesitation rang the bell.

He was surprised at the comfort and luxury of the
place. Abe had a large study to himself, pleasantly furnished, with Gauguin and Utrillo reproductions on the
wall. In one corner stood a record player on which were
records of Beethoven, Mozart and Smetana. How different
from the Boys' Room at 302. It was here that he had
first heard the *Moldau*.

"I like your room," he said self-consciously.

"Oh, it's all right."

"It must be wonderful to study here."

"I manage."

"You know, Abe, I've been thinking."

"You don't say."

"You're always talking politics to Justin."

"So?"

"About poverty and oppression."

"Yes?"

"With all this around you?"

"These are material things."

"They are nevertheless important."

"Not fundamental."

"One only realizes the value of material things when
one has never had them."

"Does one really?"

"Yes. I grew up somewhat differently. In a slum to
be exact."

"Distict Six."

"Yes, District Six. Caledon Street. I've known poverty."

"So where does that leave you?"

"It eats away the soul."

"Poverty is not your monopoly."

"But can you ever understand what I'm talking about,
Abe? The filth, the grime. Prostitutes. Street fights. People
with no aim in life except to eke out their miserable
existences on their Friday night's pay."

"I can appreciate that."

"I had three friends."

"Yes?"

"Close friends. Broertjie, Jonga and Amaai. Jonga had been to a Reformatory."

"Yes?"

"I'm sorry if I'm boring you."

"You're not, go on."

"They were my friends. I had no other choice."

"You sound as if you're apologizing."

"I existed in two worlds. I used to leave school in the afternoon to go back to District Six."

"I understand."

"Do you still accept me as a friend?"

"Don't be silly. You're being self-conscious over nothing. I couldn't care less where you came from."

"I'm glad. I thought you might be like Herby."

"Herb's O.K. He can't help himself."

"He's a play-white."

"He's a victim of this society as much as we are."

"But surely he can think for himself?"

"I think we should try and understand people like him. It's easy for Herby to cross the colour-line. He's fair and his hair is O.K. It means advantages. No abuses. Better facilities. All that goes with the divine rights of a white skin."

"Then what about you?"

"There's too much at stake."

"For you?"

"For all of us."

"Do you think this crazy set-up will ever change?"

"It must."

Andrew left feeling wonderfully refreshed. He walked home past Zonnebloem, taking a roundabout route, thinking of Gauguin and Smetana, politics and friends like Abe. District Six seemed miles away. He hummed snatches of the *Moldau* as he walked down Nile Street.

Then the examination heat was on. Swotting till three in the morning. Livy, Catullus, Cicero. Vivamus mea Lesbia atque amemus. Endless cups of black coffee. The dagger scene from *Macbeth*. Trace the importance of Gabriel Oak. Wordsworth's naturalism. Bleary eyes and a tired struggling brain. Boyle's Law, Dalton's Atomic Theory. Kipp's Apparatus provides a ready and steady supply of gas. The oppressive silence of the early hours of the morning. Pythagoras's theorem for acute angles. Diminished by twice the rectangle formed by one of the sides and the projection on it of the other. Parabola faces mouth downwards. Find Log 1.765. Logs, Catullus, dactylic hexameters, Malcolm and Donalbain. Words, words, words till the brain could take no more and he fell asleep at his table.

And then filing into examination places. Candidates will leave all books outside the examination room. Print your names on the cover and use only the right-hand pages of your answer book. It is now nine o'clock. You will stop at twelve.

And then the pace slackened till the examinations were a thing of the past, and the long, lazy December vacation stretched ahead, and the waiting for results.

18

What worried Andrew most was what was to become of him once his examination results were out. Would he have to go and look for work? Would Kenneth and Miriam be prepared to see him through University or College? What he wanted most was to become a teacher. To be able to dramatize situations, delineate characters, discuss symbolism, imagery. What he dreaded was working in an office. He knew there was no such thing as a Coloured clerk. It was a euphemism for a glorified office-boy earning a miserable salary for skilled work. The monotony of a routine job. Invoices and accounts and sitting at a desk. Miriam had never mentioned future plans to him. If she had discussed it with Kenneth, he knew nothing about it. Many times he had been on the verge of broaching the subject, but had always retreated into a confused and self-conscious silence.

The holiday season came with a flourish. He spent Christmas Eve alone as Kenneth and Miriam had gone to a party at Annette's place. Christmas dinner was the traditional poultry, roast potatoes and heavy puddings, while the

sun blazed down from an enamel-blue sky. Then came the
hot summery days before New Year with the waves of
heat rising from the tarred streets.

Late on New Year's Eve he decided to see the lights in
Adderley Street. He instinctively hesitated when he reached
Tennant Street. This was the nearest he had been to
Caledon Street since he had left home. He hated the surroundings, and unpleasant memories flooded back. People
sat fanning themselves on the pavements, pot-bellied children played in the gutter, a drunk muttered to himself in
a damp lane. Andrew felt on sense of belonging to it. He
had never really been part of it. He found that he could
not see the slum from a detached point of view, like a
tourist. At most he could take a dispassionate interest in
it.

Instead of continuing to Adderley Street, he turned
away and walked into Caledon Street. District Six wore a
carnival air. District Number Six. Coloured streamers
fluttered across grimy lanes displaying the favours of various Coon troupes. At New Year they would march. The
coons would come. A rollicking, gyrating, satiny profusion
of movement and colour. Brilliant reds, greens, oranges
and blues. Sweating, prancing, dancing and laughing to
forget the misery of the rest of the year.

New Year was always sultry and hot, even at night, and
Andrew perspired freely. He hated perspiring. At 302 it
had meant washing in cold water over the kitchen sink in
which they also cleaned the crockery and eating utensils.
People lounged in doorways, speaking in subdued, desul-
tory tones. Andrew spotted Amaai sitting alone outside the
Brigade Hall. For a moment he regretted not having gone
on to Adderley Street.

"Hello, Amaai!" They had not seen each other for nine
months.

"Oh hello, Andrew." Amaai looked up from an American comic he was trying to read under an indifferent street
lamp.

"How's things?"

"So, so."

"Where's the rest?"

"They're all in the Coons. Jonga's in the Mississippi
Darkies and Broertjie's in the Philadelphian Gentlemen
Jazz Minstrels."

"And you?"

"As usual, no luck."

"Why not?"

"No cash for my costume."

"I see."

"But what's happened to you, Andrew?"

"I'm staying in Walmer Estate now."

"You select, hey?"

"Not really."

"Real upper-class Coloured."

"Because I stay in Walmer Estate?"

"Ja Man, with your education and science and those things. One day you won't look at us."

Andrew winced and kept silent.

"You still study Latin?"

"I've finished my exams."

"You pass?"

"The results only come out in January."

"I'm sure you'll pass."

"I hope so."

"You're a bloody clever guy, even if you come from District Six."

Andrew flinched as the words cut deep.

"Don't forget us when you become a professor, hey!"

"I'm not likely to become one!"

Andrew felt an insatiable curiosity to know more about 302. After all Miriam never mentioned the family apart from telling him about Peter-boy's departure.

"How's my people?"

"Who?"

"Danny, Peter-boy and Philip?"

"Why, don't you know?"

"No."

"Don't you ever go upstairs?"

"No."

"Philip left home."

"Why?"

"I don't know. All I heard was that he left."

"Where does he stay now?"

"With your sister."

"Annette?"

"I think so."

"And the rest?"

"James had a fight with Peter-boy."

"Why?"

"I don't know."

"Who told you?"

"Jonga."

"How does he know?"

"His ma told him."

"So what happened to Peter-boy?"

"He also left."

"For where?"

"I don't know."

"Now who's left?"

"James and Danny."

"Only the two?"

"Yeah."

"Who looks after them?"

"Your Aunt Ella cooks and cleans."

"I see. What's James like lately?"

"We never see him."

"Isn't he at home?"

"Seldom."

"Oh."

Andrew felt the information depressing him. He had a kind of revulsion about hearing news of his family, yet his curiosity got the better of him. He would have preferred to wipe out their existence from his mind. He found the recollections overwhelming.

"Well, so long then."

"Going already?"

"Yeah."

"Aren't you going to see your people?"

"No."

He wouldn't have minded seeing Danny again, but the thought of re-entering the Boys' Room was too much for him, overcrowded with memories.

"Well, be seeing you."

"O.K. Don't play white in Walmer Estate, hey, remember where you come from."

Andrew made a firm resolve not to remember. He turned around abruptly and quickly walked down Caledon Street. He saw James approaching on the opposite side of the street. His skin prickled and he again broke into a clammy sweat. Andrew walked looking straight ahead of him. James cut him dead. He turned into Tennant Street, his heart palpitating. At Hanover Street corner he caught a bus back to Walmer Estate.

19

Senior Certificate results out at five o'clock to-day. Andrew knew what that meant. Students milling around in St. George's Street, the impatient queue, having to give one's number and waiting with bated breath. Then the joy and sorrow as results were announced. Would Miriam allow him to continue if he passed well? Would he pass well? Anything could happen.

He sat with Abe and Justin on their way to the *Argus* office. The bus was three-quarters empty as it was the afternoon shift. Abe had a quiet, confident air about himself. Justin looked worried, spoke rapidly and gesticulated nervously.

"You know our numbers are last?"

He referred to the system whereby candidates were identified by their numbers and not their names in answering examination questions.

"So?"

"I mean we are numbered last."

"Yeah?"

"Because we're non-white."

"So what does that mean?"

"Nothing."

"Then why mention it?"

"I was only thinking."

"Thinking what?"

"Segregation even in the bloody exams."

"What more do you expect? You go to a Coloured High School."

"I didn't ask to."

"Neither did I."

The bus passed Castle Bridge and Andrew stole a nervous glance at Aunt Ella's house. It was shut and the curtains drawn. Most probably she was cooking and cleaning at 302.

"What do you do if you pass, Abe?"

"I go to University."

"To do what?"

"Bachelor of Science, I think."

"And then?"

"Teach. What else can I do. What else is there for a gentleman of colour?"

"Yeah."

"And you, Justin?"

"Well, I don't know if I'll pass."

"If you fail?"

"I come right back."

"That'll be lousy."

"You're telling me."

"And you, Andrew?"

Andrew was confused. He didn't know what to say. Miriam had not mentioned anything and Kenneth he hardly saw.

"Well?"

"I don't really know."

"You should study further."

"I wish I could, but my position is somewhat insecure."

"Yes, I realize that."

At the City Hall they jumped off and struggled their way through shoppers and office-workers to the *Argus* buildings. Hundreds of students stood around in worried groups. A queue stretched almost right around the building into Burg Street. They joined the tail-end.

"If we all get through we should celebrate."

"Yes," Andrew agreed indifferently.

"We should get together somewhere at least."

"We should," he repeated automatically.

His home was out of the question, as he never brought friends there. He had never invited anyone to visit him, neither in Caledon Street nor in Walmer Estate. He wondered what Miriam would say if he were to invite Abe and maybe Justin to come around.

Five p.m. The queue surged forward as the doors swung open. They moved inch by inch.

"Well, this looks like it," said Justin. "Here goes. Best of luck."

Students were emerging from the far door, some hysterically gay, others sombre and long-faced. Andrew felt suddenly terribly depressed. Alone, intensely alone, in the rush of students. The way he had felt when he had stood with the Apostolics the night his mother had died. The way he had felt when he had walked along the National Road. He had sat down on a gravel heap by the side of the road somewhere near Parow, with the sun beating down mercilessly. He had glanced at his wrist-watch, and noticed that it was three o'clock. They were most probably burying her then. He had continued walking, just walking in a wasteland, solitary and completely isolated. Would he always be on his own?

Justin and Abe stood in front of the *Argus* desk. Somehow Andrew didn't care about the results. It just didn't matter a damn.

"Number?"

He vaguely saw the clerk behind the counter.

"Number please!"

"4460," he said automatically.

She ran her finger down the list.

"Dreyer? Andrew Dreyer?"

"Yes."

"First-Class Pass and Exemption from Matriculation."

"Thanks."

It refused to register. The feeling of loneliness overwhelmed him. Would he ever find a home he could call his own? Where people could accept him for what he was? Independence from the goodwill of others? His sister's and brother-in-law's charity? He left the desk, deciding to avoid his friends. Rather walk home and sleep it off. He dreaded meeting Abe and Justin.

"Andrew!"

He stopped automatically. It was Abe running towards him, wildly excited.

"How did you manage?"

"O.K."

"What pass did you get?"

"I managed a First."

"So did I. Shake, man!"

Abe pumped his hand vigorously.

"I think we're the only two Firsts at school."

"Oh," he said unenthusiastically.

"Aren't you excited?"

"Yes," he said, but his voice sounded flat.

Justin joined them, his nervousness a thing of the past.

"Well, chaps, I'm through."

"Good show!"

"And you guys?"

"We both got Firsts."

"Nice work."

"Come on. Let's spread the good news."

They jumped on a passing bus. Abe was far too excited to notice Andrew's depression. He kept up a non-stop conversation with Justin. Andrew wished he could get rid of his class-mates and be on his own. It had been drizzling the night his mother died. The pathetic group singing hymns on the Grand Parade. A little boy with white, bleached knuckles, shivering in the cold. *Onse Vader, wat in die hemel is, laat U Naam geheilig word.* Thy kingdom come, Thy will be done on earth as it is in heaven. And then James had beaten him up. The sheer humiliation of it, in front of Danny. He had walked out, softly closing the door behind him, and had tip-toed down the stairs.

At Justin's place in Eden Road he was silent and moody. He automatically smiled when congratulated. At Abe's place Andrew wanted to listen to Beethoven's *Eroica*, but Abe refused to listen to classical music at such a time.

"Let's go to your place next, Andrew."

"No."

"Why not?"

"My people won't be home," Andrew lied.

"Surely they will."

"My sister has gone out and my brother-in-law is at work."

"Oh."

It was Justin's idea to visit Herby Solomons. Put the play-white in his proper place, as he said.

"They've got to accept us, after all we're his classmates."

"So?"

"Surely he can't chase us away?"

"Did he get through?"

"Yes, I think I saw his name."

"Was he at the *Argus*?"

"Not on your sweet life. It might have been embarrassing."

"Sure he'll be home now?"

"That's what we mean to find out. Let's go."

Herby was home. They reached an enormous face-brick

house standing well back from the road. A driveway led from an impressive oak-gate. They rang the highly-Brassoed doorbell.

"Oh, come in," Herby said, completely thrown off his guard. He ushered them into a spacious, extremely heavily-furnished lounge, and invited them to sit down.

"Do you know your results?" Abe asked.

"Yes. I phoned through. And you?"

"I got a First."

"Congratulations. And you, Justin?"

"I just passed."

Andrew felt out of things. The lounge with the wall-to-wall carpet and bay-windows depressed him even further.

"Andrew also got a First."

"Congratulations. Well, you must meet my mother."

All Andrew wanted to do was to get home. Sleep it off. Get away from the nagging memories of District Six and Jonga and Broertjie. His face had burnt the way James had smacked him and he had been nauseated by the sickly smell of blood. That damn, lying Mrs. Heidemann. Reeking of cheap wine and stale breath and still daring to put her arms around him.

"This is my mother."

Herby introduced a florid, middle-aged woman whose hair was dyed a rich red.

"This is Abe, Ma. He got a First-Class Pass."

"Oh, congratulations. I must kiss him."

She giggled girlishly as she planted a moist kiss on Abe's cheek.

"And this is Justin. He just passed like me."

She kissed him also.

Andrew felt that he would explode if she touched him. He felt the way he had felt with Mrs. Heidemann. He would knock her down, swear, scream. Do anything. His body tickled all over.

"And this is Andrew, he also got a First."

"Congratulations, Andrew."

He nodded coldly, making no advance. She must have realized his hostility because she in turn made no attempt to approach him.

"Well, I think you all deserve some tea. Herby's leaving for England next week."

Late that night he left Abe and Justin and moodily

walked down Nile Street. He felt lonelier than ever,
frustrated, hating without reason. That bloody play-white
woman with her simpering idiotic son. Running away to
England. He had spared her the embarrassment of having
to kiss him.

Miriam's home was in darkness as he entered through
the back door, and he sank mercifully on to his bed.

20

Although the music had stopped for some time,
Andrew still lay back on the couch without moving. His
glass stood empty. District Six. Jonga, Amaai and Broertjie.
The way his mouth had felt after James had slapped him.
Then the warm days with Miriam and Kenneth. The
endless arguments between Justin and Abe. He was certain he would have done something desperate if Mrs.
Solomons had dared to kiss him. Her play-white son running away to England. What a past. What a helluva past.
For a long time he lay quite still, while the curtains softly
rustled in the Table Mountain breeze. If only life could
always be like this. Music, soft darkness and Ruth. Away
from a world of pass burnings and riots and baton charges.
Sharpevilles and Langas. A hawker losing his shoe. Funny
how he had run with the blood streaming down his face.
And the strong smell of urine in the toilet. Trapped like
rats. And then the stabbing in the bus. He wondered
whether they had caught the youth. Wanting a bloody
cigarette and interfering with innocent people.

He heard familiar footsteps running up the stairs. Ruth!
Yes, it was Ruth. He recognized her short nervous strides.
He heard the key in the lock and the door opening. Her
hand felt for the switch and the place was flooded with
light. She stood confused in the doorway, then threw
herself into his arms as he stood to meet her. Andrew
helped her off with her duffle-coat as she sobbed quietly.

"What's wrong, Ruth?"

"I'm so glad to find you, Andy."

"I'm quite safe, dear."

"I'm still glad."

Her mouth hungrily sought his, and they kissed for a

long time, standing in the middle of the lounge. Her lips felt warm and moist.

"Oh, Andy."

"It's all right, dear, I'm safe."

"I'm so happy, I don't know how I feel."

"Come, let me get you a drink."

She sat down in an easy chair while he poured her a gin and tonic and refilled his glass with brandy.

"I've had a terrible time, Andy."

"Don't bother to tell me now. First have your gin."

"I'm quite calm, I think."

"Well?"

"Two detectives came here."

"Why?"

"They asked about you."

"What did they look like?"

"The one who asked the questions was middle-aged with a ginger moustache."

"Bligenhout."

"You know him?"

"Yes. He visited me on Thursday morning."

"He seems to know all about us."

"I wouldn't be surprised."

"They said they are going to contact my parents."

"Hell, that's bad."

"I won't go back home, Andy."

"Don't worry about that, dear. We'll work it out later. Listen to some music?"

"If you want to."

"I've been playing Smetana."

"Yes," she said, still worried.

He replaced the *Moldau* in its cover and looked carefully through the rest of her records.

"I went to Grassy Park to try and find you."

"So?"

"I met your nasty landlady."

"Yes," he smiled.

"She said she was going to give you notice to leave immediately."

"Don't you worry. I'll be able to manage her."

"But where can you go to?"

"Leave Mrs. Carollissen to me."

"But, Andy!"

"What would you like to hear? Britten, Purcell or Rachmaninov?"

"Anything you like."

"Let's have the Number 2 Piano Concerto."

"It's immaterial to me."

He placed the Rachmaninov record on the turntable and turned down the volume. Eight beautiful, solemn chords led into the first theme.

"I've been having an orgy of sentimental recollections."

"Yes," she said, still ill at ease.

"Come and lie down next to me. And, like Enobarbus, I will tell you."

He switched off the light and they lay next to each other in the dark, the mountain breeze gently rippling the curtain. The music went into a long flowing melody swelling with the strings and woodwinds.

"I thought many things while I was waiting for you."

She nestled closer to him and he put his arms around her.

"About my childhood and youth in District Six. My mother's death. That night I ran away from home and walked for days and days along the National Road because I felt guilty. Remorse. Absolute loneliness."

The pace of the music quickened as the piano faded away and the strings hinted at the opening theme.

"Then I went to my sister's place in Walmer Estate. Miriam had a garden full of zinnias and phlox. Beautiful it was. Red and blue and green."

He could hear her breathing next to him. He gently rubbed her neck.

"And then I was in my final year at High School, and in the mornings walked with Abe and Justin along Constitution Street."

He could feel her breasts harden. The first subject of the Concerto reappeared in the strings, accompanied by the pounding chords of the piano.

"And when the results of my examinations came out, I felt lonelier than ever. Completely isolated. Like I felt on the Grand Parade when a little boy offered me a hymn-book in the drizzle. I stood listening to an Apostolic Group the night my mother died."

The Concerto moved into its beautiful second movement. He could hear her breath coming in short, quick pants.

"Ruth?"

"Yes, Andy?"

They kissed hungrily.

"Please, Ruth."

"I know."

Passion overcame him, as he felt her hanging on to him. Hungrily he sought her. Days with Miriam and little boys with hymn-books. And Rachmaninov. *Vltava?* No, Rachmaninov. Rhapsody on a theme. A nocturne movement. A long coda. Beautiful. Hysterically beautiful.

For a long time afterwards they lay in a close embrace, listening to the last movement. The music moved into the final triumphant restatement of the second theme. Then a full orchestra with the piano thumping massively. And the Concerto ends with a breathless dialogue between soloist and orchestra. The room silent with self-conscious passion.

"Ruth?"

"Yes, Andy?"

"We've done a non-European thing."

"I read that somewhere."

"Yes. Me and a white lady did a non-European thing."

"I still love you."

"I love you also."

"I don't care about the police, or my family, or what people think, I only want to be with you."

"This is South Africa, dear."

"I don't care."

She cried softly in his arms. After a long time he rose and adjusted his clothes.

"More gin?" he asked, switching on the light.

"I haven't touched the first glass yet."

"I'll have a last brandy, then I must go."

"Must you, Andy?"

"I can hardly sleep here."

"Why not?"

"With a white lady? That would be very un-South African." He attempted a wry smile.

"Where are you going?"

"I think it's time I visited my sister Miriam again. We

last saw each other two years ago after I had had a quarrel with her husband.

"She won't be expecting you."

"Dont worry, I'll manage."

"Will you be safe?"

"I'll be all right.

"But you won't be able to get a bus now."

"I'll hitch a lift somehow."

"Take my car."

"What about you?"

"I can take a bus to Varsity."

"When do I see you then?"

"I'll be free between three and four p.m. tomorrow."

"Wait for you in the Library?"

"All right, Andy. The keys are in my duffle-pocket."

"Good."

He gulped down his brandy and gave her a long kiss.

"Good-bye, Andy."

"Good-bye, Ruth."

He walked quickly down the stairs to the car park, and started the engine of the Austin. As he drove away he thought he saw Bligenhout sitting opposite in a parked car.

Part Two

Tuesday, 29th March 1960

All major building and engineering projects in Cape Town are virtually immobilized. Coal, milk and newspaper deliveries are seriously impeded. Customers are urged to call at depots for their milk. Bread is in short supply. Hotels and garages are working on skeleton staffs. Shipping congests Duncan Docks. Shops in Langa are down to their last bag of mealies and last loaf of bread, and the food situation in the Location is desperate. Over two thousand Africans return hurriedly to the Transkei. Official sources allege that agitators have warned Location people both in their homes and at their places of employment that there will be severe reprisals unless they cease to work.

1

It was nearly two when Andrew pulled up outside Miriam's house. The place was in darkness and all the curtains drawn. Kenneth's car was not parked in its usual place against the wire fence. That was good, as Andrew was in no mood for further scenes. He parked Ruth's car around the corner and then walked back to the house. He rang the bell, remembering the evening years before when he had rung the same bell. No one answered this time, although he heard the tring penetrating into every room. Miriam might not be home although that seemed unlikely. He stood in the garden, uncertain what to do. A sickly sliver of a moon surrounded by ragged clouds floated over the Bay. He rang again and thought that this time he detected some movement behind the door. Thirteen years ago. A very long time ago. The night of the funeral. A warm evening after the winds and the rain. A yellow Van Gogh moon over Table Bay. Dazzling yellow on a March night, in 1947. The air electric. Yes, long time ago. He decided to ring again. The passage light switched on.

"Who's there?" It was Miriam, but her voice sounded strange.

"Me. Andrew."

"Who?"

"Andrew, your brother."

"Oh!" There was a long pause, then he heard the key turning in the lock, and the door opened slightly.

"Come in."

"Andrew!"

"Miriam!"

He was shocked at her altered appearance. Her skin was tight and drawn and there were dark pockets underneath her eyes. She seemed more frail than before and bore an uncanny resemblance to his mother, something Andrew had hardly noticed before.

"Yes, Miriam, it's me."

She looked at him hard and her lips twitched. Then

her attitude changed suddenly and she turned away from him.

"What do you want here at this time of night?"

"I'm looking for a place to sleep."

"Can't you go somewhere else?"

"I came back to you."

"Is it because of politics?"

"Yes it is, in a way."

"I thought as much."

She sat down heavily without offering him a seat. There was something depressing about the atmosphere. He noticed that his sister was still fully dressed although it was two in the morning. Something was wrong. Something weighty.

"Miriam?"

"Yes, Andrew?"

"Is anything the matter?"

"I'm tired."

"I'm sorry to have disturbed you."

"It's nothing to do with you. I'm always tired lately. Everything gets me down, everything. It's here. Inside. Inside me. Deep down underneath my skin."

"Is it Kenneth?"

"No, it's not Kenneth." He knew she was lying. "No, it's nothing like that at all."

Andrew was not convinced.

"Miriam, may I sleep here tonight? I might have to stay for a short time."

He laughed nervously but she showed no reaction.

"I don't know. Really, I don't know. Why did you have to come to me?"

"Well, as it was, I had to go somewhere, and after all you are my sister."

"Am I still, after two years?"

"I haven't been visiting you because of your husband."

"Kenneth."

"Yes, because of Kenneth."

"Yes, because of Kenneth," she repeated almost in a whisper.

"Is he at work now?"

"I don't know."

"But, surely, you must know?"

"I don't know and I don't care."

"Miriam, there is something wrong."

"There is nothing wrong."

"Tell me. I might be able to help you."

"I'll make some coffee."

She climbed wearily to her feet and shuffled heavily to the stove.

"I'm sorry if I woke you."

"No, you haven't. I seldom sleep."

"Waiting for Kenneth?"

"Just waiting."

"Does he treat you badly?"

"Who?"

"Kenneth!"

"He's all right."

He noticed that the kitchen wasn't as tidy as it used to be. Cups were stacked unwashed in the sink, a calendar hung askew on the wall and the place wore a strained and neglected air.

"But there must be something the matter."

She poured the coffee and he wasn't sure whether she was listening to him or not. He got up to get the sugar and spoons from the top rack. They drank in silence.

"Will it be in order if I stay?"

"I can't really say."

"Miriam, you are afraid of Kenneth!"

"I am just afraid."

He remembered two years before when he had left. Kenneth's blood-shot eyes, the almost overwhelming desire to grab his brother-in-law by the throat and choke his guts out, beat the hell into the swine. A pity he had not done it then.

"How is he lately?"

For the first time she looked at him directly, her lips quivering.

"It's hell, Andrew, sheer hell. He drinks heavily now, all the time."

"I know. He was starting when I left."

"But this goes on and on. He and James."

"Oh?"

"Yes. They're as thick as thieves."

He remembered James cunningly egging Kenneth on

against him. The swine. It hurt the night his brother had smacked him when his mother had died.

"They're always together in those cheap white bars. After wine and women."

"Where is he now?"

"He should be on shift. He's still with the Tramway Company."

"I don't mean Kenneth, I mean James."

"He's separated from his wife. Boards somewhere in Observatory."

"As a white?"

"Yes, as a white."

"Does he still come here?"

"Almost every night. They drink together all the time. In bars, here, there, everywhere. I can't take it any longer. It's all inside me, Andrew, inside here."

"I'm sorry, Miriam."

She cried softly, but in an expressionless, tired way.

"It really started becoming serious last June."

"Yes?"

"I knew he was drinking heavily, but this was different."

"Go on."

"I was coming from Daniel's place."

"What's happened to him?"

"He's married. You know that?"

"No."

"Lives in Cambridge Street, near Zonnebloem. He's an Evangelist now and preaches on street corners in District Six and on the Grand Parade."

Andrew shuddered as the recollection hit him.

"Well, as I was saying, I was coming from Daniel's place. He wasn't home so I returned at once. I found Kenneth's car outside, which was odd as he should have been at work. He was on night-shift then. I came in and switched on the passage light. Then I went into the bedroom."

"Go on."

"He was in bed. Not alone!"

She sobbed on quietly, tears running down her cheeks.

"You needn't tell me."

"With a white girl. A prostitute. She couldn't have been more than sixteen."

"Don't bother to explain."

"Wearing heavy make-up and nothing else."

"All right, Miriam."

She tried to control her crying. Andrew decided to change the subject.

"I'd like some more coffee, please."

"I'll have to warm it up again."

"Please don't bother."

"I'll make some more in any case. Kenneth should be home around three or four o'clock. That is if he comes home."

"What happened to Peter-boy?"

"No one knows."

"And Philip's still with Annette?"

"Yes."

"So the family is widely dispersed."

She switched on the plate and then continued speaking without looking at him.

"Andrew."

"Yes?"

"I'm afraid Kenneth might find you here."

"Don't you worry!"

"But you know what he can be like."

"I think I can handle him."

"But can't we try and avoid trouble? For my sake?"

"Leave him to me. I would very much like to speak to my brother-in-law."

"Will it be all right, you think?"

"Quite all right, dear. Now let's have more coffee, then I would like to go to bed."

She was all on edge, jumping at every squeak of the gate. Finally his bed was ready in his old room.

"Thanks a lot, Miriam. Now you try and get some sleep."

"What time should I wake you?"

"Not too early. I won't be going to school tomorrow."

"All right, Andrew. Good night."

"Good night."

He went into his room and was gently enveloped in the smell of familiar things.

2

Andrew gazed around him but the room had not been changed much. His textbooks were still neatly piled on his table. Breasted, Bradley, Arnold, Loney's *Co-ordinate Geometry*, the Anglo-Saxon primer, *The Philosophical Theory of the State*. A bit dusty but still in the same place. He removed Bosanquet from the shelves. *The Conception of a Real Will*. The Will that wills itself is the Real Will. The Supreme Will in Hobbes and Locke. The General Will in Rousseau contrasted with the Will of All. How vague and artificial all that seemed now. He slowly replaced it. Next to the books were his records, warped and scratched. Right on top, Smetana, with the inscription on the cover "from Abe to Andrew on his intellectual coming of age." He opened the drawer and a musty smell hit him full in the face. Old University examination papers, registration cards, membership forms for the Modern Youth Association, library dockets. He removed a faded letter from its envelope. The first letter he had received from his Principal after he had heard his Senior Certificate results. Hell, that had been a close shave. He lay down on the bed re-reading the old-fashioned handwriting. As close a shave as possible. It had come a week after he had spoken to Miriam about his future. He still remembered that morning vividly, the morning after he had nearly pushed Mrs. Solomons over her own couch, the ridiculous old bitch.

He remembered how he had felt after he had left Abe and Justin that night. He had slept fitfully, but had awakened the following morning to find the sun streaming in through the window. He felt partially recovered but his anxiety about his future still gnawed inside him. Would Miriam allow him to continue to University? Who would finance his further studies? He felt it was time to speak. He was still in the bathroom when she called him to breakfast, but when he came into the kitchen she had gone into her room. He ate a silent breakfast. Did she really know the result? She might have seen it in the morning newspaper. He saw the *Cape Times* still folded

on the kitchen table. Most probably she would by now
be in the front garden. He finished his bacon and eggs
and walked down the passage into the bright sunlight and
sat on the wall. Miriam was wearing a beach-hat and dark
glasses, hosing, digging and rearranging flowers. Dahlias,
zinnias, phlox and snapdragons. He leisurely watched
people on their way to work, hurrying to catch their buses
in Sir Lowry Road.

"The results are out, Miriam."

"Oh?" she said, straightening her back. "So how did
you do?"

"I got a First-Class Pass and a Matriculation Exemption."

"That is good, very good indeed." She sounded for a
moment very like his Principal, Mr. Altmann. Then she
bent down to continue struggling with a dahlia she was
transplanting. He felt it was the right time to broach the
subject of his future.

"Miriam, what's to become of me?"

"Well," she said, spreading out the petals of the flower
and examining minutely its dewy-red texture, "Kenneth
and I have been talking about it."

He waited, not daring to breathe.

"Kenneth doesn't feel he can afford it."

He tried to cover his bitter disappointment.

"You see, it's only Kenneth working and he doesn't
earn much. So if you wish to stay on here I have no
objections, but you'll have to try and find a job. We
might be able to send you further later on."

"Thanks, Miriam, I understand."

He felt his world collapsing under his feet, but attempted
to maintain a semblance of nonchalance. His room seemed
very dark after the brilliant sunlight outside. He took *Far
from the Madding Crowd* from the pile of books on the
table and flicked idly through the pages. All over. He
would have to join the crowd of workers hurrying to
catch the morning bus in the Main Road. Office work, if
one could get such a job. We might be able to send you
further later on. How much later? The, by now, familiar
feeling of dependence and isolation crowded back on him.
Would he never be able to prove himself? Never have
the chance? Had he committed a crime to be born
Coloured? Poor, and in District Six? To have the effrontery

to rise from the slums and gain a First-Class Pass? He felt bitter and frustrated a long time afterwards.

Every evening he scanned the newspapers. Employment offered men. Professional and Business Vacancies. Clerk wanted—Europeans only; Long-established firm requires slightly-Coloured youth: what the hell was a slightly-Coloured youth? Experienced invoice clerk or one willing to learn—only Whites need apply; Office work—First class job for European youth just leaving school, pension fund available. Write Box 1807, Write *Argus* XYZ—763, Write Masons, Strand Street. Write, write, write! Europeans only, No Coloureds, Only Whites need apply.

He listlessly drafted applications for the few vacancies available. In most cases no reply, in a few cases we regret to state.

The letter from his Principal, Mr. Altmann, came out of the blue. An official buff envelope with On His Majesty's Service printed conspicuously along the top. It could be anything, most probably congratulations on gaining a First-Class Pass. He read the letter without interest and then sat bolt upright. It was short and to the point.

"Dear Andrew,

Congratulations on your First-Class Pass. The Van Zyl Memorial Scholarship, founded in 1914 under the will of Mr. Jan Hendrik van Zyl of Paarl, Cape Province, is open to students residing in the Union of South Africa under British rule, without distinction of creed, class or colour. The value of the Scholarship is £120 per annum tenable for four years at any recognized South African University. Please complete enclosed forms and reply immediately."

Hell, this could solve a lot of problems. It was signed A. G. Altmann, B.A. This was the very thing.

That night at the supper table he decided to mention it. Kenneth was buried in his newspaper.

"Miriam, if I were to get a scholarship, do you think it would be possible?"

"Would what be possible, Andrew?"

"For me to go to University?"

"Have you got a scholarship?"

"No."

"Then it would be pointless discussing it."

"But say, for argument's sake, I did get one?"

"Well, I don't know, Andrew. I really don't know. It's

not only a question of books and fees. We must clothe and feed you as well."

"I could always work during vacations."

Kenneth lowered his newspaper.

"Don't you think we've done enough for you already?"

"I would only like to study further."

"And who the hell has to support you?"

"I could try and get a job during the holidays."

"Don't you think it's enough that we have given you a roof over your head and fed you free of charge for nine months?"

"I appreciate that."

"Well then, don't talk nonsense. You go out and find a job. I've had to work for my living from the age of fourteen. Why the hell can't you?"

"I'm sorry, Kenneth."

"Well be careful or you'll be out of here on your neck. I think I've just about had enough of you."

Miriam listened to the interchange without saying a word. Andrew excused himself and went miserably to his room. Kenneth's outburst had shocked him. Maybe he should have produced the letter instead of trying to approach the subject in a roundabout way. He heard Kenneth's raised voice in the kitchen and Miriam's quiet replies.

"Well, then, you can see to that lazy, black son-of-a-bitch brother of yours yourself."

He had never heard Kenneth like this before. Up to now he had carefully avoided his brother-in-law, but considered him more neutral than hostile. Even Miriam, he suspected, was a little afraid of Kenneth. So that was the end of the Van Zyl Scholarship and a University career. An abrupt, ignominious end. He wrote a reply to the Principal, declining the offer without stating reasons, and posted it the same evening.

The days stretched ahead. No replies from jobs. School started and the University was preparing for a new academic year.

One night a week later, a sultry Thursday evening, he walked up to Abe's home. Andrew was in a bitter and frustrated mood. He found Abe studying a University Arts and Science prospectus.

"I'm trying to decide on my first courses. What the hell is Logic and Metaphysics?"

"Search me."

"It doesn't really matter. I've decided to do Science instead of Arts."

"Yes."

"What are your plans?"

"Find a job somewhere."

"That's lousy."

"What else can I do? I chose the wrong family."

"Hardly your fault."

"I haven't a doting mother to push me through University."

"Now wait a minute."

"I was born in a slum. I should have stayed there."

"If you behave this way, I'm inclined to agree with you."

"I always thought you would."

"I'm terribly accommodating. Prepared to agree with anything you say."

"How noble. It must be wonderful to be able to play the patron with those who are denied opportunities."

"I think you're being unjust."

"Smarming over people who are less privileged than you are. I suppose it's possible that you will become a white student at University."

"I have no intention of doing so."

"I suppose you will do your best to understand and appreciate the problems of oppressed blacks."

"They are my problems as well."

"You remind me of liberal whites who discuss injustices, oh so academically, from the comfort of their armchairs."

"I've never known you like this, Andrew."

"It's time you did."

"The answer is to fight situations, not retreat into cynicism and petty personalities."

"I've fought enough."

"One has never fought enough."

"I feel at times that I should never have left District Six. I should have finished Primary School and looked for a job somewhere as a street-sweeper or a messenger boy. I've tasted forbidden fruits. Now I'm aware of what I am being denied."

"Education is a right, not privilege."

"That sounds like the Modern Youth Association."

"You are not denied entrance to a University."

"Of course not. I'm quite free to go. It's my right. Nothing prevents me from using it, other than money. All I need are books, fees, clothes, food, a roof over my head. Otherwise it's easy to claim my right."

"Many have struggled before."

"And many have failed."

"That does not give you the right to be defeatist about it."

"It is very easy for you to be critical from your comfortable pedestal."

"I didn't choose my parents."

"I suppose not."

Andrew left in a fit of remorse, self-pity and frustration. He knew he had hurt Abe, but he felt justified in a sadistic way. As he walked down Nile Street he spotted a familiar car outside his house. Altmann! What the hell was his Principal doing there? He walked hurriedly along the passage to get to his room.

"Andrew!" Miriam called after him.

"Yes?"

"Come into the lounge for a moment."

He entered slowly to find Miriam, Kenneth and Mr. Altmann sitting around the table. Kenneth was poker-faced.

"Good evening, Andrew," said Altmann shaking his hand.

"Evening, sir."

"How's our little genius?"

"Fine thank you," he said, swallowing hard.

"Sit down, my boy."

Mr. Altmann was prim and proper, a martinet, but nevertheless understanding. He was feared and admired by all the students. Andrew sat down on the very edge of the couch.

"We've been discussing you, Andrew."

"Yes, sir."

"And everything is now fixed up. You'll get the Van Zyl Scholarship plus a school bursary. That should cover everything for four years."

"Thank you, sir."

"So get into a University frame of mind and treat your Professors better than you did us."

"Yes, sir. I mean no, sir," he said confused. Mr. Altmann smiled. Kenneth watched glumly.

"And if you have any difficulties, Mrs. Peters, just give me a ring at school. Everything for the best, Andrew."

"Thank you, sir."

The principal shook hands with them, and left with a final wink at Andrew. He went to his room feeling confused and lifeless. Kenneth, he realized, would not be particularly keen. Lazy black son-of-a-bitch. Well, this black son-of-a-bitch would show how he wasn't lazy. He would work like bloody hell. And, of course, he would have to make it up with Abe.

3

After that the days went by in a confused whirl spinning dizzily in all directions. English, Latin, History, Philosophy, timetables, registrations, tutorials. Days of sheer madness in which he held on tightly in case he lost his grip. The wizardry of Shakespeare and Chaucer. Gladly wolde he lerne and gladly teche. Then nestling in the arms of Titania with Bully Bottom. The ravings of mad Lear on the blasted heath. The magic of Arden. The more fool I, when I was at home I was in a better place, but travellers must be content. His first days. The Registrar must be informed of any change in the curriculum. History 1 will meet in room 27 at 11:15 a.m. Gazing with awe at the ivy-covered lecture-rooms and the students milling around him. The heart yearnings of Catullus. Vergil's *Aeneid* in heroic style. At nunc horrentia Martis, arma virumque cano. Rolling it on the tongue to capture the throbbing metre. I sing of arms and the man. Days of self-conscious adaptation with seas of faces at the tables. Black, white and brown. Abe seeming to take it in his stride. The principate of Alexander. The Great Schism. The French Revolution did not produce liberty, equality and fraternity. The gradual unravelling of philosophical theories. Descartes, Plato, Hobbes, Hegel. The brain faint and overwhelmed by words, words and still more words.

And then the days evened out and the initial excitement was over. Andrew settled down to study, taking time off only on Sundays when he could afford it. He saw to it that he made it up with Abe on the first day of the new term.

"I'm sorry about the last time, old chap."

"Fair enough, I understand."

"I didn't really mean what I said."

"I believe that."

"Can you forgive me?"

"I said before that I am adaptable."

"Arrogant swine."

"Same to you."

Miriam still bustled around busily, but Kenneth openly ignored Andrew and remained poker-faced and indifferent in his presence. It took some time to adapt himself to University life, but once he knew the ropes he took it in his stride. Arguments raged. Discussions, political theories. Socialism. Fascism. Capitalism. Non-racial democracies. After much persuasion from Abe he joined the Modern Youth Association, and attended his first lecture on "Colonialism and the African Stage." More words and arguments. Condemnations. Imperialism as the highest development of Capitalism. Secondary industry in South Africa. The dilemma of class and caste. Abe in the forefront. Parrying and thrusting. This House moves the following motion. Mr. Chairman, in reply to the last speaker. I wish to move a motion of no confidence. On a point of order, Mr. Chair. A crazy vortex of theorizing, moralizing, generalization, invectives, stock phrases, clichés. To quote Lenin. Already in the seventeenth century Spinoza said. Plato prescribes Communism for his Guardian Class. Man is born free but everywhere he is in chains. Bacon, Voltaire, Nietzsche. Mr. Chairman, I wish to review and rescind. Motions, counter-motions, amendments. Till Andrew felt part and parcel of it all and entered into the verbal fray and dogfights with fervour.

In 1948 the Malan-Havenga coalition won the South African election with the battle-cry of apartheid. Segregation. *Eiesoortigheid.* The Nationalist Party, representative of white Afrikanerdom, won seventy-nine seats in the House of Assembly to the United Party's seventy-one, although outvoted by 140,000. The first all-Afrikaner Gov-

ernment in South African history came into being, while
the largely unrepresented non-white sat back and watched
with fear and uncertainty.

"So what happens now?" Andrew asked.

"I suppose we wait and see," Abe replied.

"Do you think that now that the Nats are in, the
situation will change radically?"

"Not really. But there'll be more intensive legislation
and we'll be at the receiving end."

And very soon the Nationalist Government started
putting its programme into practice. In September, train
apartheid was introduced on the Cape Town Suburban
Line. Special seats were to be reserved for whites only.
Andrew and Abe attended a mass protest meeting on the
Grand Parade as observers from the Modern Youth Association. Speaker after speaker condemned the Government
scheme. They spotted Justin in the crowd, busy handing
out pamphlets. Finally, volunteers were called for to ride
the trains and challenge segregation. Sit where you like.
Be prepared to be gaoled for your principles. All those who
are ready to do this step up to the platform. A queue
formed. Justin was helping to sign up volunteers.

"I'm going up," said Abe. "How about you?"

"I don't know."

"We have no alternative. If we are going to fight, we
must be prepared to suffer the consequences."

"I suppose so."

"Well, I'm going to sign up."

Andrew realized with misgiving the hopelessness of his
own situation. He existed on sufferance. What would
Miriam say? Kenneth? It could very well mean the end
of his academic career, which he couldn't afford to risk. It
had been rescued only by a miracle. And now he should
jettison it all?

"No, Abe. I'm not going to."

"Scared?"

"Yes, in a way."

"Well, I'm going."

Abe joined the queue of volunteers. Andrew watched
him hot-eyed, overwhelmed by feelings of shame and remorse. Humiliation burned inside him at the thought of
Abe considering him a coward. But could Abe understand? Could any of these people understand? His very

existence was threatened. All his hopes of an academic career. To be branded a coward, gutless. He turned abruptly and walked away, tears burning in his eyes. He walked all the way up Darling Street and Hanover Street till he turned down towards home.

He read the following day that the demonstration had been called off, but that brought him no relief. For weeks afterwards he avoided Abe. He seriously considered resigning from the Modern Youth Association, but in the end merely avoided attending meetings. He threw himself into University work with a vengeance, studying till the early hours of the morning, and sometimes with bloodshot eyes he saw the sun rising over Table Bay.

Tired and suffering from severe strain, he wrote his first-year examinations. Life passed in a haze of foolscap sheets, spot questions, memorizing, paraphrasing, condensing. Then back to Nile Street to revise feverishly for the next paper. When the results appeared he had gained a distinction in English, but merely managed to pass in Latin, History and Philosophy. He determined to work harder during the following years, politics or no politics.

4

Andrew's second year at University also passed speedily. Things started to gather momentum and life took on a serious aspect. He worked furiously, so that at times he fell asleep at his table through sheer exhaustion. Abe he sometimes saw on the campus, but they merely nodded coldly when they ran into each other.

Very early in the new year, the coons still dancing in the streets of Cape Town and the houses still decorated with festival bunting, he sat eating his evening meal at the kitchen table with Miriam and Kenneth. James was expected later, and Andrew was on tenter-hooks in case he should still be eating when his brother came. Kenneth was, as usual, immersed in his newspaper. Andrew tried to gulp down his hot coffee at speed. Miriam sat quietly, a rather worried look on her face. Andrew knew that she was not very partial to James's visits. From behind the *Argus* Kenneth suddenly burst out.

"These bloody coolies, bloody curry guts!"

Miriam looked puzzled, but Andrew knew what he was referring to. At the Market in Victoria Street, Durban, an Indian had smacked an African boy who had then fallen against a plate-glass window and cut himself. That had sparked off the worst African-Indian riots in the country's history. More than a hundred people had been killed and over a thousand wounded. Shops, factories and homes had been fired and destroyed, and flames danced over Cato Manor.

"Why do you say that?" Miriam asked him, still puzzled.

"Because Indians don't bloody-well belong in South Africa. It might be a good thing if the Kaffirs murdered the whole bunch of them."

"Really, Kenneth!"

"Don't really me. If the whole bloody lot could be sent back to their country it would be healthier for decent Coloureds and whites. The Kaffirs one can deal with. Indians have always turned my stomach."

Andrew felt that he had to say something, anything to counter Kenneth, but then he thought better of it, and remained silent.

"Now, you take their women. Do they ever allow us to see their wives? Bring them into our company? Not a damn. But they want our Coloured girls all the time."

"That's not fair," Miriam insisted.

"Oh, isn't it? Since when have you become so fond of Indians? Why the hell didn't you marry a bloody coolie and rear a lot of oily, curry brats?"

They heard a knock at the door. Miriam was still looking at Kenneth in horror.

"Come on, answer it!"

"But Kenneth!"

"What the hell, don't sit there like a bloody fool!"

"I'll go," said Andrew rising.

He walked down the passage feeling as if he might explode. He opened the door to admit James and a heavily-powdered white woman. His brother mumbled a distant greeting, and Andrew then retreated to his room as fast as he could. He still felt he should have countered Kenneth's racialistic remarks. How long would he have to endure his brother-in-law? He realized that there was almost nothing he could do. Maybe one day, when he was qualified and could stand on his own two feet. Maybe then he could answer back.

From his room he heard the front door bang as Miriam went out, and soon afterwards the glasses were clinking in the lounge. For how much longer would he have to stand by helplessly?

The Nationalist Government unleashed a spate of legislation to implement their policy of segregation. Apartheid. Different races must be separated. Post office apartheid. The Prohibition of Mixed Marriages Act.

"But Kenneth," Miriam insisted on another evening, "these laws must affect you as a Coloured man."

"Do I look like a Coloured man?"

"No, you don't, but you are registered as one."

"Do you for one moment think that anyone would suspect that unless they saw my wife?"

James was now a frequent visitor, often accompanied by different white women. Kenneth resented Andrew's answering the door, and said as much to Miriam who tactfully advised Andrew to keep to his room. Best stay out of his way altogether, he finds your presence embarrassing. The moment James came Miriam would find a pretext for going out. There was obviously no love lost between brother and sister. Where she went Andrew did not know. Kenneth and James would settle down to their drinking with whomsoever James had brought along.

Early in September, months after the train protest incident, Andrew slipped into a Modern Youth Association meeting, and quietly occupied a rear seat. Abe sat at the main table, taking notes. The topic under discussion was opposition to post office apartheid. Segregation had just been introduced in all post offices in the Cape Peninsula, and the Modern Youth Association had been invited to send members to a demonstration outside the central General Post Office at noon on the 13th. At the end of a protracted and sometimes heated discussion, the students' association decided to identify itself with the anti-apartheid demonstration after adopting a weighty resolution twice the length of the American Declaration of Independence.

Andrew now regretted having gone to the meeting. Was

that further proof of his cowardice? His gutlessness? Or was it sheer apathy? He didn't know himself.

At eleven o'clock on the morning of the 13th, his mind was made up. He cut all lectures for the day and hitched a lift to Town. Outside the General Post Office he found a crowd milling about. More than a hundred demonstrators stood lining the pavements with protest posters, and at the far end he spotted Abe. This might be his chance to make it up, prove himself, salve his conscience. He pushed his way through the spectators till he stood behind his friend.

"Hello, Abe," he whispered. "I'm reporting for duty."

Abe turned around and showed no reaction when he saw who it was.

"Good!"

"Where do I find a poster?"

"There are none left, but you can share mine. Grab one end."

For the next two hours they stood, while the crowd grew larger and the police marched up and down the line. A white lady walked in front of the demonstrators waving her umbrella.

"Keep your heads up and you'll go far!" she kept repeating in a high-pitched voice.

"You agree?" Andrew asked.

"What?"

"If you keep your head up you'll go far?"

"Sure. Don't you?"

"Of course I do," Andrew said, and he meant it.

5

The second year was over and Andrew was in the hurly-burly of his final year. Hours in libraries, hours at Abe's place, hours at his table at home till the pages became blurred and the days merged into a continuous haze. He had almost no idea of what was happening around him, hardly noticing the lines deepening in Miriam's face, her increasingly frequent arguments with Kenneth, James visiting more and more often. At his sister's suggestion he avoided Kenneth and did most of his studying at Abe's place. Stay out of his way and also try not to see James, she advised.

The spate of apartheid legislation poured out unabated. The Nationalists were determined to make segregation work. Entrench white domination for at least another three hundred years. Legislation and more legislation. The Goup Areas Act: complete residential segregation. Whites, Africans and Coloureds must by law live in different areas. Suppression of Communism Act: the Minister of Justice is the sole arbiter of whether a person is a Communist or not. Population Registration Act: all people in the Union of South Africa are to be classified into racial categories. Every person must be ticketed, photographed and identified according to race. Immorality Amendment Act: any sexual relationship between Europeans and any variety of non-white becomes illegal. And still legislation poured out. Entrenching apartheid.

Andrew was vaguely aware of what was happening around him. Only on rare occasions did he read newspapers. This was his final year, and he couldn't afford to come down.

One evening early in October, he was studying in Abe's room when he realized that he had forgotten his Anglo-Saxon translations at home. The examination heat was on full blast and he had to have them. He remembered that they were in a black, spring-back file and that he had last used it earlier in the day in the lounge while his room was being cleaned. He quickly explained to Abe and walked briskly to Nile Street. He entered through the kitchen door, hoping to find the lounge unoccupied. He heard voices filtering down the passage of which he could only make out Kenneth's. Andrew was in no mood to barge into company, but he had to have his notes. If only he could find Miriam, but she was not around and her apron hanging behind the kitchen door indicated that she had gone out. He walked down the passage with vague forebodings. Kenneth was sitting with his back to the open door and James was sprawled over the couch. He spotted his file on the display cabinet. Next to it was an unopened bottle of brandy. He must have disturbed the two because there was a sudden silence.

"Excuse me, please," he said timidly.

Kenneth slowly turned in his chair to face Andrew.

"What the hell do you want?"

"My notes. They're on the cabinet."

Kenneth was sitting in such a position that it was difficult to get into the room.

"Bugger off!"

"I would just like my notes, please."

"I told you to bugger off."

"There they are on the display cabinet. It's the black file."

Kenneth got up unsteadily, breathing heavily, while James watched, poker-faced.

"Didn't I tell you to get the hell out of here?"

"I must have my notes, please."

"Are you giving me bloody orders in my own house?"

Andrew felt limp and found his legs wouldn't move.

"No," he managed to say at last, "I merely want my notes on the display cabinet."

"You black son-of-a-bitch! I'll show you! You won't treat me the way you treated James!"

Kenneth grabbed him by the chest, tearing his shirt in the process. For one hideous moment Andrew felt like squashing his fist into the palpy, white face. Obliterate the snarl around the close mouth. He was strong enough to do it, and suddenly he realized his strength.

"I only want my book," he insisted.

"Get out! You impertinent swine!"

"It's on the sideboard."

"*Voertsak!*"

Kenneth kicked at him viciously and Andrew sprawled against the passage wall. James watched without changing his position.

"Here are your f——ing notes. You're getting far too bloody smart for me."

Kenneth flung the file after him and sheets scattered all over the passage. Andrew burned with white heat as he retrieved his notes. Instead of returning to Abe's place he went straight to bed, although he didn't sleep at all.

Then the final examination began. Kenneth and Miriam lost somewhere in the background. He often slept and ate at Abe's place, sometimes not coming home for days on end. Abe's mother, Mrs. Hanslo, was accommodating and hospitable. Andrew found he never seemed to get used to examinations. His stomach always felt like jelly as question papers were handed out. His pen would refuse to write. He kept thinking of ridiculous things like the Utrillo on Abe's wall. Watching the second hand on the giant wall-clock going round and round and round, till he finally forced himself to write, his palms clammy with sweat.

Early in December the list of graduates was pasted up. Abe and he went together and they strolled slowly up the endless steps to the main notice-board.

"So today we are either made or broken," said Abe fatalistically.

"Are you as worried as I am?"

"I'm not really worried."

"Remember the night the Senior Certificate results came out?"

"And Justin all excited?"

"And Herby Solomon's mother?"

"He's in England now."

"Most probably a member of the Friends of South Africa Association."

"Well, what does one do if one gets a University degree?"

"Well, since we are both members of the Great Unwashed, we have the choice of either becoming a Prime Minister or taking a seat in the Cabinet. Which do you prefer?"

"Don't be silly."

"Well, what other choice is there?"

"Teaching little snot-nosed brats in a classroom somewhere."

"Now look, Johnny Ferreira. If you insist on eating your fish and chips in that noisy manner, I will have to ask you to leave my Latin class."

They found students milling around the notice-boards.

"You go and look," Andrew told Abe, "and come and tell me the result. I just can't face it."

"All right. Here goes."

Andrew leaned against a pillar. His head throbbed slightly and his eyes were burning. This might mean everything. At least one might be able to do something with a degree. It gave one academic status. A sense of having arrived somewhere. A frail, bearded white student with intense eyes addressed him in Afrikaans. Andrew remembered having seen him on the campus before.

"*Is jy deur?* Did you make it?" he asked without being invited.

"I don't know yet," Andrew replied.

"Not worried?"

"A friend is finding out for me."

"Well, thank God I've made it."

"Congratulations," said Andrew shaking his moist hand. Abe joined them breathlessly.

"Well?"

"May I shake your hand, Mr. Andrew Dreyer, B.A.?"

"Not really!"

"But truly!"

Andrew could feel hot tears in his eyes.

"And you?"

"You are addressing a member of the University Convocation. Baccalaureus Scientiae."

"Speak English."

"Sir, I present myself. Mr. Abraham Barry Hanslo, Bachelor of Science."

"Congrats old man. Oh, I'm sorry, let me introduce you. This is Mr. . . ."

"Braam de Vries."

"Mr. Braam de Vries, Mr. Abraham Hanslo. I am Andrew Dreyer."

"How do you do, Mr. de Vries?"

"Call me Braam. My friends call me Braam de Vreeslik. I did Honours in Nederlands and Afrikaans."

"Did you make it?"

"I was forced to."

"Well, here we go again. Let's spread the happy tidings."

"Come and have some wine at my place," Braam invited them.

"Not quite at this moment," Abe apologized. "My mother is expecting."

"Not at her age surely," said Andrew in high spirits.

"All right, another time will do." Braam looked disappointed. "Do you know Justin Bailey?"

"Of course. We went to school together."

"He's a very good friend of mine. Come and see me sometime. I'll write down my address. I board with a Jewish Rabbi."

"But I mistook you for a . . ."

"An Afrikaner? That's right. I am an Afrikaner. Uncircumcised." He scrawled his name and address on the back of a used envelope and then left abruptly.

"Queer customer," Abe remarked. "I expect we'll probably see him again."

"I have a vague idea you're right," said Andrew with misgivings.

"Let's hitch a lift back to town."

A friendly University lecturer stopped his car and offered them a lift. They accepted gratefully. Abe asked to be dropped on De Waal Drive above Zonnebloem College.

"This is where we get off. Thanks very much."

"A pleasure," said the driver.

Andrew remained behind in the car.

"Are you going any nearer town?" he asked suddenly.

"I'm going through to Sea Point."

"Well, can you drop me off at the Fire Station in Roeland Street, please?"

"Certainly."

Abe waved a puzzled good-bye. Andrew felt in no mood to face Miriam and Kenneth. After he had alighted, he walked down De Villiers Street to District Six. He spent the rest of the evening roaming around his old haunts.

6

It was only the following evening that Andrew decided to break the news of his University success. The only time Miriam, Kenneth and himself were together was at the supper-table, and that was only when Kenneth wasn't working a different shift. Whereas before he used to ignore Andrew he had now become distinctly hostile. Only one more year, Andrew thought. Then with a teacher's diploma, he would be financially independent for the first time in his life. When it was necessary to communicate with his brother-in-law he usually did so through his sister.

"Miriam?"

She arched her eyebrows enquiringly while pouring the coffee.

"I've finished my degree."

She stopped what she was doing and smiled faintly.

"How wonderful, Andrew. I'm glad for your sake. You're a B.A. now?"

"Yes."

"Kenneth!"

Her husband ignored her and went on reading his newspaper.

"Kenneth! Andrew's got his degree."

"Huh?"

"Andrew's got his B.A."

"Oh. Now I suppose he'll be able to order us around," he commented sarcastically.

"Don't be mean, dear. I think he deserves congratulations for working so hard."

"He can go to hell for my part."

She shrugged her shoulders philosophically as Kenneth returned to his newspaper.

"I have two invitations to the graduation ceremony. You may have them if you'd like to come."

"I would certainly like to come."

"And Kenneth?" Andrew asked out of sheer duty.

"A lot of bloody nonsense," said his brother-in-law, getting up and leaving the table in a huff.

"Don't worry about him," said Miriam, trying to make it up through her tears. "I'm proud of you. I'll come."

And she did turn up, watching solemnly while the Chancellor conferred the degree of Bachelor of Arts on her brother.

Their final years at University saw Abe and Andrew racing through their Secondary Teacher's Diploma. Like the previous year, 1951 was marked by political unrest.

The Separate Registration of Voters Act arose out of the fierce desire of the Nationalists to remove 48,000 Coloured voters in the Cape Province from the Common Roll. This, in effect, disenfranchised them.

It was the year of the Torch Commando. Under war-leader Sailor Malan, jeeps and cars converged on Cape Town where Parliament was in session. Ten thousand ex-soldiers with flaming torches, led by Commander Dolf de la Rey, a seventy-four-year-old Boer War veteran, paraded through the streets in protest against the disenfranchising of the Coloured voters. The Commando was, in most cases, open to white ex-soldiers only.

Abe and Andrew were posted as student-teachers to

their old school, still under the principalship of Mr. Altmann who was in his last year before retirement.

It was a strange feeling standing in front of a class for
the first time. A sea of brown, expectant faces. Words
refusing to come and sticking in his throat. A girl giggling
in a corner. Andrew was specializing in Senior History
and English. Take note, class. The Forest of Arden acts
as a catalyst. No sooner do all the parties converge on it
than their personalities are radically transformed. Sweet
are the uses of adversity, which, like the toad, ugly and
venomous, wears yet a precious jewel in his head. How
very true. There was a great similarity, students, in the
motives which compelled the Trek-boers and the Bantu
on the Eastern Frontier of the Cape during the nineteenth
century. More similarities than dissimilarities. Sipping tea
in the staff-room with his former teachers. Watching them
with curiosity from a completely different point of view.
They were well-dressed, respectable, spoke about cars and
syllabuses and discussed politics theoretically. Altmann was
always kind and helpful. After retirement he hoped to get
a post as an assistant teacher in a Southern Suburban
school and concentrate on his home and garden in Lotus
River. He seemed a neutral politically.

After the first week Andrew found things beginning to
run more smoothly. The class had got used to him, and
he was starting to pick up the little tricks of the profes-
sion. It seemed that teaching wasn't going to be so bad
after all. He tried to avoid any questions of a political
nature in the class. But the questions still came. Sir, explain Fascism to us. Why are we forced to attend separate
schools? What happens if we are taken off the Common
Voters' Roll? Andrew played safe and walked a political
tight-rope.

Then back to University to prepare for the final examination and apply for posts. Application Form E 7.
Testimonials. This is a true and certified copy of the
original. To whom it may concern. I have known Mr.
Andrew Dreyer.

He received a temporary appointment at Tiervlei High
School to start in January, 1952. Abe was going to Steenberg High as a permanent science-master.

"Do you know, Andrew, Altmann will be on the same
staff as me?"

"Where?"

"At Steenberg High."

"How do you know?"

"The Principal told me."

"Who's the Principal?"

"A Mr. De Jager. He seems O.K."

"Must be strange to be about to teach with Altmann as a colleague."

"You're telling me. But the old boy doesn't know that I know, so keep it to yourself."

"Sure."

They still attended Modern Youth Association meetings when they could find the time. One evening in the early part of October they were returning from an Executive Meeting that had carried on till eight o'clock. Lifts were impossible to get, and after trying to hitch for half-an-hour they took a train to Cape Town, intending to take a bus to Walmer Estate. They had just missed one and the next was due only in forty minutes' time. There was nothing else to do but loiter on the Grand Parade.

"Let's take a Hanover bus," Andrew suggested.

"It will mean a hell of a walk for me. But you go ahead."

"I'll wait for you."

"As you like."

On the Parade corner nearest the station a small group was as usual holding a prayer-meeting. Andrew felt an irresistible urge to go and listen to them and after some persuasion he managed to get Abe to agree to go with him.

"Come on, I find them fascinating."

"I'm not at all interested in Jesus-jumpers."

"Their sincerity is out of this world."

"You're telling me!"

"We haven't anything to do but wait for the confounded bus. We might as well get a spot of conversion."

"All right."

They sauntered over to the tiny group. Andrew realized that painful recollections would come flooding back. He was afraid of opening old wounds, but nevertheless continued masochistically. There must be a difference between the reactions of a slum-waif of sixteen whose mother was dying in a tenement building and a Univer-

sity graduate who was almost a professional man, almost
an adult, practically grown-up. He walked over as casually
as he dared.

The Apostolics for the most part consisted of intense,
banjo-strumming labourers and their thin, undernourished,
equally intense wives. They were dressed in their patchy
best, and were singing hymns in nasalized, guttural ac-
cents. Andrew wondered about the small boy who had
offered him a hymn-book on a rainy evening, a long time
ago. Must be quite a big fellow by now. Wonder if he
still hands out hymn-books or did he give that up years
ago?

A man in his late twenties, fair and good-looking, was
preaching. He spoke in a more cultivated accent than the
rest of his group. Sweat stood out thickly on his forehead
and drops of spittle flecked around the corners of his
mouth. His voice rose and fell in waves of damnation. His
eyes spotted Andrew and Abe, and he nodded recognition.

"Who the hell is he greeting?" Abe asked, a little
annoyed.

"Let's move," Andrew said suddenly.

"Do you know him?"

"No. Let's go!"

"Hang on a bit. The bus hasn't come yet."

"I feel I've had enough."

"It was your idea to watch them."

"I know. It wasn't a very good one. If I stay any
longer I'll get sick to my stomach."

"All right."

He was moody and silent by the time the bus came.
Abe was puzzled by this sudden change in his behaviour
and looked at him enquiringly. Andrew felt his insides
turning and a severe headache coming on. But how could
one explain to Abe the memories it brought back, and
tell him that the man they had watched preaching was
his brother Daniel?

7

Andrew started his first teaching post with
justifiable misgivings. He had heard from reports that
his new Principal, a Mr. van Blerk, was a boor. Those

who were more unkind called him a quisling, an in-
former, a government stooge. Miriam was up early the
first day, fussing around and seeing to his clothes and
breakfast. Andrew dressed slowly and carefully, looking
himself over several times in the mirror. He wondered
whether he looked like a teacher, whether he wore the
right air of authority. He sincerely hoped so. His reflec-
tion wasn't altogether unsatisfactory. He had grown taller
and slimmer. A shock of wavy black hair topped his
rather handsome, brown face. A square-cut chin and
heavy, bushy eyebrows. He brushed an invisible speck of
dust from his jacket and tried on his dark glasses for
effect. Then he went in to breakfast.

He had to catch a train to Tiervlei, then walk the
quarter-mile down Dirkie Uys Street to his school. The
train was overcrowded and he spotted several students
from Goodwood onwards wearing the Tiervlei High badge.
He tried to concentrate on his *Cape Times* as every
teacher should, then settled down to the crossword. At
Tiervlei he alighted and enquired of a group of students
the nearest route to school.

His first disappointment was to find that the school
was mostly pre-fabricated. The main block, however, was
built of brick. What amused him was the number of
very young Afrikaner children whom he passed. Most of
them touched their caps and greeted him politely in
Afrikaans. Clusters of students stood conversing outside
the Main Gate. This was his first test. Did he look old
enough to pass for a teacher or would he be mistaken
for a senior student? He should have lit a cigarette. They
stood aside respectfully and greeted him as he passed.
Andrew sighed with relief.

He found the Principal's office deserted, and stood waiting alone in the corridor, watching the students in the
central quadrangle through a window. Not a bad-looking
bunch, though some seemed sadly lacking in discipline.
He wondered how Abe was faring on the other side of
the Peninsula. Some of the boys and girls did look
terribly poor, undernourished, wearing broken shoes and
patchy blazers.

A small waspish man walked excitedly up the corridor.
"Good morning. You Mr. Dreyer?"

"Yes, sir."

"I'm Mr. van Blerk."

He shook hands with his new Principal and decided he didn't like him.

"Step inside. Sit down. Excuse me while I put through a phone call."

Andrew watched him closely. A peppery, annoying type of man.

"That Tiervlei Police Station? Van Blerk here. Yes, van Blerk, Principal of Tiervlei Coloured High School. There's a member of my School Committee, a Mr. De Bruyn, standing outside my school and advising new students not to enrol here because I'm supposed to be a Government stooge. Yes, the sidegate in Flinders Street. I want you to send someone up as soon as possible and have him removed. Thank you."

He banged down the phone.

"That settles his account. Trouble, trouble, trouble. People in the area call me a quisling and a sell-out just because I want to do my work without interference. I allow no politics in my school. I hope we understand each other, Mr. Dreyer, no politics."

So van Blerk was not going to prove easy. They settled down to the allocation of Andrew's classes and subjects. The Principal rattled them off.

"English and History for Senior Certificate. English, Latin and Physiology for Junior Certificate. Religious Instruction and Sports duty."

"But I've never done Physiology in my life," Andrew said, bewildered.

"It really doesn't matter, just keep the students occupied."

"I've no qualifications for the subject."

"That is not important."

"I've applied for a post to teach English and History in senior classes."

"Please don't instruct me about what you applied for."

"If I had known this I would never have accepted the post."

"You can still change your mind if you wish. The staff-room is around the corner. Good morning, Mr. Dreyer."

After his abrupt dismissal Andrew went out wondering

just what he had let himself in for. He made his way to the staff-room and sat down moodily. A serious, bespectacled teacher sat down next to him.

"Hello, you're obviously new here."

"Yes, I am. Dreyer's the name. Andrew Dreyer."

"How do you do? I'm Keith De Bruyn."

"Haven't we seen each other before?"

"Yes, I think we have. You were a year behind me at University."

"Yes, now I remember. Did you teach here your first year?"

"Yes, a year too long."

"You know, your surname rings a bell. Do you have a relation who is a member of the school committee?"

"My father is."

"Was he standing outside the gate this morning, advising children not to enrol here?"

"It could be. Sounds like my old man."

"I heard the Principal phoning the police about removing him."

"I wouldn't put it past van Blerk. He's nuts. Suffers from an acute persecution complex."

"Really?"

"Yes. Always running to the School Board or the Police with complaints."

"I see."

"Be careful about politics. If he finds out he's bound to report you. Has to maintain his position as the authorities' good boy."

"Seems like it."

"He feels he's a martyr, but the truth is he has only himself to blame. No one can stand his guts."

Andrew kept off politics to the best of his ability till April when the country celebrated the tercentenary of the landing of Johan van Riebeek, who had founded the first permanent white settlement at the Cape. Amid much pageantry and ceremony there was great talk of three hundred more years of white rule. There was also a move afoot amongst non-whites to boycott the festivities and not participate in the celebration of their own oppression. Thousands of leaflets were distributed and Andrew gave some to selected students in his class.

The following morning before school started, van Blerk

called him into the office. The Principal held a leaflet in his hand.

"Mr. Dreyer, do you know anything about these leaflets?" He handed the leaflet to Andrew.

"Yes, I do."

"They are circulating in the school. Have you any idea of their origin?"

"I'm not prepared to answer you."

"Could it be that they come from you?"

"Are you making an accusation?"

"Yes, I am making an accusation."

"Well, you know what to do in that case."

"Mr. Dreyer, you are jeopardizing your career in its infancy. You are not allowed to distribute political material on school premises."

"Thank you for your advice."

"Good morning, Mr. Dreyer."

Andrew went back to his class in a huff. During lunchtime he met Keith.

"Van Blerk knows about my distributing boycott leaflets."

"That's lousy."

"He has asked me about their appearance on the premises."

"And off the premises?"

"He didn't mention that."

"I think it is time we called his bluff. He has no control over us after school."

When the final bell rang to end the school day Keith and Andrew stood outside the Main Gate, distributing fresh leaflets. Van Blerk passed them without saying a word.

The following afternoon after school they were again outside the gates. Students queued along the pavement for leaflets. Van Blerk got into his car and drove off. Fifteen minutes later he was back, accompanied by a police officer. For half an hour the two sat in the car watching Keith and Andrew distributing the boycott notices.

On 26th June 1952, the Congresses began their Defiance of Unjust Laws Campaign. It was based on the Gandhian precept of civil disobedience and was completely non-violent. African and Indian volunteers deliberately broke some apartheid law or other, thus inviting arrest.

Andrew had read about it and discussed it thoroughly with Abe. They found far too many points of disagreement with the Campaign to entertain the idea of playing an active part.

One day late in August, as Andrew's train pulled into Cape Town Station he saw a crowd gathered near the ice-cream stalls. People were milling around and Andrew also tried to catch a glimpse of what was happening. From the conversations around him he gathered that a group of Defiers had just been arrested for deliberately occupying a whites-only train compartment and that the police were trying to lead them off. There were shouts of Freedom and Afrika and thumb-raising. Very soon Andrew found himself standing in front of the crowd. The Defiers were manacled and being pushed and shoved by the police. Among them Andrew spotted Justin walking firmly and refusing to be hurried along. He in turn noticed Andrew and half-smiled, raising his thumb in the Congress salute as he walked off to prison.

Andrew watched bewildered and stunned, unable to appreciate fully what was happening. Instead of going straight home he first went to see Abe.

"Remember last Tuesday evening we discussed the Defiance Campaign?"

"Yes," Abe replied.

"We came to the conclusion it was merely a Congress stunt?"

"Yes."

"I saw Defiers being marched to prison this afternoon."

"So?"

"Justin was among them."

"Who?"

"Justin Bailey."

"So what does that mean?"

"It makes all the difference seeing a close friend in manacles."

"Now don't be sickly and sentimental."

"I am feeling sentimental and I'm not ashamed to admit it. I felt a coward because I wasn't marching with him."

"How noble and sugary. Look, Andrew, this situation

must be opposed on a rational basis. Changes cannot be brought about by stunts jerking at people's heart-strings."

"What about train apartheid?"

"Tactics do not hold good for ever. What was suitable before need not be applicable now."

"I suppose you're right in a way."

"What do people like Justin and company hope to achieve? A change of heart in the powers that be?"

"I don't really know."

"We must hit them where it hurts most. Their pockets, not their consciences."

"I guess you're right. But seeing Justin in handcuffs did something to me. Something inside which I can't explain."

In October there were riots in Port Elizabeth. At New Brighton a white constable tried to arrest an African who had stolen a tin of paint. His friends tried to release him and the policeman fired into the crowd. Tension mounted and an S.O.S. was sent out for police reserves. Then the rioting started. Four whites were murdered, there were dozens of African casualties, seven of them fatal.

The following month there was violence in East London. Police baton-charged a religious gathering after ordering the crowd to disperse, and many Africans had their skulls cracked. People's tempers were inflamed to white heat. A European nun who had worked for Africans in East London for many years was set upon by some rioters and murdered.

Although he knew it was useless, Andrew reapplied for his post for the next year. Van Blerk must have branded him as an agitator in the eyes of the authorities for he received a reply regretting that his position had already been filled. He heard later that a non-graduate had taken his place. Things looked grim until Abe came to the rescue.

"There's a vacancy at our school in Senior English and History."

"That sounds good."

"Both Altmann and I have recommended you."

"Oh, of course. Altmann's on your staff. How's the old boy?"

"Same as ever. By the way, my Principal's sane!"

"More than can be said for dear old van Blerk. Who's your boss again?"

"De Jager."

"Yes, I remember now. Well, you can tell him that I have ten years' experience. One year under van Blerk is worth a decade anywhere else. I wonder if my loving chief will miss me?"

Van Blerk, in fact, was extremely glad to see the last of Andrew and determined to staff his school in future with non-political, pliable undergraduates.

8

April 1953 saw another General Election. Only whites were allowed to vote, the one exception being the Coloured male voter in the Cape Province. This time the Nationalist Party increased their seats in the Assembly to ninety-four, and by capturing both Houses practically eliminated any serious Parliamentary opposition.

Again there was a spate of new legislation. The Public Safety Bill: the Governor-General may declare whenever he pleases that a state of emergency exists in any one part of the country or in the entire Union. This can continue for a full year without any further proclamation. Separate Amenities Act: segregation patterns in transportation and public places will now be legalized. Criminal Law Amendment Act: penalties may be applied to any persons protesting against any of the racial laws or inciting others to do so. Bantu Education Act: the Government will take complete control over African education. Mission or church schools will fall in line with Government plans or close down. And so it went on and on.

Andrew was glad to be at Steenberg High. Abe and Mr. Altmann were there, the latter taking Junior classes and quite contented in his new role as Junior Assistant Master. Mr. De Jager was a fine man, understanding and tactful and a stickler for detail. If he had a fault it was over-religiousness. He sometimes prayed at Combined Assemblies for more than an hour, addressing the students and God in both official languages, English and Afrikaans.

It was infinitely preferable to van Blerk and Tiervlei. Life followed a pleasantly monotonous routine. After Combined Assembly, Religious Instruction for one period. Then three periods of teaching. A long lunch-break and then three more periods. A short tea-break and the last two periods. Then home with Abe. Often they got a lift with De Jager who went as far as Salt River, but occasionally they took a train from Steenberg to Cape Town and then the Walmer Estate bus home.

The train journey was dull on the whole, and they usually settled down to reading newspapers or books. There was, however, the occasional incident which livened up the dullness of the routine.

It was one of those ripe, warm afternoons which can only be found in the Southern Suburbs, those balmy September days before the Christmas heat, when people tire sooner and tempers just start becoming frayed. De Jager had informed Andrew and Abe that he would be remaining late after school, which meant that they would have to take a train.

The ticket-box at the station had the usual two windows, one for Europeans and the other with a detachable board overhead, prominently displaying the legend, "Non-Europeans Only." The latter window faced the South-Easter and the soot from the railway line, whereas the "Whites-only" window looked into a neat, though austerely furnished, waiting-room. Abe rolled his green eyes in mock despair.

"It's hard being a non-white."

"I don't see why you should grumble," Andrew replied. "You could easily pass for white if you made the effort."

"It's my mother's fault. I can't be held responsible for my charming freckles and luxurious blond tresses."

"How Coloured can you get!" Andrew replied.

The two joined the queue outside the non-European ticket-box. They had heard quite a few complaints from their students about the new clerk. Apparently he treated all dark passengers with absolute contempt. On the railway timetable someone had scrawled in pencil, "Don't throw the tickets at Coloreds like dogs, you big white gorila."

"I don't admire the style, though I appreciate the sentiments," Abe said laughingly.

"Some mute, inglorious Milton," Andrew replied. "It's obviously constructed in very free verse."

"The spelling is atrocious. Only a member of 10b could spell gorilla like that."

"All right, we can't all be English masters at a third-rate high school."

"The more's the pity."

"I believe there've been complaints about this monkey in the ticket-box."

"Yes. Serves the whites first, then sees to us black folks at his leisure."

"The insolence of office."

The queue slowly moved forward.

"I heard he swore at some of our senior students the other day."

"I wouldn't be at all surprised. This is, after all, South Africa, in case you didn't know it, and men like him are the aristocracy of labour."

"Of white labour?"

"Of all labour."

It was Abe's turn to be served. The clerk was a heavy man, sallow-complexioned and sporting a Groucho Marx moustache. The unknown bard had been right. There was something distinctly simian about his appearance.

"One first-class single to Cape Town please."

The clerk looked up slowly, puzzled by the unfamiliar accent.

"Other side, please," he said politely.

It was Abe's turn to look surprised.

"Excuse me?"

"Round the corner, sir. This is the non-European side."

"Oh, I see," said Abe, amused as he realized that the clerk had been taken in by his fair complexion.

"That's all right. I'm Coloured or so-called Coloured."

"Other side, please," said the clerk firmly.

"Now, let's not be difficult," Abe began. "I prefer to be served here."

"I'm not allowed to serve whites at this counter."

"Excuse me?"

"I'm not allowed to serve Europeans here."

"I'm not a European. I've never been to Europe in my life."

"Round the corner, please."

The clerk crossed over to serve an overdressed brunette at the other counter.

"Of all the giddy things!" Abe said, amazed.

"Damn fool," Andrew agreed.

"So I have to fight now in order to establish my non-white status."

"It's the shape of things to come."

"How crazy can one get."

The queue was lengthening behind them and people, mostly housewives and builders, were becoming impatient at the holdup. Abe tapped angrily on the counter-sill with his money.

"I'm sorry, but I'm not serving you here."

"I would like a first-class single to Cape Town, please."

"I only serve Coloureds on this side. Europeans are around the corner."

"But I am Coloured. I have a mother with bushy hair and thick lips. I teach at a Coloured high school. I am most ostentatiously Coloured. Hundred per cent pure mixed breed."

"I am not here to listen to your insults."

"Then stop acting silly. One first-class single to Cape Town."

"It's against the law to serve you at this window. I'm afraid you must go round to the European section."

"Like hell! I'm staying right here."

The clerk served three more Europeans, then sat down pretending to be engrossed in a copy of *Farmers' Quarterly*. He made a great show of being completely indifferent to Abe's hostile glare. The queue was becoming still longer and people's tempers more frayed. A train pulled in and left amidst shrieks and whistles, picking up very few non-white passengers.

"Come on, Abe," Andrew pleaded. "You've had your fun. You might as well pretend to be white and get this silly business over with."

"I don't find this at all funny, and I refuse to be anything other than myself."

"All right. I'll buy your ticket."

"I get my own, thanks."

"There is a crowd of people waiting behind us. We've caused them to miss one train already."

"They might as well miss a few more."

"Is it fair to them? We're wasting the time of innocent people."

"I'll explain to them."

Abe turned around and cleared his throat. He threw a stray lock of hair out of his eyes.

"Ladies and gentlemen!"

He had to raise his voice to make himself heard.

"My friends, may I have your attention! There is a delay here because the clerk refuses to serve me. The reason is that he has apparently taken it upon himself to declare me a European. I assure you that I have never left South Africa. He has therefore asked me to join the white queue, which I have no intention of doing. I refuse to be anything other than what I am, one of you. Therefore I'm staying right here until I'm served. Are you with me or against me?"

Those who could hear him agreed. The rest murmured sullenly. Abe turned back to Andrew.

"Does that satisfy you?"

"Your little speech was totally unnecessary."

"You asked for it."

"Pure exhibitionism."

The clerk continued to concentrate on his magazine, serving white customers only. Another half-empty train pulled in and left. The crowd was growing impatient again.

"If you refuse to come around to the other side I won't serve you," he said without looking up from his desk.

"Is it legal to serve non-whites at a non-white counter? I see a notice above my head."

"Yes."

"Well, I'm non-white."

"I'll serve you around the corner."

"And break your own laws?"

A white railway constable arrived amidst mingled boos and cheers from the impatient crowd. He entered the ticket office and had a quick, whispered conversation with the clerk. Then he peered at Abe through the window.

"Now what's all the trouble about?"

"I'm waiting to be served. I've waited over half an hour."

"The clerk says you're in the wrong queue."

"Is this the non-white queue?"

"Can't you read?"

"Is this the non-white queue?"

"Yes!"

"Well then, I'm in the right queue."

"Sure of that?" he asked suspiciously.

"Quite, quite sure."

The policeman returned to the desk and whispered intently to the clerk, then he left, pushing his way through the crowd. The protests were becoming quite loud and threatening by now. Another ten minutes passed. The clerk looked up slowly, his eyes filled with hatred. Abe met his gaze unflinchingly.

"All right," the clerk said at length. "I'll serve you."

He slowly rose and left the office. Once outside he came to where Abe was standing. Andrew wondered what the hell he was up to. The clerk reached for the "Non-Europeans Only" notice and withdrew it from its socket. The crowd watched expectantly. He reversed the sign, displaying the "Europeans Only" printed on the other side. He glared at the crowd, then slipped it back into its socket.

"What a transformation!" Abe remarked, surveying the new sign. The clerk maintained a hostile silence as he went back into his office. Then he served Abe. He left his window for the second time and reversed the notice. The crowd roared with laughter.

"So we're back where we started," Abe remarked.

"How damn silly," said Andrew.

"Next!" the clerk ordered gruffly.

"One single first-class to Cape Town," said Andrew. "It's quite safe, I'm not a European."

The clerk glared at him.

9

Life was essentially humdrum and a matter of routine during the years that followed. Kenneth was drinking heavily and Andrew avoided him whenever possible. Only on rare occasions did they meet at the supper table. James often visited Nile Street and even tried to be friendly with everyone, but Andrew cut him

dead. Miriam was showing the effects of Kenneth's treatment with dark rings appearing around her eyes and the
lines in her face deepening. Sometimes Annette visited
them, but Miriam judiciously warned Andrew well before-
hand, which gave him a chance to be out when she made
her appearances.

Andrew was attending more and more political meetings, public and private. Protests, motions, resolutions.
Sometimes with Abe, more often alone. Nationalism
must be opposed. South Africa and neo-colonialism. All
shall be equal before the law. Non-racialism, multiracialism. The boycott as a tactic or a principle. Meetings,
discussions, symposiums.

As Andrew became more and more emotionally involved, Abe seemed to become more academic and distant.
He still read avidly, argued convincingly and impressively,
but Andrew sensed that he was weak at translating his
political theory into practical, militant terms.

"I don't believe that teachers can afford to take a
political stand," Abe would explain.

"Why not?"

"As semi-civil servants we are more vulnerable."

"Wouldn't it then be more honest for us to give up
political leadership altogether?"

"As the most educated members of the community
we are also the most aware politically, and therefore leadership is thrust upon us. We haven't chosen it."

"But all within the framework of our vocational limita-
tions?"

"I'm afraid so. The situation is paradoxical. We cannot afford to accept the responsibility yet circumstances
give us no alternative."

In 1954 Dr. Malan retired from the Premiership and
Hans Strijdom, the uncompromising Lion of the North,
took over the mantle of apartheid. Ever since 1952 the
Nationalist Party had made efforts, even at the risk of
wrecking the Constitution, to remove the Coloured male
in the Cape Province from the Common Voters' Roll. As
his right to vote was a clause entrenched in the Act of
Union, they had to have a two-thirds majority of a joint
sitting of both Houses in order to deprive him of it. In
November 1955, the Senate was enlarged from forty-eight
to eighty-nine to make this possible. In February of the

following year, the South African Act Amendment Bill validating the Separate Representation of Voters Act was passed. Coloured males were removed from the Common Voters' Roll and transferred to a separate roll which would permit them to elect four Europeans to represent them in the House of Assembly.

On 26th June 1956, the five Congresses, the African National Congress, the South African Indian Congress, the South African Coloured People's Organization, the Congress of Democrats and the South African Congress of Trade Unions, met at Kliptown outside Johannesburg and formed the Congress of the People, adopting the Freedom Charter as a minimum programme of demand.

"We who have come from every corner of our land, chosen by our people to meet together in this great assembly, believe that the Freedom Charter we have adopted contains in it the most just desires of the overwhelming majority of the South African people. We declare for all our country and the world to know that South Africa belongs to all who live in it. . . ."

Abe was highly critical of the Congress of the People. He refused to accept the concept of national groups, as he saw it in the perpetuation of racialism; and he therefore strongly disagreed with the five pillar structure of the Congress which seemed to him to imply a tacit acceptance of racial patterns. He was critical of the concept of the will of all the people, regading it as a meaningless, unassessable quality aborted from the philosophy of Rousseau. Andrew listened to him carefully, and although he found difficulty in countering the arguments, he felt that something was wrong somewhere in Abe's whole approach. Maybe it was because of its over-theoretical and impractical nature. Whatever it was he could not define it.

On the 5th of December there were dawn raids throughout South Africa. One hundred and fifty-six suspects were finally picked up all over the country and flown in deadly secrecy to Johannesburg to face a preparatory examination on charges of high treason. The penalty could be death. Justin Bailey was awakened at seven in the morning, even before his milkman came, by three uniformed policemen bearing an arrest warrant. He was hastily brought before a magistrate in the police gymnasium at Caledon Square which had been converted into a

special Court. Together with thirteen others he was re-
manded to Johannesburg and put aboard a military air-
craft at Brooklyn Airfield.

Andrew heard the news at school. For the rest of the
day he was morose and upset. Abe seemed indifferent and
completely divorced from the situation. Andrew couldn't
help remembering Justin marching to gaol with the Defiers.
How long ago was that? Three, four years? He still saw
it clearly. Justin's quiet half-smile, the thumbs-up salute.
Like Abe, he had never entirely agreed with Justin's
politics. Puerile political exhibition as Abe called it, but in
some confused way Andrew felt something in common
with Justin's attitude, a vague kinship which he could
not share because he was a teacher. Justin's practical
politics made sense to him, although he did not of necessity agree with them. He could understand his attitude,
and more than merely understand, he could feel it. It was
tangible and sensuous. He never for one moment doubted
Justin's sincerity in spite of his objections to exhibitionism.
Or was it Abe's objections?

Andrew was quite surprised when a week later he was
invited to speak at a mass protest meeting on the Grand
Parade. There were certain uncomfortable implications. It
was true that as a teacher he was vulnerable. The Special
Branch would obviously be present. He might get kicked
out of his post, be thrown out of school, rendered jobless.
What would Miriam and Kenneth say? His Principal? He
discussed it with Abe who strongly advised Andrew not
to expose himself. It was far too dangerous. A teacher's
position was insecure.

"I feel you'll be taking too great a risk."

"I realize that."

"Also you'll be identifying yourself with Congress
policies and stunts."

"I can't believe that this meeting is a stunt. I might
disagree with their policies, but I admire the stand they
are taking on this issue."

"I know your views, but will everyone else?"

"Does everyone else matter? I'm not going to make a
case for Congress policies. I shall be speaking against
what I, and every right-thinking person, consider an injustice. I don't believe that people like Justin are guilty
of high treason."

"Neither do I."

"Therefore on that count alone I am prepared to identify myself with anyone who thinks like me. I shall speak on Sunday."

"Well, you know your own mind."

"Will you be at the meeting?"

"When is it?"

"Sunday on the Grand Parade."

"I might and I might not."

The Parade was crowded when Andrew forced his way to the platform. A choir from Langa was singing freedom songs in the background. Over and over again the lilting melodies were sung. *Asikhathali noba siyabatshwa, sizimisel inkululeko.* We are not afraid of being arrested, we will work for freedom. Not afraid of being arrested, we will work for freedom. Voices blending beautifully. *Unzima lo mthwele, unfunamanima.* The burden is heavy, the burden is heavy. Andrew nervously took his seat. He hoped he might spot Abe in the crowd. That was if he turned up. He hoped to God he would. *Zibetshiwe, zibetshiwe, inkokeli zethu, zibetshiwe.* Our leaders are arrested, our leaders are arrested. Justin is arrested. Justins are arrested. He spotted Braam de Vries grimly holding up a poster. We stand by our leaders. Hell, he was taking a risk as a teacher. A hell of a risk. But what could he do? What else could he do? What did Martin Luther say? Here I stand, I can do no more. Something like that. Here I stand. A sea of faces, and the Special Branch most probably somewhere in the crowd. Taking down every bloody word he said. Running back to their bosses with it. Please sir, there's a naughty teacher at Steenberg High who says nasty things about the Government. I think he should be given lines, sir. Andrew felt he mustn't allow his thoughts to wander. Pull himself together. High treason was a serious, a capital offence. Write out a hundred lines. I must not speak against the Government. Show it to me in the staff-room during the second interval. He wished Abe could be with him, sharing the same platform, prepared to take the same risk.

Andrew began speaking nervously, but after a time he warmed up. The crowd listened intently in spite of the hot sun.

"Those who would divide us in fact draw us closer together. We must pledge ourselves to oppose all things that divide man from man, group from group, people from people!"

The choir sang softly. *Asukhathali noba siyabatshwa, sizimisel inkululeko.* We are not afraid of being arrested, we will work for fredom. We are not afraid of being arrested.

"By high treason, Ladies and Gentlemen, I understand racial incitement, discrimination and domination. It is the perpetrators of these who are on trial before the rest of the world."

Weee-e Strijdom, uthint abafozi, wayithint imbokodwe uzakufa. Strijdom, you have struck a rock, you have struck a rock.

"I sincerely believe, and I'm sure you'll agree, that the sufferings of those arrested, and of their families and dependants, will inspire and stimulate to keener action all those in South Africa who are concerned to remove every vestige of racial discrimination!"

If only Abe could be with him. He felt isolated on the platform in spite of the huge crowd. Justin's half-smile and thumbs-up sign.

"I quote from the United Nations Declaration of Human Rights. . . ."

If only he didn't feel quite so lonely and cut off.

" 'All human beings are born free and equal in dignity and rights. They are endowed with reason and conscience and should act towards one another in a spirit of brotherhood.' "

Abe might be in the crowd. Should be in the crowd.

"I quote finally. 'Let all who love their people and their country now say, as we say here, these freedoms we will fight for side by side, throughout our lives, until we have won our liberty!' "

He finished his speech amidst prolonged applause. As he left the platform part of the crowd milled around him, shaking his hand, slapping him on the back. He felt he was in another world, divorced from the one around him. He hardly recognized people. There were tears of frustration in his eyes.

"Still remember me?"

He tried to concentrate on the man vigorously pumping his hand. A common labourer in a dirty-brown overall who smelt of stale sweat.

"Yes," Andrew said automatically.

"You must remember me. Amaai. From Caledon Street."

"Yes, sure, sure. I remember you."

He forced his way through the crowd searching. He wasn't sure what he was searching for. Then he realized. He was searching for Abe. That's right, Abe. If only he could find him. He reached the stop, weary and moody. He took a bus home although the meeting wasn't quite over.

The following evening at the supper-table Kenneth was more sarcastic than usual. The meeting was prominently displayed on the front page of the newspaper he was reading, and he was making adverse comments throughout the meal. Andrew felt so listless and enervated that he had not even bothered to glance at the headlines. He felt that Abe had let him down badly.

"I see here you spoke at a Kaffir meeting," said Kenneth without looking up.

"Excuse me?"

"It says here you spoke at a Kaffir meeting."

Andrew felt every nerve tingling.

"What do you hope to achieve with those barbarians?"

Andrew realized the absolute importance of controlling himself. He breathed deeply.

"If you go on speaking at these meetings we'll have the bloody police on our door next."

"Don't be mean to Andrew," Miriam cut in.

"Well, I won't have the bloody cops in my place!"

Andrew felt that this was getting too much for him.

"Do I understand that you would like me to leave your house?" he asked in an even voice.

"It doesn't matter a damn to me. All I'm saying is that I'm the boss here and I'm having no bloody Communists in my home."

"I'm not a bloody Communist!"

"If you carry on this way, people might very well think you are."

"Please, Kenneth, leave Andrew alone!" Miriam pleaded.

"No one is going to tell me what to do in my own blooming house!"

"But you are being so unfair," she insisted.

"May I be excused from the table?" Andrew asked, rising.

"You may go to hell for my part!"

Andrew felt like ramming his fist into Kenneth's face. Better not lose his temper. There was Miriam to consider. He sensed his sister's pleading. He left quietly, showing no visible reaction and went to his room. He felt like doing nothing. No use walking or going to Abe's place. He would most probably quarrel with his friend. Best to go to bed, alone as usual.

10

In 1958 the white voters went to the polls to elect the Twelfth Parliament of the Union of South Africa. The Nationalist Party further increased their majority in the House of Assembly to one hundred and three, the United Party opposition being reduced to fifty-three. Strijdom died and a new Prime Minister was elected by the caucus, Dr. Verwoerd. The Treason Trials ground on wearily in Pretoria. Some of the Trialists occasionally came home when the court was adjourned and Justin Bailey was able to maintain personal, albeit intermittent, contact with his wife and friends in Cape Town. Just before the General Election, Coloureds had been allowed to vote for the four European candidates to represent them in the House of Assembly. Enormous controversy raged about this. The Congresses were all for putting up a candidate, but a considerable and influential body of opinion was against it and called for a total boycott of the elections.

Justin, Abe and Andrew sat in Khayyams after having been to see Norman Wisdom in *The Bulldog Breed*. The restaurant was softly lit, as Abe remarked suspiciously, to prevent one from seeing the food. After the meal they sat smoking over their coffee, discussing the coming elections.

"I don't agree that it is important to put up a candidate," said Abe, addressing Justin.

"Purely for propaganda," Justin began, inhaling deeply.

"We'll be assured of a platform in Parliament. It's time they heard the Freedom Charter." Abe started getting annoyed.

"Whom do you hope to convince? The present Government?"

"If possible, yes," Justin said with assurance. "And more important the outside world in general. Imagine if our candidate gets in," he continued enthusiastically, "don't you think it will embarrass the Nats?"

Abe found his enthusiasm just a bit too much.

"Your candidate can only constitute high nuisance value." He looked moodily into his coffee. "We've got to fight outside Parliament."

"But if we can gain a foothold in the lions' den, then why not?"

"Because it smacks of political opportunism to me. And I mean it. By accepting this separate representation you are working the system of your own oppression."

Justin started losing his confidence.

"But, Abe, can't you understand that the move is purely tactical?"

"No, because we cannot afford to accept less than the full franchise on the Common Voters' Roll. The full right to elect and be elected."

"Universal franchise?" Justin asked with slight sarcasm.

"Yes," Abe said, looking him squarely in the face. "The franchise should not be a reward for educational qualifications or for colour qualifications. It is a right, Justin, not a privilege. The right of citizenship," he emphasized. "Those who are denied the franchise are denied citizenship."

Although he did not participate in the discussion, Andrew sided wholeheartedly with Abe. He accepted unconditionally the principle of boycotting the separate elections and threw himself into the work enthusiastically. Canvassing, speaking to people, knocking on doors. We call upon everyone not to participate in the elections. Don't go to the polls. Do not accept semicitizenship in the land of your birth. Abe remained aloof from all activity. Andrew attended and spoke at meeting after meeting. Mr. Chairman, we cannot accept a separate voters' roll. Nothing less than the full franchise. Ladies and Gentlemen, we demand the inalienable right to govern and be governed. Apartheid cannot be fought with apartheid. Night after weary night. Mass meetings, house meetings, private discussions. Boycott! Don't go to the polls! Stay at home! Boycott! Boycott! Boycott!

The morning of the separate election dawned. Andrew was at the polling booth when it opened. Together with his compatriots he strung up banners. Posters were handed out. Very soon the police were on the scene, taking down names, confiscating placards, charging them with trespassing. Twice Andrew was ordered off the lawn in front of the hall. A white lady who was assisting the Congress candidate phoned up city councillors and got permission for the boycotters to remain. Abe turned up for a brief moment in the afternoon, then left again. Andrew stood wearily outside the booth till it closed in the evening. He had supper at Abe's and never during their discussion was the campaign referred to. In spite of all that, Andrew never doubted Abe's sincerity for one moment.

It worried him as he walked home, Abe's apparent indifference. Completely inexplicable. It couldn't be that he was scared of positive action, or was he? Andrew entered through the kitchen door and found Miriam was there, waiting to see him. She looked worried and completely upset.

"Andrew, the police were here this evening."

"What on earth for?"

"They came to look for you."

"Did they say anything?"

"They searched the whole place and took some pamphlets from your room."

"Was Kenneth home then?"

"Yes, he's still here. In the lavatory at the moment."

"That's lousy, damn lousy!"

"I thought I'd better warn you."

"Miriam!" Kenneth called from the toilet. "Is that your damn brother?"

"No, it's someone else," Miriam replied.

"It's me. Andrew."

"Wait! I want to see you."

Andrew heard the chain being pulled forcefully and the water gurgling in the pan.

"Don't you worry, Miriam, I think I can deal with him."

"Please be careful, Andrew."

Kenneth entered still buttoning up his trousers.

"What the hell is the meaning of this?"

He stared at Andrew with blood-shot eyes.

"The meaning of what?"

"Blooming police around the place."

"I understand from my sister that they wished to see me."

"I don't allow that sort of thing in my house!"

"As you like."

"It might be a damn good thing if you decided to get out altogether."

"That's fair enough."

"Get the hell outta my place!"

"I'll leave in a few moments."

"We'll be better off without the black son-of-a-bitch," he said to Miriam, somewhat surprised at Andrew's reply.

"Please, Kenneth, don't be silly. Andrew, he doesn't really mean it."

"Shurrup!"

"Please, Kenneth!"

"Shurrup! Or I'll ram my fist down your bloody throat!"

"If you dare to do that," said Andrew coolly, "I'll have no alternative but to give you the hiding of your life."

"What's that?"

"I'll be forced to thrash your miserable hide!"

Kenneth summed him up, looking at him in amazement. Andrew had grown much taller and heavier than himself. For the first time he realized that his brother-in-law was now a full-grown man. He had not noticed that before.

"So it's reached the stage where I'm threatened in my own house!"

"Yes, if you dare touch that woman."

"She's my damn wife."

"You don't deserve her."

"So you really think you can threaten me?"

"Why not test me?"

"And what do you propose to do?"

"Give you the hiding you've deserved for a long time."

"You'd better leave," said Kenneth, defeated.

"I'll do so at my leisure."

"The bloody nerve!" he burst out after Andrew had left the room. "Did you hear that black bastard threatening me in my own house?"

Miriam put on her coat and left for Annette's. Later that night Andrew packed and left without saying goodbye to anybody.

Abe allowed him in without asking any questions. Andrew slept fitfully, all night, worrying about Miriam. He awoke the following morning, his eyes all red and raw. At school he was out of sorts and remained so throughout that week.

There was a boy in one of his Junior Certificate classes he had always noticed. Good looking with greenish-grey eyes. Intelligent as well. He stopped Eldred Carollissen in the corridors one day.

"Tell me, where do you stay, young man?"

"In Grassy Park, sir."

"Where on earth is that?"

"You take a bus from Plumstead Station."

"Does one have to swim crocodile-infested rivers and fight Zulu impis on the way?"

Eldred chuckled deeply.

"Well, young fellow, you go home and ask your parents to find out whether they know of anyone who needs a boarder. I'm thinking of shifting."

"Yes, sir."

First thing the following morning Eldred reported back, his eyes sparkling.

"My mother wants to know whether you would like a room in the house or have the garage converted."

"I'll take the room in the house." He regretted it for years after.

"Now tell me exactly where you stay."

"It's not difficult to find, sir. It's in First Avenue off Lake Road, and the house is called 'Semper Fidelis.'"

"Hell. Tell your mother to change the name and I'll shift in on Saturday afternoon."

"Yes, sir. We'll be ready."

He shifted into Mrs. Carollissen's household and had been there ever since. How long he would stay on now was problematic, especially after the two raids in one week. This was the first time he had seen Miriam for a long time. Hell, what a change. She looked like an old woman. Kenneth was most probably threatening her more than ever. He wondered what Ruth was doing. Hoped it wasn't Bligenhout he had seen parked in the car outside her flat. He hummed De Little Black Bull as he switched off the light.

11

The following morning Andrew woke feeling as if his head would burst. Funny, he couldn't possibly have a hangover. Only two brandies at Ruth's flat and that was all. The sun streamed in through the window and he could hear the voices of children on their way to school. Under normal conditions he would now be on the train to Steenberg either talking to Altmann or reading his *Cape Times*. He usually took a bus to Plumstead and then caught the 7:50 train. Altmann always sat in the same compartment and would greet him with the same "Morning, Mr. Dreyer, and how are we today?" Altmann would most probably miss him and suspect that something was wrong. For a long time Andrew lay quite still, his head throbbing. He could hear Miriam's slow shuffling in the kitchen. Then he got out of bed feeling bilious and sick. He felt for his shoes and then painfully buttoned up his trousers.

"Morning, Miriam," he said as he entered the kitchen.

"Morning," she said without looking in his direction. He made his way to the bathroom-cum-toilet, feeling like vomiting. He glanced at himself in the mirror above the washbasin. Red, puffy eyes and dishevelled hair. There was a small, yellow pimple on his nose. He pressed it between his fingers, forcing the pus out. On the shelf he found a bottle of aspirins and gulped down two. Then he swilled his face in the cold water, but even that brought no relief to his throbbing head. There was only one remedy which would help. He had used it ever since he had been a child in District Six. He carefully bolted the door of the toilet, then forced his fingers down his throat. After he had finished retching he felt tremendously relieved. A cold shower, then a brisk rub-down and he felt fresh. Miriam still used the same scented soap and the bath-

room still smelt of lavender and old newspapers. He
cleaned his teeth and combed his hair. Andrew already
felt considerably improved. There was Ruth to meet between three and four, wait for her at the University
Library. He still had a book outstanding from his student
days. Eight years outstanding. No, nine. What the devil
was it again? *The Hero* by Raglan, or Spencer? *The Man
versus the State*? He remembered it had a brown cover,
and Abe had recommended he should read it. He
wondered how Abe was getting on at school. Hoped De
Jager would understand. He was O.K. Politically neutral
but dependable in a crisis. Yes, Abe would have to tread
warily. His cautiousness must have been merely a transi-
tional stage. Political soul-searching. Fortunately, or un-
fortunately, he had begun to play a more positive role,
had even spoken at odd meetings although he sometimes
reverted to his academic ivory-tower. He had also been
raided on the 24th, and Andrew had been surprised at the
way he had taken it in his stride. Mere routine check-up,
you know. In fact Abe had shrugged off the whole business with a quotation from Hegel, or was it Spinoza,
and had peered over his dark glasses and coughed like a
grammarian. Wonder whether De Jager knew that they
had bunked the Sports Meeting. Hell, he had forgotten
all about that. Should have asked Eldred how the school
had done. He wasn't really interested in sport. Had tried
the half-mile once and had played centre for his school's
rugby team. Now Justin had been a fairly good athlete.
First-class sprinter and idol of all the juniors. Yes, there
was a possibility of seeing Justin today. Usually took his
lunch at Khayyams between one and two. He could
just make it, if he went to Grassy Park fairly early. His
head still throbbed slightly, but he was already feeling
much better, even had an appetite.

Andrew returned to the kitchen just as Miriam was
dishing up his porridge. *The Times* lay unread on the
dresser. He attempted to make conversation as he reached
for it.

"Kenneth still in bed?"

"Yes," she said resignedly, after a long pause.

"Working night shift?"

"Yes."

"Does he know I'm here?"

"I don't think so. I never told him."

He sensed that the whole situation was proving too much for her. He unfolded the newspaper and glanced at the headlines. WIDESPREAD RIOTING IN RAND TOWNSHIPS. ATTACKERS TRIED TO DERAIL WORKERS' TRAINS. The whole bloody situation was getting completely out of hand. CHURCHES, SCHOOLS AT WORCESTER LOCATION BURNT. ERASMUS WARNS DO NOT BURN PASSES. Yes, the whole damn situation was becoming crazy. Completely uncontrollable. TEAR GAS CLEARED THE PARADE. POLICE SHOW RESTRAINT. It seemed a hell of a long time since the baton charge. That garrulous old woman in the train had complained about her lost bag. Just like Mrs. Carollissen. "Mr. D., I lost my bag when the police attacked us, wasn't that nasty." He could imagine Mrs. Carollissen running in her Sunday best, modestly tucking in her skirts. Well, he would have to see her soon. Maybe get to Grassy Park after breakfast. He could imagine what had passed between her and Ruth. The strong smell of urine and the frightened, wide-eyed people in the Public Lavatory. A young man leading in a shivering Moslem. His father, maybe, or his uncle. Seeking shelter from the batons and tear gas in a urinal. That seemed ages ago, not just the day before.

Andrew tackled his porridge with appetite. After he had finished a silent breakfast he turned to his sister.

"Miriam?"

She looked up slowly from the coffee she was pouring.

"I think I will have to stay here for a short while."

"I don't think that will be possible."

"Because of Kenneth?"

"Yes, because of Kenneth."

"I'll manage him."

"It would be better if you could find some other place. What about Abe's?"

"He's suspect. He was raided last week."

"And Grassy Park?"

"They're watching my place."

"I'm afraid of Kenneth."

"You have nothing to fear."

He got up decisively.

"I'll be back late tonight. Keep some coffee warm."

"Please be careful, Andrew."

"Don't worry about me."

He put on his jacket and adjusted his tie.

"I'll be back at about eleven. If Kenneth objects tell him to go to hell!"

He pecked her on the cheek and walked down the passage, slamming the door unconcernedly.

12

Andrew had scarcely shut the door when Miriam heard Kenneth stirring in the bedroom. She sat down heavily on the kitchen bench. Thank God the two had not met face to face. A husband and a brother. She was afraid of Kenneth, and Andrew also seemed obstinate. This was a different Andrew from the one she had known, more mature and self-assured. There was no knowing what could happen were the two to meet.

"Miriam!"

She rose dutifully to her feet.

"Miriam!" Kenneth called again from the bedroom. "Who the hell were you speaking to?"

"It's nothing, nothing at all, Kenneth."

She could visualize him at that moment sitting up in bed and fumbling for his trousers. Thin, white, spider-like arms feeling across the bedrail. He would find them and after putting them on, sit picking at his teeth with a broken match, his raw, red feet thrust out in front of him. She had always found his feet physically repulsive.

"It's nothing, Kenneth. It's not important."

"It's blooming important to me!"

He entered the kitchen bare-footed, struggling to get into his shirt.

"Who was here this morning?"

"No one, Kenneth."

"Whose dirty plate is that?"

"Please, Kenneth!"

"Was it that black swine Andrew?"

"My brother's not a black swine!"

"Was Andrew here?"

"It's not important!"

"Was he here!"

"Yes, he was here," she said as she sank resignedly into her seat.

"You mean that you allowed that bastard into my house?"

"He was looking for a place to sleep last night."

"And you had the nerve to put him up?"

"Yes."

"Who gave you the right to?"

"He had nowhere else to go."

"So the worm came crawling back here?"

She felt it best to remain quiet. Better gather the dirty plates and cups and remove them to the sink.

"Who gave you the right to let him in?"

She turned on the tap, allowing the water to run over her hand till she felt it was hot enough.

"I'm asking you a question!"

She reached for the soap and rubbed it into a wet cloth.

"I'm speaking to you, damn it all!"

She emptied Andrew's leavings into the dirt-bin then soaked the plate in the water.

"Answer me!"

"Please forget it, dear."

"I refuse to forget it!"

It came so suddenly that she was momentarily thrown off her guard. He knocked the plate out of her hand and it crashed to the floor. She stared after it stupidly.

"When your husband speaks you bloody-well answer!"

"What do you want from me?"

"Why did you allow Andrew in here?"

"He's my brother."

"That doesn't matter a damn to me."

"It does matter to me."

"You have the impertinence to answer back!"

She turned to the sink and began rinsing a cup. He grabbed it out of her hand and flung it viciously against the wall. The pieces scattered on the linoleum.

"I'm not staying here while you're in this mood!" she said, starting to untie her apron-strings.

"Where the hell do you think you're going?"

"That's my business."

"You're staying right here!"

For a brief moment they challenged each other with their eyes.

"You had the nerve to let that black swine into my house?"

"I let my brother in."

"A bloody mother-killer. Maybe that was the best thing that could have happened. She might have spawned more like him."

"Please leave my mother out of it!"

"Don't tell me what I can and can't say."

"My mother has nothing to do with this."

"She spawned that little black squirt."

"Please leave my mother alone!"

"If he comes here tonight I'll put the police on to him, the damn Communist."

"If you do that I'll also make a report to the police."

"What!"

"I'll report your white prostitutes. You've heard of the Immorality Act?"

"What!"

"I said I'll report your white girl-friends."

"You're a lying bitch!"

"Why not call me a black lying bitch?"

"You're a black lying bitch!"

"There's no reason for me to lie."

"What do you know about white prostitutes?"

"They're already been in my house."

"You lie!"

"In my bed!"

"You lie!"

He grabbed her, pinning her arms behind her back and forcing her to the wall.

"It's true!"

"You're a lying bitch!"

"You know I'm speaking the truth. If you inform the police about Andrew I'll tell about your white women."

"You mean to tell the police!"

"If you don't let me go."

"You're a dirty little slut!"

He smacked her hard across the mouth with his free hand, drawing blood.

"Please, Kenneth!"

"Admit you're lying!"

"You know I'm telling the truth."

"So you mean to report your husband to the police?"

"You deserve it!"

He smacked her again and again. His finger-marks stood out red against her cheeks.

"Let me go, Kenneth!"

"Not until you admit you're a lying bitch."

"I'll say anything you like, only let me go."

"Admit it!"

"Please Kenneth!"

"Admit it!"

"I'll admit it."

"You never saw white women here!"

"Let me go!"

He twisted her arms tighter.

"You never saw white women here."

"I never saw white women here."

"And you'll never let that bastard in again."

"No, Kenneth!"

"You'll never let him in!"

Miriam gulped down hot blood, choked and coughed helplessly. Kenneth loosened his grip.

"If I find him in my house I'll break his bloody neck. You hear that?"

She wiped her mouth on her sleeve.

"Hear that?"

"Yes, Kenneth!"

"Now get my damn breakfast. I'm hungry."

She dutifully placed the pan on the hot stove and poured in the cooking oil.

13

On Tuesday, March 29th, Mr. William B. Freijohn arrived late and annoyed at his office because the suburban train services had been disrupted. He heard later in the day that a lightning bolt had struck a 33,000-volt transmission line near Salt River.

Ruth Talbot had to leave early to catch the 8:15 bus in order to get to the University in time for her first lecture.

Pampoen of Springs won £30,000 in the Southern Rhodesian State Lottery.

Braam De Vries tried unsuccessfully to get a permit to enter Nyanga Location.

The Minister of Defence told the Senate that the Union's one hundred and seventy-five Commando units consisted of 2,640 officers and 56,803 men.

Abe Hanslo drove to Steenberg High School full of misgivings. It might have been wiser to have stayed away like Andrew.

A trawler operating off Cape Town hauled up a rare *Oreosoma atlanticum* from 300 fathoms.

Miriam Peters packed her bags tearfully but realized that she had to make a break finally.

The 114th performance of *Son et Lumière* was conducted in Afrikaans at the Castle.

Justin Bailey realized the importance of leaving home soon, as he expected mass arrests at any time.

Eldred Carollissen bunked the first period as he had not prepared his science homework for Mr. Hanslo.

A Coloured youth of sixteen was wanted to learn manufacturing as a trade. Pleasant work conditions for the right applicant.

Mr. Altmann couldn't solve 2 across in the *Cape Times* crossword. "The rare bad garment is worn? Ten letters. Must be an anagram of 'the rare bad.'"

Five pounds was offered for information about the present whereabouts of Louisa Adams, late of Kloof Street.

Mrs. Millicent Carollissen took off her shoes and relaxed on the sofa after seeing Charmaine and Jeremy off to school at the bus-stop. She really felt like resting after having been on her feet since half-past six. The children were becoming more and more difficult. What a to-do about the lunches in the morning. Vincent doesn't like cheese. Paul won't have tomatoes. Charmaine insists on having peanut-butter and refuses jam. And as for Eldred, that boy was really becoming too much for her. She was certain that it must be Mr. D.'s influence. She would have to speak to her husband about him, but that man never did anything. Completely useless. Always reading his confounded *Cape Times* or *Argus* and leaving her to manage the children. Eldred was getting completely out of hand. Take that very morning. He wouldn't even greet his own mother, made no appearance at the breakfast table and left without taking his school lunch. Mr. Carollissen must really do something. There was no reason, no reason on earth, why she should be struggling alone like that. After all he was the father of a family. Look how rude Eldred had been in front of that white woman, Ruth, something or other. Mr. D.'s girl-friend. Searching for him in Grassy Park. But that was final. Mr. D. would have to go. She couldn't have detectives all over the place.

"Minnie!" she called. The girl never answered one.

"Minnie!"

"Yes, Mrs. Carollissen?"

"Warm up the coffee for me."

Mr. D.'s room would suit Eldred and Vincent. It was obvious her family was growing up and she needed more space. He wasn't a bad boarder, that she had to say for him, but she couldn't have white girls all over the place. She now felt tired and the corns on her toes ached.

"Minnie! Wake me up when the coffee's ready."

She wondered whether the girl had heard. Nobody ever paid the slightest attention to her. And when things went wrong to whom did they run?

She was just dozing off when she heard a car stopping outside her gate. Who could be coming at that hour of the morning?

"Minnie! Who is it, girl?"

She heard the door opening and Minnie speaking to someone in the passage.

"Minnie! Who's there?"

"It's all right. It's me. Good morning!"

Mr. D. Oh Lord! What was he doing away from school at this time of the day? Andrew entered breezily.

"How are we today, Mrs. Carollissen?"

"Fine, thank you," she replied somewhat stiffly.

"Nice weather outside, a bit overcast though."

"Yes," she replied, trying to control herself.

"It's warm in town, but I must say, quite pleasant out here."

"Mr. D.," she decided to come straight to the point. "Mr. D., I'm very sorry, but I'll have to give you your notice."

"Certainly," he agreed. His ready compliance threw her off her guard. She had expected some form of opposition at least.

"I can't have detectives all over the place."

"Of course you can't."

"Also my family's growing up and we need more room."

"That's fair enough."

Mrs. Carollissen felt the situation was becoming embarrassing and she found herself apologizing and making concessions.

"I don't expect you to leave at once, if you haven't found a place yet. The end of April will do."

"I'll call for my stuff within a few days."

"There's no hurry, Mr. D."

"Thanks."

"As long as we can get your room fairly soon."

"I'll try my best."

"Have you got a place already, Mr. D.?"

"At the moment I'm with my sister in Nile Street. You know where she stays?"

"I have an idea."

"It's the third house on the right going up towards Windsor Street."

"I think I know where it is. By the way, Mr. D., two detectives came here yesterday."

"Eldred warned me about it."

"They asked all sorts of questions about you, but I put them in their place."

"Good show!"

"They're supposed to catch criminals, not interfere with educated people."

"Quite correct."

"A decent, respectable Coloured teacher like yourself."

"Don't flatter me."

"I'm not flattering you, believe me, Mr. D., if I had more room I'd certainly keep you on."

"I appreciate that from the bottom of my heart."

"Interfering with respectable people! But I told them their fortunes."

"I believe Ruth came here last evening for me."

"Yes. She's a nice girl. Pity she's white."

"She can hardly help that."

"I like her. She's steady. Mr. D., you mustn't think I'm chasing you away from here."

"Oh no, no, no, no, no."

"You must always come and visit us whenever you are in this area."

"I'll certainly do so."

"Only the family's getting far too big and the house is rather small."

"Yes, I appreciate that. Well, I'll be off now. In the meantime Eldred and Vincent may use my room."

"Thank you very much, Mr. D."

"Well then, see you sometime soon."

"Stay for some coffee before you go. Minnie's just warming some. Minnie!"

There was no reply.

"Minnie! Really, that girl must be deaf. You must have some coffee before you go, Mr. D. You mustn't think I'm trying to get rid of you. Only. . . ."

"Only the family's getting too big. I quite understand. I'll certainly stay for some coffee if I may."

14

Having some time to spare, Andrew drove slowly along the Main Road to Cape Town. There was every possibility of meeting Justin at Khayyams at about one. All along the way he saw evidence of the success of the African stay-at-home. Whites and Coloureds selling newspapers, sweeping out offices, loading trucks. Not a black worker in sight. In Sir Lowry Road he pulled up at a garage for petrol. A white attendant bustled over.

"Good morning," said Andrew. "Could I have three gallons of regular, please?"

The attendant clumsily unscrewed the petrol cap.

"Usual chap not on duty today?" Andrew asked.

"You mean the native boy? No, they're all on strike."

"Any chance of their returning soon?"

"I hope to God they will. But they're scared as hell other Kaffirs might beat them up."

The attendant spoke in an Observatory English accent.

"You really believe that?"

"Look, chum, a guy comes here last Wednesday, let's see, yes, last Wednesday morning. Flashily-dressed native with a brief-case. You know the type, one of those impertinent Kaffirs. Talks to my two boys in their own language. What the hell he told them, I don't know.

Can't understand their monkey talk. He wouldn't clear off when I told him to, so I had to phone the police. He was gone by the time they came, so were my bloody boys."

"You think there are agitators at work?"

"Like hell there are. Bloody Kaffir Communists."

"Wouldn't you agree that African grievances are legitimate?"

"Come again?"

"You don't feel that Africans suffer so much under this system that they are bound to react?"

"Not a damn, the ungrateful bastards. My boys got three pounds ten a week, which is a hell of a lot, more than they'll get anywhere else. They can live on it, eat, have a roof over their heads."

"You consider that a living wage?"

"Why the hell not? I earned three pounds a week when I started working."

"Had you a family to support on that?"

"No, but I could do a lot with three pounds then."

"Could you manage on that now?"

"What do you mean?"

"Could you live on three pounds ten a week with a family to support?"

"Jeeesus, I'm a white man."

"I think I realize that."

"You know, we'll have to stand together. The white man and the Coloured man. We're in this together."

"Sure of that?"

"What the hell do you mean?"

"I mean that everyone who is living below the breadline, whether white, black or brown, must have grievances and I consider a family living on three pounds ten a week to be below the breadline."

"If it were yours or mine, yes. But that's more than sufficient for Kaffirs."

"How much do I owe you for the petrol?"

"Twelve shillings."

"Thanks a lot."

Andrew got into the car and switched on the engine. He was about to drive off when the attendant thrust his head through the window.

"You know, you might be right, chum. Come to think

of it three pounds ten a week is bloody little, but what can I do? I have a business to run."

"Sure, you have a business to run."

Andrew put the car in gear and drove off.

He parked outside Khayyams in Hanover Street. The stay-at-home seemed to have had almost no effect on District Six. Life still continued in its normal, carefree way. He found a table in the far corner and ordered samosas and coffee, as well as a copy of *New Age*. He settled back to read. The weekly contained graphic reports on Sharpeville and Langa. MASS SLAUGHTER BY POLICE. BLOODY REPRISALS AGAINST ANTI-PASS DEMONTRATORS. LANGA'S NIGHT OF TERROR. He carefully read the A.N.C. statement on the Pan-Africanist campaign. *A Congress statement issued on Monday night expressed severe shock at brutal police violence which serves only to incense and inflame the people. Could not methods be used to disperse crowds without killing and maiming people?*

The waitress reappeared with coffee and hot samosas. *The authorities are keen to use any excuse to shoot fear into the hearts of the people.*

"And what are you doing out of school?"

Andrew looked up.

"Hello, Justin. I was hoping to find you here. Have a seat."

Justin looked tired and worn, and there were dark pockets under his eyes.

"Doing a bunk from your class?"

"Yes. For obvious reasons."

"And Abe?"

"He went to school."

"That was indiscreet."

"I agree. By the way, would you like some samosas and coffee?"

"No, thanks, I have no appetite lately."

"Please have something."

"All right, if you insist."

Andrew signalled to the waitress to bring an extra cup of coffee and more samosas.

"So, Justin, how successful do you think the stay-at-home has been?"

"Beyond my wildest dreams. If only the Coloured workers would come out."

"That's always been the difficulty."

"We're working hard, very hard, but they're afraid to budge." Justin looked tired. "It's understandable, they have so much more to lose."

"Yes, I suppose so," Andrew replied. "But how do you think the Government will react?"

"Let's not fool ourselves. This is a last ditch stand. The twilight of three hundred years of white rule." Justin attempted a smile. "They will throw everything they have into it. There will be more raids, arrests, baton charges, gaolings. But what I'm most afraid of," he looked up at Andrew, "is that they might declare a state of emergency."

"And that means?" Andrew asked the question although he really knew the answer.

"A hell of a lot. For instance, the armed forces are called out and anyone can be detained without a warrant for as long as the Minister of Justice decides."

"Yes, I realized that."

"No redress to courts, and I think one can be kept in solitary confinement for thirty days. Anyone can be picked up for questioning, and God help you if you refuse to answer their questions."

"So," said Andrew breathlessly, "these boys can get really tough."

"Yes, and they certainly will. I advise you to get away while the going is good. You and Abe. Disappear. You might both end up in gaol for a long, long time."

"But what about you?"

"I still have some work to do here trying to persuade black workers to stay out on strike and Coloured workers to come out in support. Tomorrow I have pamphlets to distribute in Langa. After that I might lie low. If you can, come along and help."

Andrew remained silent.

"You know," he said after a time, "there is just a chance that they might not declare a state of emergency."

"True, they might not. But don't build up false hopes. Prepare for the worst. Get away before you are caught."

"I suppose so."

"Warn Abe as well. Things are getting pretty serious."

"I'll try and phone him this afternoon."

"Fine. What's your programme today?"

"Well, I'm not quite sure. I have Ruth to meet at the University this afternoon and that's about all I hope."

"I'll be at Braam's place this evening. Come along and try your best to bring Abe with you. We might need you two."

"Yes," said Andrew hesitantly. "Does Braam still stay in Bree Street?"

"Yes. His front door works now. Try not to be spotted. His place might very well be watched."

"O.K."

They sipped their coffee in silence, then lit cigarettes. After a long pause Andrew spoke.

"Justin, I think I'd like to give you a hand."

"We can discuss that tonight."

"All right, see you then. Let me pay for the coffee. I'll be at Braam's place about eight."

"O.K."

15

Andrew parked the Austin near the top of Adderley Street, then glanced at his watch. 2:45. Still plenty of time before meeting Ruth. Wonder what she feels like after last night. Abe should be leaving school just about now. Mustn't forget to phone Abe. There was a public telephone-booth outside the Library. Tell him about the meeting with Justin and Braam. Andrew slowly walked up Government Avenue. A strong detachment of police were guarding the Houses of Parliament, although people passing seemed unconcerned and uninterested. Strolling in the sun, buying peanuts and feeding the pigeons and squirrels.

Andrew found the Library deserted except for a female attendant who ignored him. He settled down at the far table with his back to her. He might as well read while waiting. Damn it! He had left his copy of *New Age* in the car. He walked over to the shelves. Economics; Economic History; Economic Geography; Ethics; Logics and Metaphysics; Political Philosophy. He removed Bosanquet from the shelves. *The Philosophical Theory of the State.*

It seemed years ago that he had done Political Philosophy. He remembered how the Professor would enter, Malherbe it was, cough a dry academic cough, wipe his glasses and rustle through some yellowed pages. The argument, class, is basically that between monism and pluralism. Is the state merely a corporation among corporations or is it in reality the paramount body? Dry as dust. There used to be a giddy blonde who sat just in front of him and sucked wine-gums all through the lecture. One day she turned around and offered him a sweet. He refused self-consciously. She giggled and said, "Segregation in reverse?" He had avoided her after that. Wading one's way through Lippmann, Hsaio and Bosanquet. But the State *de facto* (which is also *de jure*) is the society which is recognized as exercising compulsory power over its members and as presenting itself *qua* a single independent corporation among other independent corporations. Boring to an incredible degree. Thank God that was all over now. He read without taking in anything, familiar phrases ringing vague bells. Even the B.Comm. Degree he was studying for was vaguely in the past. Left in the balance somewhere about the time of Sharpeville and Langa.

Then he spotted Ruth coming through the turnstile. She seemed pale and her face looked drawn, not her usual self at all. She sat down opposite him without showing a hint of recognition, then picked up a copy of *Popular Mechanics* from the table. He noticed that she shivered slightly as she took hold of it.

"I see you're studying philosophy," she said.

"And I'm curious about your new-found interest in *Popular Mechanics* which you are reading upside down. Spent a good night?"

"No. I was frightened to death after you left."

"Why? What happened?"

"Nothing. I was just frightened."

He lowered his book. "Ruth, I hope you won't feel bad about this, but I've been considering things and I think it would be wise for us to part temporarily, maybe permanently."

She took a long time to reply.

"Must we?" she said simply, clenching the magazine and not looking up at him.

"Yes. Things are going to get a lot tougher. I spoke to Justin Bailey before I came here."

"Yes," she said, her voice quivering a little.

"He paints a gloomy picture of the future. He feels they might declare a state of emergency quite soon."

"What does that mean? I'm stupid, you know. I don't understand these things."

"That means arrests without charges, solitary confinement without redress to courts. Gaolings."

"I'm not afraid while I'm with you, Andy."

"They won't allow you to be with me. Please understand, Ruth. We are both suspect. Bligenhout knows all about us and where we both stay. If a state of emergency is declared he can pick us up without bothering to find any reasons."

"I'm not afraid."

"But I am, for your sake, dear. Why don't you get away? Get leave from lectures and go back to Vereeniging. Remain at home for a time."

"That's out of the question. My father would want to know why I left University. Besides, he has enough trouble with his business."

"Ruth, go home for your own sake."

"I can't leave you, Andy."

"You must, Ruth."

"Are you trying to get rid of me?"

"You know I'm not. I'm thinking only of you."

"I've given you everything, Andy, everything I could." Her eyes were dry. "Even . . . even last night. Why must you chase me away now?"

"Because I'm convinced that sooner or later they'll come for you. Gaol is no joke for a white woman."

"Have I suddenly become a white woman? I was just a woman last night."

"Please, dear, let's not argue. Try and understand what I'm trying to say."

"I'm staying in Cape Town, Andy."

"All right, if you insist. I've tried my best."

"I'm staying in Cape Town!"

She got up decisively. "Good-bye, Andy."

"Where are you going?"

"I have an appointment to keep. I mean another lecture. Please, Andy, I must go now."

"Here is your car key. The Austin is parked opposite the old Supreme Court."

"Keep it just in case."

"In case what?"

"You need a white woman again."

"Ruth, you don't really mean that."

"It'll be quite easy for you to get in."

"Please, Ruth."

"Good-bye, Andy."

She neatly placed the key on the table, then walked out unsteadily, trying to control herself. He heard the turnstile creaking. For a long time Andrew sat toying with the key. She knew he hadn't meant to hurt her. She must know. After all she wasn't a woman without principles. A common slut. What a situation. He felt like running after her, but he knew it would be useless. The librarian watched him curiously. Hell, what a damn situation. Had she now permanently walked out on him? Would she have left her key if she had? In case he wanted a white woman. He hoped she hadn't really taken it quite so badly. He shut Bosanquet, slipped the key into his pocket and walked hurriedly to the telephone booth to phone Abe. What the hell was the number again? 25215. The phone rang and rang on the other side. Then a click as someone picked up the receiver.

"Hello? Is that Mrs. Hanslo? Andrew here. Andrew Dreyer. Is Abe home yet? Oh thanks. May I speak to him, please? Certainly, I'll hang on."

He would have to make it up with Ruth somehow. Prove to her that he acted entirely in her own interest. Didn't intend to get rid of her.

"Oh, hello, Abe. Andrew here. I'm speaking from a public booth in Cape Town. I'd very much like to talk to you, but I can't do it on the phone. I can come up to your place. Yes, I have transport. I have Ruth's car. I'll be there in about twenty minutes. O.K.? See you quite soon."

He rang off. What a damn situation. Wonder if she really had a lecture or had she just wanted to get away from him? Walking out on him. Well, drama students did have classes at the oddest times. If she had walked out she wouldn't have left her car key. Oh damn. Better see Abe and try and unravel all complications. Cool off first.

He re-entered the library and opened Bosanquet a second time. It may be observed at this point that the conception of a law of nature. . . . Might as well see Abe. When sorrows come they come not single spies. He got up and slammed the book back on the shelf.

16

Andrew drove slowly along De Waal Drive, half-noticing the houses spread-eagled below him and the long sweep of Table Bay. The air was fresh and exhilarating and he opened wide the car windows. What a life away from landladies and detectives and possible states of emergency and brothers-in-law and Ruth. No, he didn't really mean that. He would really miss her. Miss her a hell of a lot, maybe more than he realized. He drove at a steady thirty miles an hour, drinking in the green slopes, the crackly pine trees and the giant purple mountains looming overhead, Devil's Peak stretching out towards the Constantia Mountains. He turned off at Woodstock and pulled up outside Abe's door. Mrs. Hanslo answered the bell. Abe resembled her quite a lot, the same light, freckled face, green eyes and shock of light-brown hair. She looked unwell. Trouble with her heart, Abe had said.

"Hello, Andrew. Step inside. Abe's busy in his study."

He entered the polished dining-room, and was at once assailed by the feel of familiar things.

"Have you eaten yet, Andrew?"

"Yes, thank you."

"Are you boys in trouble again?" She looked him squarely in the face and he noticed a nervous twitch around her mouth.

"Not just yet, Mrs. Hanslo."

"Are you expecting any?"

"Well, things are a bit unsettled just at present, but don't you fret."

"I hope for your sakes things will be all right."

And for yours, Andrew thought. He knocked on the study door.

"Come in," Abe called.

Andrew entered to find him rummaging through masses of papers, notebooks and files.

"You seem busy, old man."

"Run off my feet I am, getting rid of incriminating material."

"The Great Scare gathering momentum?"

"Caution is always very advisable, especially if one is *persona non grata*."

"What a job."

"I'm destroying everything. They won't find a damn thing if they decide to raid again. Minutes, resolutions, pamphlets."

"I can see that."

"I had no idea I had so much material. I think I'll take a break now."

He sank down in a chair feigning exhaustion.

"Have a cigarette," Andrew offered.

"Not now, thanks. Let me get my wind first. I'm not as young as I was."

"What price senility."

"I have news and news for you. They were at school today."

"Who?"

"Three detectives."

"For us?"

"How right you are. I was busy in the lab at the time. Apparently they walked into the office without removing their hats and De Jager gave them a ticking off."

"Just like him."

"I got this from Altmann who was there at the time. They then asked to see Dreyer and Hanslo. De Jager replied that he had no such persons at his school. There were, however, a Mr. Dreyer and a Mr. Hanslo on his staff."

"Good for him."

"He requested their business, but they refused to tell, so he walked out of the office, leaving them standing. Altmann said that they left in a high temper."

"That was a tough line for De Jager to take. Now he has committed himself. I always thought he was a neutral, you know, a typical school principal. I can imagine what van Blerk would have done in similar circumstances."

"The old man sent a message to me with Altmann, explaining what had happened and requesting me to take sick leave at once. I left school immediately and got home before twelve."

"But won't they find you here?"

"Let them. I am not going simply to give myself up, but I'm certainly not going to panic. I mean to leave, but leave when I'm ready."

"I wonder."

"Before I left school Altmann offered the two of us sanctuary in case we needed it. You know where he stays in Lotus River?"

"I think so. It's somewhere off the beaten track. Round about 11th Avenue somewhere."

"He said his wife cooks well. I have his address and his phone number in case."

"Good."

"I've decided to fix up things at home and then leave tomorrow. First sort out all this junk."

"By the way, I met Mr. Bailey today."

"Justin? I hear married life hasn't treated him very well."

"Oh, trouble with Florence?"

"Yes. My ma told me about it. Apparently his wife is a good friend of hers. She phones the old girl regularly and comes here for doses of comfort."

"I don't blame her."

"So what did Justin have to say?"

"He feels they might declare an emergency at any time now."

"Hell. You know what that means."

"The lot. And you and I, dear Abe, might very well be at the receiving end."

"That's grim."

Mrs. Hanslo knocked softly at the door and brought in hot coffee and biscuits. There was a pregnant silence until she had left. Abe resumed the conversation.

"Ma's taking the whole thing rather badly."

"I can appreciate that."

"The last raid upset her. She had a slight heart attack as a result. After the detectives left I had to get a doctor. That's why I'm half-inclined to stay. However, I'll accept Altmann's offer. I've suggested to Ma that she should go somewhere for a rest, but she won't leave me. For her own sake it's best that I leave her. I've tried to persuade her."

"I've tried to persuade someone to leave me too."

"I think I can guess who."

"Yes, Ruth. I saw her before I came here. She reacted strangely."

"Lots of people are reacting strangely these days."

"These are strange times."

"Well, then, what do you say? Do we retire to the sanctuary of Lotus River?"

"It might be wiser. We can leave in the morning. There's no state of emergency declared yet."

"No. Not yet."

"Justin wants us to meet him at Braam's place this evening."

"Is that wise? Isn't Braam's place likely to be watched?" Abe asked hesitantly.

"There's no state of emergency yet, as you said. I think we are still allowed to visit friends."

"After supper we can talk about it. You'll stay for supper?"

"If you insist."

"Ma!" Abe called, after opening the door. "Andrew's staying for supper."

"All right, dear."

"It might be the last supper for a long time."

He shrugged his shoulders fatalistically. "Well, there's no need to be morbid. Back to work."

For the rest of that afternoon Abe sifted and destroyed papers, while Andrew smoked endless cigarettes and played the *Moldau* over and over again.

17

Justin had not arrived by the time Braam let Abe and Andrew in. His room hadn't altered much since they had last seen it, except possibly for the worse. There was still the odd assortment of clothes, books and food on the floor in the centre of the room. A new addition was a surrealistic reproduction of three female nudes, by some unknown painter, which Braam called The Three Disgraces.

"Have some wine while you're waiting. Wine while you're waiting." He rolled it on his tongue. "Notice my alliteration. Native woodnotes wild."

He fetched half a gallon of Tassenberg from the kitchen and searched amongst his clothes till he unearthed two cups and a mug. They drank in silence.

"What have you been doing with yourself since I last saw you?" Andrew asked.

"I'm busy running a business for someone. I've become a capitalist!"

"How degenerate. What kind of business?"

"Cape Town's only Astrobolic Bookshop!"

"What!"

"Cape Town's only Astrobolic Bookshop."

"Ye Gods!"

"It's quite a nice place really. Top of Long Street. Know Mervyn Langdowne?"

"No. What is a Mervyn Langdowne?"

"He owns this joint, but he's temporarily indisposed. Got caught under the Immorality Act with a dame from the African Jazz Bohemians."

"Oh yes."

"He left me the keys when he went to Roeland Street. Do come and see the joint some time. Bring your own wine."

"Do you sell any books?"

"On odd occasions. We sold one last week but the cops are chasing away my customers. They check up far too regularly. They don't seem to like the set-up."

"I promise to drop in sometime."

"It's easy to find. Near Steinberg's. You know, the top righthand corner."

"I know where Steinberg's is."

"Well, two doors away from it, farther up. We have a good selection of leftist literature if you're interested. Have some more wine."

"Thanks."

Abe kept up a frigid, contemptuous silence. He was obviously not partial to Braam's pseudo-Bohemianism.

"So how are you affected by all this unrest?" Andrew

asked in an attempt to keep the conversation going, since Abe refused to make any contribution.

"I'm writing a poem about it."

"In heroic couplets?"

"No. That went out with Chaucer. Free verse. I've already finished three cantos. The first is on the dead of Sharpeville. Like to hear it?"

"Not quite yet. Let's have more wine."

Justin arrived just as the conversation was petering out again. Abe revived instantly.

"Hello, Andrew. Hello, Abe, nice to see you again."

"Have some wine," Braam invited.

"Thanks."

"Use my mug. I'll take the can."

"I believe that you have forebodings for the future," Abe said to Justin, turning his back on Braam.

"Yes," Justin replied, "though I wouldn't quite call it forebodings. Let's say things are becoming more serious."

"Think they'll declare a state of emergency?"

"It's highly likely. But meanwhile, since the P.A.C. started all this, our job is to carry the situation to its logical conclusion."

"And that is?"

"Press hard for the total abolition of passes and a minimum wage of a pound a day."

"And how do we do that?"

"Bring out the Coloured workers in support of the strike—in the Cape at any rate. They're doing it at Worcester. Some of us are working night and day at it."

"Continuing in this adventurism?" said Abe sarcastically.

"What do you mean by that?" Justin asked sharply.

"The P.A.C. started this campaign in a spirit of bravado and political opportunism."

"So? I'm not a P.A.C. man."

"All this was somehow intended to bring freedom to the so-called African people by 1963."

"You must admit that there wasn't any lack of response to their call."

"I don't for a moment think that people responded to the P.A.C. call as such. I don't think that they were aware of its policy then or that they are aware of it now. They were simply prepared to attend any meeting critical of the Government."

"Is it their programme you don't agree with or their methods?"

"I don't agree with either. Quite apart from their Africanist orientation which is as bad as white racialism, they haven't even begun to consider fundamental problems such as the kind of society they envisage. They don't take into account, or even understand, the nature of the oppression they're fighting against. One of their chief spokesmen in Cape Town said, if I remember correctly, that all the Africans could do was to exert pressure on the industrialists who have the vote and could, with enough pressure behind them, appeal to the Government."

"I think it was Kgosana."

"I'm not sure who it was. But surely it was a manifestation of political *naïveté* that is almost criminal. At the outset they hand the responsibility over to the enemy."

"You sound like a teacher in front of a classroom," Braam sneered.

Abe ignored him and continued addressing Justin.

"The people must at the very start be made to recognize the indivisibility of oppression. They must look upon themselves not as Africans, Coloureds, Indians or whites, but as a people seeking to abolish national oppression. Racialism cannot be fought with racialism, or with localized stunts."

"Hear! Hear!" said Braam contemptuously.

"That's all very well," Justin replied impatiently, "but where does it get us? Where do we go from there? Do we sit on our backsides discussing the finer points of political theories?"

"Don't underestimate the importance of political theories."

"Very fine phrases. But exactly how does one translate your views into practice?"

"By educating people."

"In classrooms?" Braam interjected.

"No, in life. Education, not learning. On the level of ideas firstly. A people that wants to bring about its own emancipation must understand that the acceptance of racialism is a negation and a repudiation of our common humanity."

"So how do we educate people in practice?"

"By rallying them on every issue which affects them."

"Who's being opportunistic now? With localized stunts, I suppose?"

"Yes, as long as one sees things in their context and doesn't lose sight of the over-all situation."

"You know," Justin said irritably, "I've listened to you intellectuals, or so-called intellectuals, long enough. All you do is talk, talk, talk! You never *do* anything. Your whole outlook on life is negative. You oppose everything. Haven't you ever thought that you might not be the only ones in step?"

"Before we can *do* anything, we've got to understand what we are going to do and its implications. Choose our moral weapons carefully and our battlefields."

"And where are they?" Braam cut in. "In the class-room?"

Abe ignored his remark.

"If our struggle is a principled one we cannot go wrong."

"Principles be damned!" said Justin angrily. "You talk of principles while people are starving, gaoled and banished. You talk about humanity in high-faluting academic terms while the dead of Sharpeville are crying for revenge. Does the other side bother about humanity and principles?"

"Don't get hysterical. It's unaesthetic."

"I have every right to get hysterical and I don't care if it's aesthetic or not. I'm working on a united non-European strike. Am I wrong and unprincipled?"

"Yes, if you're working on a *non-European* strike you are in fact accepting racialism."

"You know you're just plain bloody reactionary!"

"Why not call me a police spy as well?"

"Have you always thought in this way?"

"Well, not always, but ideas develop."

"You were raided. Agreed? You are suspect. Agreed? If they throw you in gaol tomorrow, how will you react?"

"Physically, I cannot say. But mentally, I fully realize that I am a victim of a society which will try to deny me most things, but cannot deny me the right to analyse and understand its nature."

"Of course, of course, of course. Now let's look at practical things for a change. Tomorrow, as usual, I will be working on the strike; I thought at first that I could depend on the two of you for assistance. Are you prepared to help?"

"No. Not on your conditions."

"Scared of doing something practical?"

"Not in the least. I am prepared to canvass workers, not Coloured or African workers as such."

"Workers then. What the hell does it matter! Are you prepared to canvass workers?"

"For what purpose?"

"Oh hell. Must we go through all that again?"

"I think it is important."

"Will you assist, Andrew?"

Andrew was in a difficult position. He vaguely agreed with Abe, but felt that he was making far too great a fetish out of what seemed to him an essentially academic issue. He realized that, like Justin, he was getting more and more emotionally caught up in the urgency of the situation.

"Will you assist, Andrew?"

"I'm prepared to canvass workers."

"I'm distributing stay-at-home pamphlets in Langa tomorrow. Coming along?"

"Yes, I'll come along."

Andrew felt that somehow he had betrayed Abe.

"How do I contact you?"

"That might be difficult. I'll most probably be at a new place. But you can leave a message either at my sister's or at Ruth's flat."

"Ruth Talbot?"

"Yes," Andrew said heavily. "Ruth Talbot. She's on the phone. You'll find my sister's number under Peters. Kenneth Peters."

"Thanks. I'll phone you."

For the rest of the evening the atmosphere was tense and hostile. Abe drank glass after glass of wine in silence. Andrew felt guilty about him. Justin continued expounding on the situation with odd digs at intellectuals and armchair politicians, ably abetted by Braam. Andrew and Abe left just as Braam was threatening to read his unfinished poem.

"I'll contact you tomorrow," Justin said to Andrew.

"Good."

"So long till then."

"So long."

They did not say good-bye to Abe, and he left maintaining his frosty silence.

18

Abe didn't say a word until Andrew pulled up outside his home. Andrew also thought it wiser not to attempt any conversation. Not while Abe was in his present mood. He felt that he had been disloyal to his friend in agreeing to help Justin give out pamphlets. But then it was imperative to take a stand some time or other. A practical stand. Theory was all very well but one couldn't theorize all the time. Abe's behaviour had become inexplicable. He wasn't scared as Justin had tried to accuse him of being. Cautious maybe, but not scared. Discreet. Polemical. A trifle too academic. A born controversialist. Andrew felt that he had better make some attempt at conversation to break the deadlock.

"Good night," Abe said curtly as he started opening his gate.

"By the way, what happens tomorrow?" Andrew asked from the car. "Do we go to Altmann's?"

"I suppose so."

"Good. Shall I pick you up?"

"It might be better if I have my own transport."

"I promise not to bite."

"It's not that. I'll obviously need my car. I'll meet you there."

"Know where it is?"

"I think I can find it."

"All right. See you tomorrow. If you need me before then, I'll either be at Miriam's or at Ruth's."

"Good night."

"Good night."

Hell, what a strange attitude. Almost puerile, Andrew thought as he pulled away. As if he were to blame for what had happened that evening. What a strange person. There was no doubting his sincerity, but he did behave oddly at times. Couldn't bear to be crossed. Must dominate

every discussion. No, that wasn't quite true. Oh well.
Now for Miriam's. A hot bath and straight into bed. He
felt a bit heady after all the wine and smoke at Braam's
place. He hoped Kenneth wouldn't be home yet. He
didn't care for a row after such a day. He drove slowly
down Nile Street and was glad to see that the lounge
light was on. Miriam was obviously expecting him. He
knocked loudly and lit a cigarette while waiting for her
to answer the door.

"Hello." It was Kenneth. Andrew was thrown off his
guard for a moment. Kenneth stared at him with slightly
blood-shot eyes.

"Good evening," Andrew stammered. "Is Miriam
home?"

"No, she is not in yet, but she left a message that you
were to come in and make yourself comfortable. Step
inside."

Kenneth sounded cordial enough and this confused
Andrew even more. He stood undecided in the doorway.

"When will she be back?"

"Any minute now. Come in and wait."

"All right," said Andrew after some hesitation.

He felt suspicious of his brother-in-law's attitude. This
was most unlike the Kenneth he had learnt to know.

"Come and join us in the lounge while you're waiting."

"Us?"

Andrew's second surprise was to find James drinking at
the table. Two opened bottles of brandy and a bottle of
gin were standing on a tray.

"Have a seat."

He sat down uneasily, not quite knowing what to say.
Kenneth was obviously in a good mood.

"You know James?"

Andrew smiled weakly.

"We've met before," James said coldly.

"I want you to make yourself quite at home. Let bygones be bygones. The past is all over and forgotten."

"I hope so."

"I would prefer us to forget what happened before,"
Kenneth added genially.

"Sure."

"Have a drink," James offered.

"No thanks, if you don't mind."

"Come on, be sociable. We're all pals now," Kenneth insisted.

"I would prefer not to."

"Just a small one."

"All right, I'll have a small one."

"Let me get you a clean glass."

Kenneth left slightly unsteadily for the kitchen, while James toyed with his glass of brandy without looking directly at Andrew. If only Miriam would come. He had no wish to sit drinking with these two, friendly as they might appear to be. Kenneth re-appeared wiping the glass.

"Brandy or gin?"

"Gin, please."

"Tonic?"

"Yes. Plenty."

"Say when," Kenneth said and proceeded to pour it out.

"When."

It happened so suddenly that Andrew had almost no time to realize it. Kenneth flung the gin into his eyes, temporarily blinding him. As he tried to wipe it out, a fist crashed into his jaw. He fell to the ground clutching the leg of the table. Kenneth stood over him.

"You bloody black bastard! You won't upset my home again."

Andrew tried to focus his stinging eyes. A shoe landed viciously against the side of his head. He wasn't sure who was attacking him. Blows and kicks rained from all sides. He struggled to get to his feet feeling a dull pain all over his body.

"Chase my bloody wife from my house and you have the cheek to come back?"

He winced as a blow from Kenneth's shoe caught him full in the stomach. He managed to get upright although it was very painful, steadying himself against the leg of the table. He heaved with all the strength he had left, overturning the table. Glasses and bottles crashed to tiny fragments on the floor. Kenneth had hold of his jacket. Andrew pulled away, tearing his clothes. Kenneth lunged at him and the two rolled in the glass splinters. Andrew scrambled to his feet and ran for the door. He struggled with the knob for what seemed an age until it yielded, and he ran down the garden path with Kenneth in hot pursuit. Andrew vaulted over the gate. James was attempting to hold Kenneth back.

"You black bastard! It's because of you that my wife left home. Come back and I'll rip your guts wide open."

He was brandishing the broken gin bottle in his bleeding hands.

"Get the hell away from here!" James shouted at Andrew. "Don't put your bloody face in here again or you'll get what you damn-well deserve!"

Andrew half-ran to the car, his body hurting all over, his clothes wet with blood. His eyes were burning and he squinted trying to find the lock in the car door. Get to Ruth. Get to Ruth, kept drumming through his head, get to Ruth. Away from people, far away from people. Get to Ruth. He got into the Austin and switched on the engine. Every part of him ached. He vaguely saw Kenneth trying to force open the gate and James holding him back. He couldn't concentrate on anything other than getting to Ruth. Get to Ruth. Get to Ruth as fast as possible. Away from people. Get to Ruth.

Part Three

Crowds gather early in the morning in the locations of Langa and Nyanga when it becomes known that many of their leaders have been arrested in pre-dawn raids. Around 11 a.m. they converge on Cape Town led on by the student Kgosana. After protracted discussion with the police, they start the march back to the Locations, and Kgosana is raised shoulder-high by his supporters. Later in the day, in the name of the Governor-General, a state of emergency is declared.

1

Andrew tossed restlessly on the couch. The night was stifling without the slightest trace of a breeze. In his twisting and turning he had thrown off the blankets which Ruth had provided. Every muscle in his body ached and every movement was sheer agony. He wasn't sure whether he was dreaming or awake. It hurt in the places where Kenneth had kicked. Vicious kicks like a stallion's hooves. No, a bull's hooves. De little black bull went down de meadow. No, it must have been a big bull, a damn big bull. Why the hell should a bull go down de meadow? Maybe bulls liked to go down de meadow. His side was aching like the devil. The heavy thud of shoe-leather against his ribs and then the dull pain spreading upwards. The body cringing as it anticipated the next dull thud. Twisting and straining to avoid it. Kenneth breaking the end of a gin bottle and holding the neck while the spirits spilt over the carpet, filling the room with a nauseating, sickly smell. He had felt like retching, but there had been no time to push his fingers down his throat. Must prevent Kenneth from coming for him with that broken bottle. Someone trying to tear him away. Mrs. Carollissen. Please, Mr. D.! The smell of urine and brandy always nauseated him. The crunch of material tearing as Mrs. Carollissen tugged at him. Cold fear as Kenneth came again with the broken gin bottle. Sweat running out of every pore, his body wet and greasy. Sweat soaking through his shirt. Damp patches of perspiration pricking him all over. Every part of his skin itching and a ringing in his ears. Like someone ringing a doorbell endlessly. Ringing and ringing, impatient to get in.

Better get out before they caught him. Ringing and ringing. He felt like shouting out, come in for God's sake if you want me. That was peculiar. The Special Branch never rang. They usually knocked. Hard knocks thundering through his head. Throbbing and pulsating till he felt he would burst. Christ, he felt thirsty. Thirsty as hell. O for a draught of vintage that hath been cooled a long age in the deep-delved earth. Tasting of Flora. Now class, Shelley's life was one of passionate devotion to intellect, and this ardour explains how his ideas were transmuted into poetry. Oh, to hell with intellect and poetry. He wished Minnie would bring him some water. Tasting of Flora. How did the Keats go? With beaded bubbles winking at the brim. Minnie or Miriam? What the devil did Miriam know about poetry? But maybe she could stop that crazy ringing at the door. Tring-tring; tring-tring. Maybe hell was like that. Hell. Purgatory. Eternal damnation. Dante's *Inferno*. Waiting in a room forever with a bell ringing all the time and no one to answer it. No one ever to answer it. Like Sartre's *In Camera*. Working on your bloody guts. And again, tring-tring; tring-tring.

Like sounds rising to a crazy crescendo. Swelling and gaining volume till the whole room pulsated with the ringing. His body tortured and convulsively keeping time. Tring-tring. One enormous tring-tring.

As Andrew dimly became aware of his surroundings, he realized that the ringing was not only inside his head. Slowly his scattered thoughts returned, consciousness stealing over him. The room began to take shape. He could dimly make out the white record player next to the couch, and the moonlight filtering softly through the French windows. The phone rang on unmercifully. He struggled to sit upright, but the pain burned through him and forced him to lie back. He felt like shouting for someone to answer the damn ringing, then he heard movements. He could hear Ruth crossing over to the bookshelf, and the click as she switched on the corner-lamp. He lay back sweating profusely as he heard her picking up the phone.

"Hello? Hello? Yes, this is Ruth here. Who's speaking? Oh. No, not at all. I was half-asleep. Yes, he's here, but I wouldn't like to wake him. He seems to have had a nasty accident. No, I don't quite know what happened. What's that? Well, all right, if you think it's urgent."

Andrew felt her hand gently shaking his shoulder.

"Andy?"

"Yes?"

"Are you awake?"

"Yes."

"Abe on the phone for you."

"What does he want?"

"I don't know. He says it's urgent."

"What's the time now?"

"I think it must be something to two."

"What a bloody hour to phone. O.K. I'll speak to him."

He sat up in great pain and eased himself against the table. Every step was agony, and he felt he would never reach the phone.

"Hello, Abe?" he said, panting heavily from the effort.

"That you, Andrew? Sorry to ring you at this ungodly hour."

"It's all right. What's wrong?"

"Ruth says you've had an accident."

"It's nothing serious. What's wrong?"

"Listen, Andrew, there's trouble, serious trouble. I can't explain anything over the phone."

"Yes, I think I can guess."

"We have to get to Altmann in a hurry."

"I follow."

"Get some clothes and wait for me in the car. Not directly outside the flat. Round the corner. I'll circle around the block. Tell Ruth to come along as well."

"O.K."

"See you in about fifteen minutes' time."

"Right."

He couldn't ignore the urgency in Abe's voice. Something serious must have happened. Get some clothes. How damn funny. How ridiculously funny. Where the hell did he get clothes from? What a bloody joke. A torn jacket and blood-stained trousers. He must compose himself. Things seemed serious.

"Ruth."

"Yes, Andy?"

"Something has happened. It seems urgent."

"What is it?"

"I don't know. Abe wants us to get away from here as soon as possible. We have to meet him round the corner in your car."

"We're not moving, Andy, you're in no condition to go."

"Do as I say! Get some clothes on!"

"Please, Andy."

"Shurrup and do as I say!" He had never shouted at her before and she turned pale with shock.

"All right, Andy."

Ten minutes later, wrapped in Ruth's dressing-gown, he eased his way down the stairs of the flat. She helped him in silence.

"I'll get some clothes in Grassy Park. It's on the way."

"Where are we going?"

"That's not your business."

"All right."

When they reached the car she searched for the keys.

"I'll drive," she said.

Without replying he handed the keys over and then eased himself into the backseat.

2

Long after Andrew and Abe had left, Braam and Justin sat finishing another gallon of wine. Justin had not found Abe's reaction altogether unexpected. He had had tastes of it quite recently, and had mixed feelings about his old school friend.

"But in spite of all that, Braam, I still like him a hell of a lot. In an odd sort of way I admire him. We were pals at High School and have met on and off ever since. It's only when he becomes so damn academic and obstinate that he rubs me up the wrong way."

"I can't stand any of these pseudo-intellectuals."

"I don't think he is a pseudo-intellectual."

"Isn't he?"

"No. In his own peculiar way I think he's trying to discover himself."

"Then why doesn't he shut up and let those who can get on with the practical work?"

"I don't think we can blame him. In any case I think it's important that we should be big enough to take criticism."

"Yes, but only from those who are prepared to do something. Now, Andrew seems all right. There's a guy I can admire."

"Well, he did vaguely promise to help. Mustn't forget to phone him. What about you? Coming along to Langa tomorrow?"

"That's a bit risky. Haven't you any contacts there?"

"Yes, but they're being very closely watched, so it's out of the question using them."

"How does one get in without a permit?"

"There's a long unguarded fence along Vanguard Drive. Come along with us?"

"All right. I'll close the bookshop. Business has been bad lately, so the place is more closed than open anyway. Don't know what Mervyn will say when he comes back from gaol."

"That's settled then. You, me and Andrew. Just the three of us. I think Andrew has a car. I'll contact Abe as well—just to show there's no ill-feelings."

"Tell him to go to hell."

"Be kind to him."

"Bloody reactionary."

"Well, I have to be off now. See you tomorrow afternoon."

"I'll be home all day. Don't think I'll go to the shop. Which way are you walking now?"

"I'll catch a Hanover bus opposite Garlicks."

"All right, I'll walk you there."

Braam searched for and found his duffle-coat in the kitchen. The two then proceeded down the stairs. Braam left his door unlocked. In Adderley Street the two parted.

Braam turned away undecided whether to return to his room or not. Going back to Bree Street seemed extremely uninviting. Alone in his room above a bar. It was the loneliness that ate into him. He had to have people around him, lots of company, the hub-bub of conversation. But friends seldom came unless they were specially asked. It had always been like that. He had grown up an only child in the Bethlehem district of the Free State. At school he had always been on his own. At University he had hardly met any students other than his political contacts. Women found him difficult. Initially they were attracted by his strange intensity,

but they always dropped him soon afterwards. He realized
only too well that people found his pseudo-Bohemianism
odd, and his acute self-consciousness usually came out
as aggressiveness. His political friends found him suspect
emotionally and regarded almost with cynicism his attempts at identifying himself with them. Take Ruth
Talbot for example. After their first meeting in the
University Library Braam felt that he had at last solved
his problems. They had gone out a few times until Ruth
found his intensity too much for her. She had walked out
of his life into Andrew's. Not that he grudged Andrew
anything. No, not a damn. But why did so many women
do that to him? After a week, or even one night? Why
didn't anyone take permanently to him? They just
tolerated his friendship and this made him escape more
and more into aggressive make-believe. Sublimation by
rebellion.

He decided against returning home, and walked aimlessly along Dock Road. The street was almost deserted;
dark, dreary and unattractive. Sordid, menacing dark
lanes filled with garbage cans, old newspapers and filth.
Only one place was still open, a dimly-lit, fly-spotted
café owned by a Greek. As Braam entered a juke-box
was blaring,

> You say that you love me
> And swear that to be true,
> You say that you love me
> And swear that to be true. . . .

He chose an inconspicuous table as far from the music
as possible, and sat down moodily. It was the indescribable
loneliness that made a tight ball inside him. Nights of
walking the streets, just walking the dark, seductive lanes
off Signal Hill. Just walking and maybe talking to himself.
Himself and the dreamy unattractive night.

> But if you can come over here,
> And make me know you do,
> If only you come over here,
> And make me know you do. . . .

Walking along greying Darling Street just before the
sun rose over Kloof Nek. The pale neon signs and the

unnatural quiet. Newspapers whisked about by pre-dawn breezes. Returning to his room and falling down exhausted on his sleeping-bag. Friendless nights, hostile and woman-less.

> Come on baby make me know it,
> Go ahead and really show it. . . .

The Greek owner looked up from the till where he was counting his takings.

"Yeah?" he enquired heavily.

Braam ignored him. The only other occupants of the café were three heavily-rouged Coloured girls sitting next to the juke-box. Obviously prostitutes. No conversation. Just sitting around their greasy table, half-listening to the crooner.

"You want anything?" the owner asked.

Braam did not reply.

"Coffee? Doughnuts? Cigarettes?"

"Coffee," he replied, although he didn't really want any.

"One coffee!" the owner shouted through a hatch into the kitchen. Braam felt desperately like company, he had to speak to someone, anyone, even the Coloured girls.

> You say you've got kisses
> And swear to me they're new. . . .

Two of the prostitutes got up and started dancing with each other.

> I bet that's fine if you ain't lying,
> So make me know they do. . . .

Female bodies pressed close in a slow shuffle. A dreary and hopeless kind of dance, almost somnambulistic with sad, expressionless faces. The remaining one stole sur-reptitious glances at Braam.

"Hello?" he invited.

She looked carefully at her fingernails. They were dirty under the bright red polish.

"Hello?" he repeated.

"Hello again!" she said slowly, looking at him.

"Care to dance?" he asked.

"Sure."

She got up and stood waiting. Braam walked over and they started moving stiffly. At close quarters she looked far older than she had seemed at first. She was ugly. High cheekbones and a wide nose under a broad, over-painted mouth. Her breath smelt stale.

> You say you want to hold me,
> And stick to me like glue. . . .

Braam felt every muscle tingling. He could feel her warm flesh under her thin blouse.

> Well hearing is deceiving
> So make me know you do. . . .

The two prostitutes continued dancing together ignoring the couple.

"Hey you!" shouted the Greek owner. Braam looked at him.

"Cut that out."

"What?"

"It's not allowed here."

"What is not allowed?"

"You want me to lose my licence?"

"What the devil are you talking about!"

"You can't dance with Coloured girls here."

"Go to hell."

"You want me to call the police?"

"Go and drown yourself."

They stopped dancing and sat down at the table. Braam was fuming.

"You angry?" the girl said.

"Just bloody crazy!"

"You not cross with me?"

"Not a damn."

"You know, I like you. Tell me your name."

"John. John Coetzee," he lied. "What's yours?"

"Call me Gladys."

"O.K. Gladys. Like some coffee?"

"No, thanks."

"Then what would you like?"

"Just talk to me."

"What do I have to talk about?"

"Yourself."

"There's nothing to say really. I'm just a lonely guy who likes company like you."

"Jesus, you're funny."

"Am I?" he asked, hurt.

"Yes," she smiled.

"Would you like something stronger to drink?"

"Where do you stay?"

"Not far from here."

"Where?"

"Lower Bree Street. Above the Gloucester Bar."

"Opposite the fruit shop?"

"Yes, right opposite the fruit shop."

"See you there later."

"Come along with me now."

"Don't be silly. There might be cops around."

Braam winced under the reprimand.

"All right. See you later. But for goodness' sake come alone."

"Sure, Johnny-boy."

He walked out, giving the proprietor a dirty look.

"Hey," the Greek called after him, "here's your coffee."

"Shove it up your backside!" Braam replied. As he left, the juke-box was finishing the blues.

> Make me know it, come on now
> Go ahead and really show it
> I say seeing is believing
> So make me know it's true. . . .

Braam was still angry as he mounted the steps to his room. He switched on the light. No, that was far too bright. He lit the paraffin lantern, then cleared a space on the floor and spread out his ground-sheet and sleeping-bag. For twenty minutes he lay back staring at the patterns on the ceiling, waiting for the knock on the door. He wondered whether she would come. Hell, if she didn't, the dirty, double-crossing whore. He was still smouldering over the café incident. No mixed dancing, no mixed drinking, eating, sleeping. What the devil could one do? He didn't hear the knock at first. Then it came again, softly. He jumped up trembling with relief and lightly ran down the stairs.

"Come on in," he said almost gaily as Gladys stood before him. "I thought you might not turn up."

"I always keep my word, Johnny-boy."

"Johnny-boy?"

"You said your name was Johnny-boy, didn't you?"

"Sure, sure. Come inside."

"I know your name ain't Johnny-boy."

He could smell her bad breath. He latched the door as she felt her way up the stairs.

"Why is your place all dark?"

"I prefer it that way."

"You're funny, but I like you."

"Do you?"

"Yes, even if you're a white man."

"Who said I'm a white man?"

"Of course you are."

She sat down on the sleeping-bag, kicking off her shoes. Braam switched on the light.

"Jeesus, your room's in a mess."

"I know."

"Looks like a rummage sale."

"Now, don't be rude, Gladys. I'm waiting for a nice girl to come and clean it."

"Who?"

"You."

"Hell, your're funny."

"Am I?" he said, slightly hurt. He pecked her lightly on the cheek.

"Some wine, beautiful?"

"Sure, Johnny-boy. I'll call you Johnny-boy even if that's not your name."

He fetched a fresh bottle of Tassenberg from the kitchen and found the two glasses used by Andrew and Abe. They were still dirty and wine-stained. Braam filled them to the top.

"Here you are, beautiful."

"Don't call me that. I know I'm not beautiful."

"But I think you are. Here's your wine."

They both drank deeply. She spilt some wine on her blouse.

"More?"

"Sure, Johnny-boy."

Braam refilled the glasses.

"Where do you stay?"

"That's my business."

"Now, don't be difficult, Gladys."

"Everywhere in Cape Town. Where's there's men there's me."

"I see."

They drank on for a long time. She was becoming more drunk and Braam found the longing raging inside him. There were two open sores on her leg, but that didn't matter.

"Too much light?"

"Yes, too much light."

He switched off and then blew out the lantern. He lay back on the sleeping-bag, pulling her next to him. She felt warm and sweaty.

"You want me?"

"Yes," he said hoarsely, feeling for her clothes. The room became uncomfortably hot and he perspired profusely. Afterwards, when he lay back exhausted and dissipated, a feeling of revulsion came over him. Now that it was all over he wanted to get rid of her, but she was snoring gently next to him. Braam turned away from her in disgust. Wished like hell she would go. He shook her gently, but she mumbled in her sleep and rolled on to her side. It was then that he heard loud knocking. Who the devil could it be? It must be after one o'clock. Maybe Justin. He buttoned up his trousers in the dark and walked quickly down the stairs. He hoped it would be Justin. Anyone to talk to, to get the bad taste out of his mouth. He was beginning to suffer acutely from a feeling of guilt.

"Hang on!" he shouted as the banging increased in volume. He unlatched the door to find two white detectives staring at him.

"You're Braam de Vries?" the elder asked. He was heavily moustached with a scar above the lip. The younger man was fresh and blond with a nervous twitch around the mouth.

"We've a warrant for your immediate detention under the Public Safety Act."

"Go to hell!"

"Come on, don't be difficult."

"Dirty swines."

"Shurrup!"

"Bloody fascist!"

He felt an open palm landing heavily on his cheek, jerking his head back. He choked and coughed helplessly. The blond detective pinned his arms behind his back.

"Let's search the place."

"You bloody Gestapo."

The younger man twisted his arm tighter so that Braam winced with pain. He was half-pushed up the stairs.

"Where's the damn switch?"

He found it and the place was flooded with light. Gladys was lying on her back again, breathing heavily, her mouth open. Her unbuttoned blouse exposed one half-bare breast.

"So you were having a nice time, hey?"

"Mind your own damn business!"

"High treason and immorality."

The senior detective nudged Gladys none too gently with his foot. She sat up squinting in the light.

"Hello, madam, enjoying yourself with white men?"

She looked up with horror at the two strange men, clutching her blouse to cover herself.

"Caught beautifully. Come on, you've got a date with us."

"Please, baas."

"Get up!"

She climbed unsteadily to her feet. Suddenly she ran to the older of the two men, pummelling him weakly with her fists. He jerked her arms behind her back with ease.

"Black bitch!"

"Let me go, baas."

She struggled and slipped her hands from his grip. He held her tightly around the breast. She looked up and giggled coyly at him. The detective could feel her warm flesh. For a second a brief smile flickered across her face, then he looked away self-consciously.

"Come on. Bring the white bastard and his *Hotnot meid!*"

They frog-marched the two down the stairs into the waiting patrol-van.

3

Justin always came away from arguments with Abe feeling slightly puzzled. It had happened over and over again. They had parted after Matriculation, Abe going to University and Justin to an office job at two pounds fifteen a week. But in spite of that they had not altogether lost contact. During the four years of the Treason Trials, he had seldom seen him. But then he had lost contact with so many people during those years, including Florence. She had changed completely by the time he had come back. Four years of it. The dawn raid. How could he ever forget the loud banging at the door? The fifth of December 1956. Yes, that was it. A Wednesday morning. Funny how things always happened on a Wednesday morning, unpleasant things. Was sentenced to gaol as a Defier on a Wednesday morning. The knock at the door at four o'clock. A chilly December day well before dawn. Then in a police-van racing to Caledon Square. Preparatory examination on an allegation of high treason. Leaving Florence behind, shocked into a stunned silence. Then in the bleak dawn aboard a military Dakota to Johannesburg. Locked in The Fort and singing in the cells. *Nkosi Sikelel 'i Afrika.* God bless Africa. And the wonderful feeling that came over him when he felt his oneness with Africa. The Africa of the future. Glimpses of the vision splendid. More than a vision, the feeling of inevitable realization. And then the trial opening in the Drill Hall. The singing mass of supporters surging outside. We stand by our leaders. Shouts of *Mayibuye Afrika.* Let our people go. The police firing. The sharp staccato of the guns. My God, they can't be shooting them. A woman trialist fainting near him. And the droning voice of the Prosecutor going on and on. Years of argument, cross-examination, learned discussion, evidence, reams of papers, pamphlets, books. Four lost years and coming back to find a changed Florence.

Justin had just parted from Braam when a Hanover Street bus rounded the bend. He jumped on and eased himself into a vacant seat. Must life always be like that? He wasn't really a political masochist. Imprisonment wasn't his idea of fun. No wonder Florence couldn't take it any longer. In fact she was becoming distinctly aggressive, openly hostile. She had shown studied indifference to his strike activities, and had turned to soap-box operas on the radio and Mrs. Hanslo for consolation. He couldn't cope with that. Sometimes she showed signs of really caring, but these were slight and far between. He couldn't cope with that type of behaviour. Maybe it was the absence of a child. It must have been four lonely years for her. If only they could have had a boy with his mother's eyes and light-brown hair. Something to ease her loneliness. Only had Abe's mother as her friend. Years older than she was. Her nights of waiting for him to come from meetings. Having to bail him out constantly, bringing food to Roeland Street. Oh well, he thought fatalistically, life was like that. Jobless for four years. Hounded by the Special Branch. Forced to give up their home in Eden Road because they couldn't afford the rent. Shifting to two rooms and a kitchen at the back of a house in Arundel Street, in the heart of District Six. He didn't really mind, but Florence did. Married five years and still he didn't understand her. However, it was good to see Andrew again. They had seldom met since Andrew had moved to Grassy Park. Or was it Southfield? Well, one of those places on the Cape Flats.

At the Star Bioscope, Justin alighted and walked along deserted Hanover Street till he turned up at the doctor's surgery. He walked down a dimly-lit lane and opened his yard-gate. The next-door dog barked. He noticed that his kitchen light was still burning. The door creaked as he opened it and he hoped he hadn't disturbed Florence, but she was obviously awake as the radio was playing.

"That you, Justin?" he heard her voice from the bedroom.

"Yes, dear."

He desperately wanted to be nice to her. Should have thought of a present or something. He found her sitting up in bed, combing her hair. She was not unattractive, fair and buxom. When she was in a good mood he called her his fräulein.

"So, how is my little wife tonight?" he asked cheerfully.

"Are you really interested?"

"Come now, little fräulein. Be nice to me."

She combed her rich hair carefully, admiring herself in a hand-mirror.

"You'll never guess whom I met today."

"I'm not interested."

"Guess."

"I'm in no mood for guessing."

"Someone you know."

She continued combing her hair and avoiding him.

"Now who do you think?" he persisted.

"One of your political cronies."

"None other than Andrew Dreyer."

"I don't remember him."

Justin knew that she was pretending.

"Andrew, man, he was at school with you. Abe's friend."

"Oh, him."

"He's a teacher at Steenberg High School now."

"I know. Mrs. Hanslo told me."

"Then you do remember him."

"Please, Justin, I'm in no mood to argue."

He was determined not to allow her to dampen his spirits.

"I also met Abe tonight."

"How absolutely thrilling."

"We had a bit of a quarrel."

"And you won, of course."

"How did you guess?" he laughed.

"You're infallible. How can you ever lose?"

"Now, don't be nasty."

She started to plait her hair deftly.

"You look beautiful tonight."

"First time you noticed it?"

"No, I noticed it the first time we ever met."

"Was that also the last time?"

"Come on, darling. Hold that pose. You remind me of a German lass. Flaxen hair, blue eyes and apple-red cheeks. You were singing lieder to the strains of an accordion in the Black Forest."

"Don't be sickly. Get into bed."

"With a waterfall behind you high up in the mountains. I once had a mouth-organ which came in a cardboard box and on the lid there was a picture of a German peasant complete with leather shorts, floral braces and rucksack. You should have been next to him laughing."

"Have you had too much to drink tonight?"

"A few glasses of wine at Braam's."

"Oh, you were with that dirty white? Why don't your political contacts have baths?"

"My political contacts are important to me."

"Yes, so important that I always have to play second fiddle. I have to sit up at night waiting. Just waiting and waiting. Waiting in two poky rooms in District Six. No wonder Mrs. Hanslo won't visit me. When you go to gaol who has to do the worrying? Me. Who has to bring your food? Me. Who has to go out and work? Me. Who was kicked out of Eden Road because the rent wasn't paid? Me! All you talk about is politics, but I have to do the worrying."

"Florence!"

"I've just about had enough of this nonsense." She turned over on her side and pulled the blankets over her head. "Put out the light when you're finished and switch off the radio."

He was about to say something but decided it was useless. He undressed slowly, saw to the light and the radio and got in beside her. He desperately wanted to remain friendly.

"I have to give out pamphlets in Langa tomorrow." He paused, waiting for the reply that didn't come. "Andrew's promised to help me. But I won't go if you don't want me to."

She turned over, lying flat on her stomach and with her head away from him.

"I've hidden the pamphlets under the oven."

"It's none of my business."

"Please, Florrie."

"I want to sleep."

"All right, darling."

He tried to put his arms around her, but she pressed down tightly against the mattress. After a time he gave up and tried to sleep.

It was the barking of the next-door dog that woke him. It seemed as if he had just dozed off, but the luminous dial of the alarm said 1:30. Then he heard loud knocking.

He hoped it wouldn't wake Florrie or the landlady. He got up and tip-toed to the kitchen, cautiously opening the door. Three detectives shone their torches into his face.

"Justin Bailey?"

"Yes?"

They shoved him into the kitchen and searched with their torches for the light switch. Justin had a wild impulse to run, but thought better of it and remained calm. They switched on the light.

"What do you want?"

"We're detaining you under the Public Safety Act."

"I see," he said flatly.

That might mean months in gaol. The dirty, flea-ridden cells. Inhuman conditions, rough treatment.

"Has a state of emergency been declared?"

The detectives ignored the question, and one walked into the bedroom while the others guarded the door. Florence woke and sat up in bed.

"I'm sorry, Florence," Justin said.

She stared hostilely at him. The detective was searching in the wardrobe, poking under the bed. Hell, they mustn't search the kitchen. Florence watched dispassionately.

"Get dressed," the detective ordered Justin.

Experience had made him used to this type of thing. He selected a thick jersey and a pair of khaki jeans. He sat on the bed lacing up his shoes.

"Florrie, I might be away for some time." She said nothing. After he had finished he stood up resignedly. "Good-bye, darling. My regards to Andrew, Good-bye, my little fräulein."

He attempted to kiss her, but she turned her face away. One of the detectives smiled.

"All right," Justin said. "I'm ready."

After they had left Florence got out of bed and peeped through the kitchen window to make sure. Then she checked under the oven. She would have to warn Andrew, but where could she find him? Abe would know. Phone Abe. She opened the door leading into her landlady's section of the house. Useless to ask permission to use the phone at this hour of the morning. Just use the damn thing. Luckily it was in the passage.

"Hello? That you, Abe? Florence here. Florence Bailey.

Yes, Justin's wife. I believe he saw Andrew and you this evening. I mean last night. Detectives have just raided us and taken him away. He left something for Andrew. No, I'm all right. Please try and warn Andrew. Thanks. Good night."

She replaced the receiver and stood undecided for a long time. Then she slowly went back to the room and threw herself down on the bed. She lit a cigarette, and for a long time she lay smoking in the dark. She was annoyed because the station was off the air.

4

Mrs. Lucille Hanslo usually slept lightly. On Tuesday, March 29th, she had gone to sleep early and had slept more lightly than usual. She was awake in the early hours of the following morning when Abe came home. The boy was acting strangely of late. She couldn't quite fathom what was wrong. Well, Abe wasn't really a boy, twenty-nine in June, and still no girl-friend. Actually, that was the only thing that pleased her, that he had no girl-friend. She dreaded thinking what would happen once he transferred his affections. He always sat moodily around the house, reading or listening to records, seldom going out except to political meetings. Those meetings also worried her. Ever since the death of her husband, over twenty years before, she had nothing left in her life except her son. Just Abe and herself. She lived only for him, ate, slept, and breathed Abe. But somehow the boy never responded. Seemed never to notice her hair greying and her heart weakening. It was useless complaining to him about the pain in her chest, the near-asphyxiation, her breath coming in short, sharp gasps, with the sweat pouring down her face. It seemed that Abe didn't notice these things. Lived in his own world of books and music. He never went out with her unless she asked him. Even then he looked at her strangely as if resenting the imposition.

"Let's go for a nice, long drive, Abe, just you and me."

"Is there anywhere in particular you have to go?"

"No, I just feel like a nice drive."

"You're quite sure you want to go?"

"Yes, Abe, just the two of us."

He would take her and drive at speed towards Hout Bay and Chapman's Peak, not saying a word throughout the journey. She would come back feeling nervous and frustrated, realizing that something had gone out of her life. It was then that her heart would start. He would lock himself up in his study and play endless records. Some evenings he went out and only came back in the early hours of the morning. Could he be deceiving her? Was it really a girl-friend? He never answered her enquiries. Otherwise he spent the evenings alone in his room listening to music.

She heard a car stopping in the road. Her senses were suddenly all sharpened. A key turning in the latch, then the familiar footsteps.

"Abe?"

"Yes, Ma?"

"Come into my room."

She heard him in the bathroom, the tap running. Then he came in wiping his hands on his handkerchief. She could see at a glance that he was angry about something.

"Come and sit on the bed and talk to me."

He sat down in an armchair without saying a word.

"What's wrong, Abe?"

"Nothing."

"I know there's something the matter."

"Nothing, Ma. Please don't fuss."

"Has it to do with politics?"

"I'm tired and would like to go to bed."

"Can't you spare your old mother a few minutes?"

"I'm very tired."

"All right, Abe."

She turned her face and he pecked her coldly on the cheek.

"Good night, my boy, sleep well."

"Good night."

For a long time afterwards she could not sleep. She suspected that another heart attack was coming on. If only the boy could come closer to her, become more intimate, more understanding. Now why couldn't he be like Andrew Dreyer? There was a really nice person. Well-mannered, solicitous. Must have come from a very good home. Well, each person must bear his or her cross.

Sleep was now out of the question. Another night just lying back and staring at the ceiling. She was still awake when the phone rang. She heard Abe switching on the light and speaking to someone. Then he in turn made a phone call. She couldn't make out what he was saying or to whom he was speaking. For a long time she lay there tense and expectant. Something must be wrong. He had looked worried when he came in. A soft knock at her bedroom door.

"Are you awake, Ma?"

"Yes, Abe."

He opened the door and switched on her light. He was fully dressed with an overcoat slung over his arm and a suitcase in his hand.

"I have to leave at once, Ma."

"Why? Where to?" she asked, confused.

"That telephone call was to warn me that the police are picking up political suspects. It would be wiser if I got away at once."

"But where will you go?"

"It's better if you don't know."

"But I have a right to know, my boy."

"Please, Ma, leave things to me. Good-bye. See you soon."

"Look after yourself, Abe."

"Don't worry. I'll phone you tomorrow."

He kissed her lightly, then she heard him starting his car and driving off. Her first reaction was to try somehow to stop him from deserting her. Plead with him to return. Then she realized the importance of keeping calm, as the pain shot across her chest. Her heart started to pound furiously and her breath came with difficulty. Why must her only son treat her like that? She had sacrificed so much for him. Concentrated all her attention on him. Where was he off to? With whom would he stay? She lay back trying to breathe evenly. Why couldn't he treat her as a son should? Phone you tomorrow. What if he forgot to? She heard loud knocking at the front door. At the same time the bell rang. She got up heavily from her bed, searching with her feet for her slippers. Then she put on her dressing-gown, panting with the effort. The knocking and ringing continued unabated, re-echoing through the house. When she opened the door, she found two plain-clothes detectives standing in the entrance.

"Abe Hanslo stay here?"

"Yes?" she said, feeling her chest tightening.

"Where is he?"

"He's not here. He's gone away. He hasn't come home yet," she said, all in the same breath.

"Get out of the way!" one of them commanded her.

"You have no right to march into my house!" She tried to shut the door. The detective shoved it back, sending her sprawling to the floor. She gasped for breath, turning white as a sheet. The second detective, a younger man, helped her to her feet and guided her to the armchair in her bedroom. Her chest felt like bursting, her body clammy and wet. They started searching methodically, going from room to room. She had no idea of anything. Only the pain twisting in her chest. If only she could breathe more easily. Sweat poured down her cheeks. After a time the two men reappeared.

"So? Where's your son?"

"I don't know," she panted.

"When did he leave here?"

"He never came home tonight."

"Stop your damn lying."

"He never came home."

"Then who the hell slept in his bed?"

"I don't know."

"Why is his wardrobe open?"

"I don't know."

"Why is there a light in his room?"

"I don't know, I don't know, I don't know."

"Better tell us or we'll bloody well lock you up. Where is he?"

"I don't know."

"Want to think about it in a cell?"

"Leave her alone," said the younger detective. "She's useless."

"All right, but God help him when we do find him. You seeing him tomorrow?"

"I don't know," she repeated.

After they had left she remained sitting in the armchair, almost doubled up with pain. Her breathing came now in short, feeble gasps and her head throbbed dully. Her whole body was sweating. She made weak attempts to raise herself from the chair to phone Florence, but fell back exhausted.

"Please God, it's true. I don't know. It's true, Abe, I don't know. I don't know. I don't. . . ."

She never completed the sentence. She slumped back, wide-eyed with a shocked expression on her face, staring at the ceiling.

During the rest of the day people knocked at the door and went away. Twice the phone rang, but the dead woman remained sitting in the chair, staring at the ceiling with a shocked expression on her pulpy face.

5

Andrew tried to settle himself in the back of the car, but his body was still hurting all over. His eyes were smarting and he tried to focus them on Ruth. She looked straight ahead without saying anything. Andrew shifted around uneasily. He felt uncomfortable in only his underwear and Ruth's far-too-tight dressing gown. A low mist was hanging like a blanket over the Common, and he shivered slightly. Strange that he had felt uncomfortably hot in Ruth's flat or had it only been his imagination? A draught played through the open front window.

"You all right, Andy?"

Jeesus, he hoped the woman wasn't going to fuss over him.

"I'm O.K.," he said sharply.

"Shall I turn up my window?"

"Please don't mother me."

"I was only trying to be helpful."

For a long time they sat in an uncomfortable silence. Andrew fully realized that Abe wasn't given to melodrama. If he said things were serious, then they were serious. Damn it. To have to face any situation in this condition. Dressed in underwear and a lady's dressing-gown, with a body that ached all over. His knee was also hurting. That swine Kenneth must have planned it all. Premeditated it with James. And he had fallen beautifully into the trap. Simply asked to be beaten up. He wondered what could have become of Miriam.

A car swung around the corner, flashing headlights on them. Could it be Abe? No, it didn't sound like his car. Might be cops. He ducked instinctively and his head began to spin. He clutched the seat tightly.

"What's wrong, Andy?"

"I'm fine, just fine. Please don't fuss."

Ruth looked back at him questioningly. Hold on, he thought, can't start getting giddy now. This situation was serious. Can't have Ruth looking at me like that. Another car pulled up behind them with screeching brakes, and Abe jumped out. He hesitated for a moment then climbed in next to Ruth.

"Hello, folks!" he said breathlessly.

"Hello, Abe," Ruth repeated coolly.

"What the hell's wrong with you, Andrew?" he asked, not detecting Ruth's aloofness.

"Oh I had a bit of an accident after I left you."

"Serious?"

"No, nothing to write home about, just surface wounds. I'm all right. Now tell me what's this all about?"

"The police are on the war-path. The raids have started."

"How do you know?"

"Justin's been arrested. Florence phoned me."

"Hell."

"There might be more treason arrests."

"That's not very pleasant."

"That's why I thought it wiser to get away fast."

"Will Altmann be expecting us?"

"I don't think he'll mind. I'm sure he'll understand that the situation is urgent."

"O.K. On the way we can pick up some of my clothes in Grassy Park."

"Right. Mrs. Carollissen first stop."

Andrew still seemed hesitant. Ruth looked straight ahead of her. Abe stared at each in turn, completely puzzled.

"Well, do we go?" he asked.

"What about her?" Andrew asked.

"Who? Ruth? She'll have to come along. Haven't they already been to her place?"

"Yes, on Monday evening when they were searching for me. Ruth, you'll have to come along."

"I'm staying right here."

"Please be sensible, dear."

"I'm not moving from the flat."

"Please, Ruth."

"I'm not going to run away."

Andrew looked appealingly at Abe. Ruth sat tense in the front seat.

"Look, Ruth," Abe began. "They'll come for you as true as God. If a state of emergency is declared you can be locked up indefinitely."

"Surely I'm not so important."

"They'll come for you."

"I'm not afraid."

"It's not a case of being afraid. It's a case of being sensible."

"Please, Ruth," Andrew renewed his appeal to her. "I need you badly." He could feel her relaxing slightly.

"I might want to mother you."

"I'm sorry I said that. It's true. I need you."

For a long time she continued to stare through the window.

"All right," she said finally. "I'll come."

"Good," said Abe taking over the situation. "We'll take your car, Ruth. I can park mine here." He got out to lock his doors and returned with his overcoat and suitcase. "Shift over, beautiful, and let Mr. Cape Peninsula take over the controls." He attempted a smile.

"Come and sit in the back, Ruth," Andrew suggested.

"I'm quite comfortable in front, thank you," she said.

6

They drove along Prince George Drive in silence. Andrew sat slumped in the back seat pretending to sleep. Ruth stared straight ahead of her.

"Say something," Abe said.

"Like what?"

"Oh, anything to keep me company."

"I'm not in a talking mood."

"Come off it. You can ignore the Philistine in the back seat, but it's difficult to ignore me."

"You're sweet, Abe."

"Am I? I wish my mother thought so."

"Doesn't she?"

"On very special occasions. She's most probably in bed right now, oblivious of her son gallivanting around the Cape Peninsula."

"Don't be unkind. I'm sure she must be a charming woman."

"Maybe she is."

"And . . . and motherly."

"I suppose she is. Only there is so much of her. Sometimes I wish that I might never see her again."

"I don't believe it."

"On my Christian oath."

"You're just teasing me."

Then it happened. Suddenly the road-block was in front of them, and scores of torches trained on the car. Abe had to swerve and apply the brakes hard. They found the road intersection swarming with police. All had lights and some had Stenguns slung over their shoulders.

"*Waar die duiwel gaan jy?* Where the devil do you think you're going?" said a raw, guttural voice in Afrikaans. Abe turned his window down and peered out.

"Sorry, sir, we didn't notice you," he replied in his best English.

"Couldn't you see the damn torches?"

"My humblest apologies."

"Get out of the car."

Abe climbed out hesitantly. Andrew felt a weak sensation in the pit of his stomach. He always felt that way when he was in contact with police uniforms. So that was it. Caught beautifully. Red-handed. Two Coloured men and a white girl heading God-knows-where. And one Coloured man in his underwear and wearing a white woman's dressing-gown. That would need a hell of a lot of explaining. A torch shone through the window.

"Come on, get out, all of you."

Ruth turned a frightened glance on him. He nodded and she followed Abe. Andrew, himself, decided to remain seated.

"Come on you, get out."

A torch shone full on his face, temporarily blinding him. Andrew felt the dizziness coming on again. He clutched the door-handle tightly and eased himself into the open. The cold air blowing in from Princess Vlei smacked him wide awake. He was afraid to breathe deeply lest his head should spin. The last thing he was interested in was a cross-examination. All he wanted to do was get away and sleep. Life had become too crowded lately, far too crowded. A lieutenant walked over to where they stood in a group, his face hard beneath his peaked cap. He passed a cursory glance over the three, then reached for his note-book and pencil. An ordinary constable shone a light over his shoulder.

"Name?" he asked Abe.

"Mr. Abraham Hanslo."

"Address?"

"Arden, Grand Vue Road, Woodstock."

"Spell it."

"Arden is A-r-d-e-n. Grand Vue is G-r-a-n-d-V-u-e."

The officer wrote it out slowly.

"And your name?" he turned to Ruth. She stared blankly at him, too afraid to speak.

"She's my wife, sir."

The lieutenant looked at Abe and Ruth carefully. Then, apparently satisfied, he turned to Abe.

"Your wife's name?"

"Mrs. Lucille Hanslo. Same address."

He wrote that down.

"Race? European, I presume."

Abe and Ruth kept silent as he noted it down. Andrew felt the cold air cutting through the thin dressing-gown. His breath came out in cloudy puffs. He felt his head spinning and the police-officer's face started whirling round and round, then he slumped down in a heap. Abe lifted him up and half-carried him to the car. The policeman watched impassively.

"And who is he?" the officer asked when Abe returned.

"He works in my business, sir. He met with an accident late last night, and my wife and I are taking him home to Grassy Park."

"At this hour?"

"We've only just come from the doctor. He was injured at about eleven o'clock."

"What happened to him?"

"He was apparently beaten up by skollies."

"Has it been reported to the police?"

"I think so, sir."

"Whereabouts in Grassy Park does he stay?"

"Lake Road."

"What's his name?"

"Andrew Dreyer."

The officer seemed satisfied with Abe's demeanour and ready answers, and relaxed slightly. He pushed his cap to the back of his head. Abe felt that he had the situation in hand and took out a cigarette. He offered the lieutenant one.

"No, thanks, I'm on duty."

"Why the road-block, if I may ask?"

"We're expecting plenty of trouble, so we're checking everyone passing through here late at night. Even Europeans."

"Even Europeans?"

"Yes, even you people. These are very unsettled times."

"They sure are. If everything's in order may we go now?"

"We have to search your car first."

"Go right ahead."

The lieutenant and a policeman walked over and flashed their torches about inside the car. Andrew lay huddled in a corner, either unconscious or asleep. Abe's suitcase was next to him on the back seat. The lieutenant opened it.

"Hey you, Hanslo! Come over here."

"Yes, sir."

"Whose clothes are these?"

"Mine, sir."

"What are they doing packed in a case?"

"I'm a commercial traveller. I'm supposed to leave in the morning."

"Didn't you say this fellow worked for you?"

"He's my co-driver."

"All right," said the policeman suspiciously. He continued searching in the boot and under the seats till he opened the cubby-hole. Inside it was a profusion of cosmetics and tissues, as well as Andrew's copy of *New Age*.

"Whose is this?"

"What?"

"The lipstick and the powder-puffs?"

"My wife's."

"Does she use your car?"

"Sometimes."

"And this newspaper?" the officer asked coldly.

"Mine."

"Are you one of those white agitators?"

"Certainly not."

"Then what's this doing here?"

"I'm interested in all points of view. I read the *Times*, *Argus* and *Burger* as well."

"*Kan jy Afrikaans verstaan?*"

"*Ek praat die taal taamlik, al is my woordeskat beperk.*"

The policeman noted down the number of the Austin.

"Get into your car and bugger off fast. We'll check on you."

"Thank you, sir."

"What's that?"

"*Dankie, Meneer.*"

The officer stared hostilely as Abe started the car and drove slowly through the road-block. The remaining policeman stared at him dispassionately.

It was only when they had turned down Klip Road that he breathed a sigh of relief.

"We live again. Hell, that was close."

"You were wonderful," said Ruth.

"My imaginative genius. My ma would have been proud of me."

"I was so frightened I thought I would faint."

"How's young Dreyer?"

"Asleep I think."

"I'm very much awake, folks, but I was forced to throw a faint. Couldn't stand there practically naked. I'm modest and conservative by nature."

"Are you sure of that?"

"Sure of what?"

"That you threw a faint?"

"Damn sure. Positive. Why do you ask?"

"Oh, I only wondered."

7

      In the early hours of Wednesday morning all was quiet and peaceful at "Semper Fidelis." The lady of the house herself had retired shortly after nine with a slight headache, having first delivered herself of a homily around the supper-table on the demerits of having political agitators as boarders in respectable, Christian households. Eldred had held his tongue although he was dying to voice his opinion. Mr. Carollissen had grunted his agreement and had then retired to his room with his newspaper and pipe. It was Minnie's night off, so after supper Eldred had helped Vincent with the washing and drying up. He had then locked himself in Andrew's room to do his homework. Latin made no sense to him and English grammar was dull. He wondered whether he should do Mr. Dreyer's home work since it was unlikely that his English teacher would be at school. Oh, well. He opened his grammar text-book. Express the essential matter of each of these groups of sentences in a single well-constructed sentence. Combine the following adjectives with a suitable noun. He gave up and got undressed. He might as well sleep in Mr. Dreyer's room. He went through the books on his teacher's shelf and selected *Engels on Capital*. He glanced through the contents. Synopsis of Capital. Chapter I. Commodities and Money. The Transformation of Money into Capital. The Production of Absolute Surplus Value. He got into bed, deciding to start at Chapter I. The wealth of societies in which capitalist productions prevail consists of commodities. He gave that up also and switched off the light.

      "Eldred!" he heard his mother calling from her bedroom.

      "Yeah?"

      "Where are you?"

      "In Mr. Dreyer's room."

      "What are you doing there?"

      "I'm sleeping here tonight."

      "Have you finished your homework?"

      "Yeah."

"What are you doing now?"

"Studying for a Biology test."

"All right, good night."

"Good night," he answered, and was soon fast asleep.

It was the noise of someone banging at the door that awakened him. Eldred stirred in his sleep, and was about to doze off again when the knocking came even louder than before. Mr. Dreyer. Hell, and he was using his room, sleeping in his bed. Eldred hoped his teacher wouldn't mind. He switched on the lamp and then walked barefooted down the passage to open the front-door. The shock of seeing three strange men wakened him thoroughly.

"Andrew Dreyer live here?" asked the man in charge, who stared at him coldly.

"Yeah."

They pushed him aside and stomped into the passage.

"Which is his room?"

Eldred stood shocked, unable to speak.

"Come on, open your jaw."

"He's not home," the boy managed to say.

"Stop lying!"

"He hasn't come home this evening."

"Where is he then, at this hour?"

"Eldred!" Mrs. Carollissen called from her bedroom, "who's there?"

"Three white men, Ma."

"Oh, dear. Wait, I'm coming."

They could hear her switching on her light and shuffling for her slippers. She appeared in her dressing-gown looking anxiously at the three men.

"Yes?"

"I'm a detective-sergeant of the political branch. We're looking for Andrew Dreyer."

"Yes?"

"You his wife?"

"No. He was my boarder."

"So he stays here?"

"He stayed here."

"Where is he now?"

"I don't know. I had to give him notice. He left yesterday."

"Did he take his things with him?"

"What do you mean?"

"His clothes and stuff."

"No, they're still here."

"Where does he sleep?"

"In that room," she said, pointing to Andrew's door. The detectives marched in followed by Mrs. Carollissen and Eldred. The sergeant surveyed the room carefully.

"I thought you said he wasn't in?"

"I did," Eldred volunteered.

"Stop your bloody lying!"

"I'm not lying," the boy said, stoutly.

"Eldred, keep quiet," admonished his mother.

"But he keeps calling me a liar."

"Shut up!" the sergeant said.

"I won't," Eldred replied. He stood shivering with rage, his green eyes blazing.

"Who slept in that bed?" the sergeant demanded from Mrs. Carollissen.

"My son did," she replied timidly.

"This is your son?"

"Yes."

"Well, teach him manners."

The other two detectives searched the room thoroughly. One of them reached for Eldred's school satchel, and started undoing the straps.

"Leave my stuff alone!" he shouted, charging over to the detective. He grabbed his bag and attempted to wrench it from the policeman's hand. The strap broke and Eldred fell to the ground with a thud. In a moment the other detective was on him, jerking him roughly to his feet and pinning his arms behind his back.

"You must be taught some manners, young man," said the sergeant walking over to him. "You should learn to control yourself."

Eldred tried to avoid the smack, but could only struggle feebly. Mrs. Carollissen watched, too horrified and frightened to intervene. The detective shook out the contents of the satchel, books, manuscripts, mathematics instruments, an athletics programme. He dumped it all contemptuously in a corner.

"Now then, where's Dreyer?"

"I don't know," said Mrs. Carollissen tearfully.

"Are you going to talk or do we have to take your son away?"

"Please leave the boy alone."

"Where's Dreyer?"

"He's at his sister's place."

"Where's that?"

"Don't tell, Ma," said Eldred struggling.

"Shut up!" said the sergeant, raising his hand threateningly.

"Don't tell!"

"Shurrup!"

Mrs. Carollissen looked nervously from the detective to Eldred.

"His sister stays in Nile Street, Cape Town."

"Where in Nile Street?"

"I think it's the third house on the right-hand side going up. It's before you get to Windsor Street."

"What's her name?"

"Mrs. Peters, I think."

"Search the rest of the house," the sergeant ordered the other two.

After they had released him, Eldred sat down on the bed, rubbing his burning cheek. Mrs. Carollissen went over to him and attempted to put her arms around his neck. He struggled to avoid her and pushed her away rudely.

"What's wrong, my boy?"

"Leave me alone."

"I'm sorry they were so nasty to you," she said, attempting to fondle him.

"Please leave me alone," he said, avoiding her eyes.

"I had to tell them, Eldred, otherwise they would take you away."

He shivered with indignation and she could see a red flush burning through his bronzed skin.

"You told them where Mr. Dreyer was."

"I had to, for your sake, my boy."

"Leave me alone."

She got up heavily, trying to maintain her authority.

"I'll speak to your father about you!"

"Go away!"

The detectives returned, having obviously been unsuc-

cessful. They could hear that Mr. Carollissen was awake.
Charmaine was crying in the children's room.

"We'll check Nile Street. If you've been lying we'll come
back here."

Eldred stared hostilely at the sergeant. The officer met
his gaze.

"You'd better learn to control yourself, young man, or
you'll find yourself in the cells pretty soon."

Eldred was about to reply, but balled his fists and kept
silent.

"We'll come back if we don't find him. God help
you all if you've been lying."

"I told you what I know," said Mrs. Carollissen.

They left immediately without saying another word.
Eldred threw himself on the bed and cried convulsively,
his shoulders heaving. Mrs. Carollissen caressed him
tenderly. He pushed her away.

"Never mind, my boy, we'll see that nothing happens
to you."

"Get away. You told them. I hate you."

"What's that?" she said, shocked.

"I hate you! Get away from me!"

She looked at him horrified. Eldred sat up, his eyes
blazing at her.

"I hate you, get away!"

There was something in his voice which made Mrs.
Carollissen obey at once.

8

Eldred lay in bed wide awake and still burning
with resentment. He could hear his mother quieting
Charmaine and his father grunting in his bedroom. For a
long time voices filtered through to him, then all was
silent. Eldred tried to sleep, but his mother's infidelity
troubled him. She shouldn't have told the police, she
shouldn't have told, kept milling through his head. His
pillow was burning hot and he turned it over several times
to find a cool spot on which to rest his head. She had no
right to tell where Mr. Dreyer was. They might find him
now. He heard a soft knock at the front door. He sat

bolt upright in bed, his body shivering. Could it be the police again? Coming for him? He could make a run for it. Get out of the window and make for the bicycle shed. Another knock. He sat up tensely in the dark, the whole room alive and vibrant. He didn't dare breathe. He heard the heavy crunch of footsteps under his window. He jumped up and cautiously drew the curtains apart.

"Mr. Dreyer!"

Eldred almost wept with relief.

"Mr. Dreyer," he whispered.

"That you, Eldred?"

The familiar voice made him want to laugh and cry at the same time.

"I'll open the front door in a minute, sir."

He ran down the passage and struggled nervously with the lock.

"Come in, Mr. Dreyer."

Andrew limped along the passage and into his room. Eldred followed, a worried look on his face.

"What's happened to you?"

"Nothing serious, Eldred."

"You're hurt."

"A bit."

"Did the police beat you also?"

"What do you mean, also?"

"Did the police beat you?"

"No, not at all," Andrew attempted a smile. "I just had a slight accident."

"It must have been the police."

"What put that idea into your silly head?"

"I'm sure it's the police."

"You can take my word for it. The police have done nothing to me, yet."

"All right," said Eldred suspiciously, "in any case I'm glad you're back."

"I'm not staying. I've only come to pick up some clothes."

"Yeah, come to think of it, why are you wearing a dressing-gown?"

"I messed up my shirt and suit in the accident."

"What accident?"

"That's not important."

Andrew started rummaging in his drawers, collecting underclothes, shirts, handkerchiefs, socks. He tried to get his trunk out from under the bed, and as he did so felt the dizziness coming on again. He held tightly on to the bed, hoping that Eldred had not noticed.

"Be a good lad and get this trunk out for me while I get a blazer and flannels from the wardrobe."

"Sure."

Eldred struggled and dragged out the dusty case, then carefully wiped it with his handkerchief. Andrew proceeded to put in clean clothes, his blazer, two pairs of flannels, his toilet-set and satchel.

"The poliice were here a short while ago."

"Oh?" said Andrew, stopping in his work.

"Three detectives came for you."

"What, again?"

"But I wouldn't tell them where you were."

"Good lad."

"Ma told them where your sister stayed."

Andrew wondered how Mrs. Carollissen knew, then realized that he must have told her the previous morning.

"Ma told them!" said Eldred angrily.

"So she did, did she?"

"Yeah. It was damn lousy of her."

"Well, they won't find me there. What else did they ask?"

"Nothing more."

Andrew looked the boy squarely in the face and saw that his eyes were swimming with tears.

"Eldred, what did the police do to you?"

"Nothing."

"Come on, out with it."

"I wouldn't tell them."

"So what did they do?"

"One held my arms while the other smacked me."

"Christ!"

"They also said they would come back."

"And?"

"Never mind."

"So they threatened you because you wouldn't tell where I was?"

"Yeah."

"The swines. Picking on kids."

Andrew shut the case firmly and stretched himself up-right. His back and knee still hurt, and he could feel a dull ache in his head.

"Could you help me with this to the car?"

"Sure."

"Get your shoes on."

"O.K."

This was worse than the baton charges or the tear-gas. To beat a youngster who was only trying to be loyal to him. Andrew felt the same way as he had when he had seen Justin marching to prison as a Defier. It was the personal element which always affected him strongly. Smacking a mere schoolboy because of him.

"I'm ready," Eldred said, lacing up his shoes.

"All right, let's move."

He walked behind the boy so that Eldred would not notice his limp. He had never really been aware of the extent of the youngster's attachment to him. True, Eldred had always been around. Just around, simply just there. Now that Andrew was leaving it was different. He would miss the boy's inane questions, over-enthusiasm, his physical presence. Up to now he had not given Eldred a second thought. He had never suspected his strong attachment and loyalty. They paused on the stoep.

"By the way, how did the Sports go?"

"Our school came second."

"Nice work. And how did you do?"

"I won the 220 yards final but I was badly beaten in the 100 yards."

"Good show! So do you think you'll make the Senior School's side?"

"I hope so. I'm training like a bugger."

"Keep it up. Train like a what-did-you-call-it?"

"A bugger."

"Yeah, like a bugger." They smiled at each other. At the car Andrew paused while Abe took his trunk from him and packed it into the boot.

"Well, Eldred, I don't quite know when I'll see you again."

Eldred stood silent, tears clouding his eyes.

"Good-bye and best of luck."

"Yeah."

"And make that Senior Schools' side. Train like a . . . bugger."

"Yeah."

"*Totsiens.*"

"*Totsiens.*"

They shook hands firmly and then Andrew got into the car and Abe reversed into Lake Road. Andrew was strangely silent and thoughtful for the rest of the journey to Altmann's.

9

The following morning Andrew woke up to find the sunlight streaming in through the bedroom window. Abe lay snoring gently beside him, his mouth slightly open. Andrew only vaguely noticed him. He felt bilious and his head still ached slightly. He sat up stiffly, feeling for his shoes. Ruth's dressing-gown was lying over a chair. He slipped it on slowly and then proceeded to the bathroom. He didn't like what he saw in the mirror. There was a bruise at the side of his head, his eyes were blood-shot and his lips puffy. There was only one thing to do to cure his head and stomach. He pushed his fingers down his throat and vomited. After that he felt a good deal better. Then he had a warm shower.

His bruises burnt as the water poured over them. He remembered the shower he had had the previous night at Ruth's flat. No, it was the Monday night. What a hell of a lot had happened since. He began to feel better, his body responding to the warm water. He started humming De Little Black Bull to himself. Then a quick wash-down and he stepped out partially refreshed. He rubbed himself down and then slipped on the dressing-gown and went outside into the open. Altmann's property stretched for over three hundred yards towards the Lotus River. Fresh and green, smelling of grass and the damp soil. Andrew breathed in deeply, the clear, cold air tickling his nostrils. The ground underfoot was wet with dew, the soil rich and moist. Why couldn't life always be like that? Why

should life all labour be? *L'Allegro*. The Happy Man. Yes.
Like the first movement of Beethoven's *Pastoral*. Tribute
to the dawn. But look the morn in russet mantle clad,
walks o'er the dew of yon high Eastern hill. *Hamlet*. Now,
class, it is imperative for you to understand and appreciate the use Shakespeare makes of sympathetic natural
background. Take *Julius Caesar*. When beggars die there
are no comets seen. Hell, school was so far away. It
seemed ages since he had last stood in a classroom. Poor
old Eldred. The bastards, holding the boy responsible for
his teacher's political activities. He had had no idea that
the youth had been so attached to him. Should have
noticed it long before. Long time ago. When de little
black bull went down de meadow, long time ago.

He walked back into the bedroom humming, to find
Abe awake and sitting up in his underwear.

"Morning."

"Morning, sir."

"You seem peculiarly happy."

"I'm only humming."

"So, how are you feeling today?"

"A bit stiff and sore, but considerably improved since
last night. I've been outside answering the call of nature."

"Why outside?"

"Don't be rude. I mean I went to admire the grass
and trees and dew and birds."

"How very pleasant and extremely aesthetic."

"I've got a soul, you know."

"Now who would have thought it? By the way, Andrew,"
said Abe, now turning serious, "I've got an apology to
make."

"Yeah?"

"I'm sorry about last night."

"I don't understand."

"Braam's."

"Oh, I see."

"I know I acted rather childishly."

"You did behave rather odd."

"I get that way sometimes and I don't find that pseudo-
politician and pseudo-bohemian exactly a tonic."

"Yes, Braam seemed to be baiting you."

"I wonder if he's been picked up?"

"He'd be most disappointed if he wasn't."

"Well, Justin's had it."

"That's bad."

There was a soft knock at the door. Andrew became tense, expecting Ruth. He wondered whether her mood had changed since the last time he had seen her. Abe quickly got down under the blankets.

"Come in," he said.

It was Mrs. Altmann who entered with two cups of coffee on a tray and copies of the *Cape Times*. She had a pleasant face, with a shy, ready smile. Neither of them had ever met her before.

"Good morning," she said softly.

"Morning. Mrs. Altmann, I presume?"

"Yes."

"I'm Andrew Dreyer and the person hiding under the blankets is Abe Hanslo."

"I've heard a lot from my husband about both of you."

"Is Mr. Altmann still here?"

"No. He's already left for school, but he left a message that you should all make yourselves at home."

"Thanks. Sorry to have disturbed you people in the early hours of the morning."

"No trouble at all; we understand."

She left as quietly and shyly as she had come. The two sipped their coffee and glanced at the newspaper headlines. Abe suddenly put down his *Times*.

"Have you bothered to think what we should do?" he asked.

"Huh?" said Andrew without looking up.

"We can't stay on here indefinitely."

"Have we any alternative?"

"Yes, we can get right away."

"Where to?"

"Basutoland."

"The three of us?"

"Why not?"

"You seriously think that we can travel together over a thousand miles without getting caught?"

"We could try."

"I'll have to think it over. At the moment I'm quite prepared to stay where I am."

"Maybe you're right."

Abe stared at him helplessly and then got out of bed.

"I'd better get cooled off under the shower."

Abe left. Andrew unpacked his suitcase and dressed carefully. He felt quite composed after combing his hair, and was humming as he walked into the kitchen. He still had a slight limp. Ruth looked attractive in matching blouse and slacks, frying bacon and eggs over the stove. Mrs. Altmann could be heard dusting somewhere in the front of the house. Andrew tiptoed up behind Ruth and pecked her lightly on the cheek.

"Morning, darling."

"Morning," she said coolly.

"How are you?"

"Fine."

He waited for her to enquire about his condition, but she concentrated on her frying.

"I'm feeling wonderful this morning," he volunteered, determined that his spirits would not be dampened.

"Yes."

"And I'm dying for those bacon and eggs."

"They're almost done."

"What's wrong, darling?"

"Nothing," she said, looking away.

"Why am I getting the cold treatment?"

"Don't you know?"

"Do you mean last night?"

She bit her lips without saying anything.

"I apologize if I in any way offended you."

"It's all right."

"You know that I wouldn't like to hurt you needlessly."

"All right."

"Not now or at any other time."

She continued frying in silence. Andrew settled down uncomfortably at the table to read his newspaper. Abe entered looking worried.

"Morning, Ruth."

"Morning, Abe." She attempted a smile at him.

"I've just been trying to phone my mother."

"So?"

"The phone just rings and rings. It's most unusual."

"Couldn't she have gone shopping?" Andrew suggested.

"Not at this hour. Well, it's best if she doesn't see me for quite some time. I'll ring her again later in the day."

10

After breakfast the three went into the lounge. Mrs. Altmann went to her room after she had been assured that they were not in need of anything. Ruth kicked off her sandals and snuggled between cushions on the sofa with a formidable pile of *Readers' Digests*. Abe switched on the radio and settled himself with cushions on the carpet. Andrew eased himself into a deep armchair and opened his *Times*. A band played a jazz rhythm softly in the background. Andrew read the headlines. LOCATION SHOPS CLEARED OUT OF STAPLE FOODS. TRIBUTE TO POLICE ON THE RAND. UNION'S QUIET DAY AFTER VIOLENCE.

"Nothing in here about the raids," he said, leafing through his newspaper.

"Too soon," Abe commented. "Unless they're throwing a blanket of silence around it."

"I wonder how many people were picked up."

"Your guess is as good as mine. But I should think they're far from finished."

"Which means we remain on the run indefinitely?"

"Seems like it. What about my suggestion?"

"What suggestion?"

"Of getting right away."

"To Basutoland?"

"Yes."

"Why on earth?"

"We'll be safe once we're outside South Africa. There's no extradition for politicals from there."

"You sound desperate."

"The situation is desperate."

"If I have any choice in the matter, I think I would prefer to stay right here."

"You're all right, but what about Ruth? Are you being fair to her?"

"Ruth must decide for herself."

Andrew stole a quick glance at her and noticed that she was not concentrating on the magazines.

"Don't think I haven't thought about her."

"Have you really?" she asked.

"Yes, I have. Now what would you suggest we do, dear?"

"Are you interested in knowing?"

"Please, Ruth."

"If I have any choice in the matter and if what I say counts for anything, I would prefer to go back to my flat."

"But look," Abe began, "it's foolhardy to do that. The Special Branch is raiding. If a state of emergency is declared you can be held in prison indefinitely. You are suspect because of your relationship with Andrew."

"I realize that."

"Think of your parents, your career, yourself."

"I have."

"You can ruin all your chances. Why not go back to Vereeniging for a short time?"

"I heartily agree," said Andrew getting up.

"Are you still trying to get rid of me?" She turned on him.

"No, it's for your own sake. You must understand, Ruth, that one doesn't know what might happen next."

"I'm well aware of that."

"The newspaper says that things are quiet now, but it's just a matter of time before the next explosion occurs, the next Sharpeville, the next Langa."

"But in the end things must return to normal."

"You're wrong, Ruth, it will never be the same again. We've reached the turning point. On the surface it might look calm again, but there'll always be cracks, and more cracks. Now and then there'll be small explosions like Langa and Sharpeville, then one day everything will blow up, and we might be in the middle of it."

"So I will be safer in Vereeniging?"

"Safer than here."

"Sharpeville is near Vereeniging."

"You will be with your parents."

"Which is preferable to being with the man I love?" Andrew sat down helplessly.

"Please try and understand, Ruth," he began again.

"Shhhh!" said Abe who had been listening with his ear glued to the radio. He turned up the volume as the voice of the announcer finished a broadcast. There was an expectant hush.

"What is it?" Andrew asked.

"Keep quiet!" he said tensely.

The broadcaster's voice came on again, even and emotionless.

". . . I repeat this news-flash just received. Thousands of Africans are marching from Langa to Cape Town. It is reported that columns are converging along De Waal Drive. Police reinforcements are rushing into the city. It is believed that the Africans are heading for Caledon Square Police Station to demand the release of their leaders who were arrested in pre-dawn raids this morning. That is the end of the announcement. We now return you to our programme of Latin-American music. . . ."

Abe switched off and looked at the others in astonishment. There was a moment's silence.

"I'm going," Andrew said decisively.

"What?"

"I'm going to Caledon Square."

He got up from his armchair.

"Don't be a fool!" Abe almost shouted.

"I'm going into town!"

"But you're in no fit state," Ruth pleaded.

"I'm perfectly able to drive."

"Please don't go, Andy," she said anxiously.

"I'm leaving right now!"

Abe and Ruth exchanged helpless glances.

"Please Abe, stop him from doing something stupid."

"Andrew," Abe tried to reason with him, "things look dangerous. It's much wiser to stay here."

"I'm going at once. May I use your car, Ruth?"

"Please, Andy!"

"Coming along, Abe?"

"You're as crazy as hell!"

"Coming along?"

"All right, I'd better come."

11

Abe drove through the suburbs at speed. Beside him Andrew sat tense and silent. All along the main road there were whites and Coloureds doing menial jobs in the face of the mass strike. Selling newspapers, delivering milk, sweeping offices. Petrol-pump attendants, messengers, cleaners. They were struck by the ominous quiet in the southern suburbs. Rondebosch and Rosebank were funereal. Everything seemed dead until they came to Mowbray, where they spotted a helicopter whining overhead in the direction of the Castle.

Then they started meeting the crowds. Everybody heading in one direction, the Caledon Square Police Station. Along Darling Street, from Sir Lowry Road, down Longmarket Street, up Plein Street. Buses full of Africans, cars filled with black faces. Trains, lorries, carts. Thousands upon thousands. And all heading for Caledon Square to demand the release of their leaders. From Langa and Nyanga they poured to demand the release of their leaders. Along De Waal Drive 15,000 people marched to demand the release of their leaders.

Abe found a parking spot on the Parade with difficulty. A long line of policemen with Sten guns was drawn up outside the station. Neutral faces betraying no emotion and looking straight ahead. Part of the machinery, cogs in the wheel. Oblivious of the surging humanity jostling past. Release our leaders. Freedom in our lifetime. *Izwe Lethu!* God bless Africa! People pouring out of trains and passing a long row of Sten guns on their way to Caledon Square. Remember Sharpeville. Remember Langa. They raid us in the morning, they raid us in the evening, when do we rest? Yes, when do we rest? All heading for the Police Station. Give us back our leaders. *Mayibuye, Afrika!*

At the bottom of Buitenkant Street the two had to pass through a cordon of tanks and Saracen armoured cars. Andrew was limping badly. Then struggling through the seething, sweating humanity. Voices around them. English, Afrikaans, Xhosa. Let us all go to gaol. No bail, no defence, no fines. It is death to have a pass. They raid us in the morning, they raid us in the evening. We can never rest.

And then someone speaks over the microphone. It is the voice of authority. Craning of necks to see, but it is useless. Will those not involved in the demonstrations leave the area! There is fear in the air. The country is frightened. The white faces peering from the windows are frightened. There is an angry fear beneath the black faces in the street. Some ask, is this the reckoning? Others say, this is the reckoning. But is it? Is this what has been expected for so long? More than three hundred years? Black hands raised in clenched fists with erect thumbs. *Mayibuye Afrika.* Palms facing outwards. *Izwe Lethu.* Our country. The women weep. Outside Parliament they hold their heads in their hands and weep for Sharpeville and Langa. The mothers weep for their sons and the wives weep for their husbands.

A youth in faded blue shorts is raised shoulder-high. Kgosana, they shout. It is Kgosana. And then he speaks. Let us be silent like people going to a graveyard. Then they argue with the policemen about the men in gaol. Let us be silent for the men in gaol. For those in the graveyard.

And then they march back to the Locations. Column after column along De Waal Drive. Mile after mile of black humanity. Hardly speaking, hardly saying a word. Silent like people going to a graveyard.

Andrew and Abe finally reached their car on the Grand Parade and got in with relief. Abe sat back, looking out of the window.

"Well, so that's that," he said.

Andrew sat upright, still tense and nervous.

"I hope you are satisfied," Abe continued.

"I am more than merely satisfied. I felt part of it all. That was me. I was the crowd milling outside the Police Station. I felt for the first time in my life that I was Africa. They might gaol our bodies, but they can never break our spirits."

"And our souls go marching on."

"Please try and understand. This is no time for cynicism."

"Don't be sickly."

"But you must have been impressed. Think of the discipline behind the demonstration; the absolute obedience; the political consciousness."

"And the absolute *naïveté*. Did that fellow . . . what's his name? . . . Kgosana, really think that the Minister of Justice would at one stroke of his pen release everyone in prison?"

"He had a perfect right to demand it."

"Really?"

"Also he's young and in an invidious position."

"Then save us from the indiscretion of youth."

"You're being completely unfair, Abe."

"Let's get away from here, for Chrissake!"

"I want to see Florence."

"Who?"

"Florence Bailey."

"But why?"

"I would like to see her."

"I would prefer not to go there."

"Why not?"

"She sickens me every time she comes whining to my ma."

"Let's go and see her."

"She can't stand my guts, but that's mutual."

"I must see Florence."

"Why on earth must you go now?"

"I want to know what happened to Justin. Do you know where she stays?"

"Well, vaguely. In Arundel Street somewhere."

"We can find it."

"Do you insist on going?"

"I insist."

"All right. We might as well drop in at my mother's on the way back to Lotus River. I might not see her again for a long time."

Abe was forced to drive slowly through the crowds moving up Hanover Street until they reached Arundel Street.

"Here we are," Abe said. "Now where's the damn house?"

"Ask someone," Andrew answered shortly.

Abe looked up, surprised at the tone of his voice.

"Come off it. You're not in a bloody revolution yet."

"You don't understand."

After enquiring they were shown the back entrance. The radio was blaring. Abe knocked somewhat impatiently.

"Come in!" they heard her voice from inside.

"Shall we?" Abe said, looking distastefully at the yard.

"You lead the way."

They walked gingerly through the untidy kitchen into the bedroom. Florence was sitting on the bed painting her toenails, and listening to the radio.

"Yes?" she asked, without looking up.

"Hello, Florence."

"Oh, it's you," she said, giving both a casual glance. "Take a seat somewhere. I'm busy listening to a request programme."

They sat down on the bed. She ignored them until the crooner on the radio had finished a sugary number.

"What do you want?" she then asked, without turning the volume down.

"Turn that damn thing off!" Abe shouted above the din.

"No need to be rude," she said, softening it slightly. "That better?"

"It'll do. Andrew insisted on coming here to find out what had happened to Justin."

"But I told you on the phone."

"So?"

"What else is there to tell?"

"Did they say anything when they took him away?"

"No, nothing."

"Did they say why they were arresting him?" Andrew asked nervously, speaking for the first time.

"Hello, Andrew. Nice to hear you can still talk."

"Did they give any reasons?"

"I don't think so."

"Did they take anything away?"

"No. Which reminds me. He left some things for you. I think he hid them under the stove. Please take it all away."

"Go and get it."

"Who you think you're ordering about?"

"Get it!"

"All right. What's come over both of you?" She first admired her toenails, then got up slowly and pattered on bare feet to the kitchen. They weren't sure whether her nonchalance was deliberate or not. She returned with a loose parcel. Andrew took a pamphlet out and read it hurriedly.

"I suppose it's political stuff?" she asked.

"Yes."

"It's because of politics that he is always in trouble." She suddenly turned on both of them. "You people encourage him, but you stay out of trouble yourselves and

I am sick and tired of keeping quiet about it. It's time you all listened to me."

"Shut up!" said Abe.

"I'm the one who has to suffer!"

"Shut up!"

"These are the Langa pamphlets," Andrew said, ignoring her and passing Abe one of them.

"I hope you don't mean to go."

"We're going straight back to Lotus River after you've seen your mother."

"Good, I could do with a bath. I feel dirty after this."

"Get out and leave me alone! I'm sick of the lot of you."

Abe looked at her in disgust.

"You've gone down a long way since I knew you at school. Do you like sitting here listening to muck on the radio?"

"Yes!"

"While your husband's in gaol?"

"What am I supposed to do, sing hymns until he comes out?"

"It might be preferable."

"You say I've gone down a long way. You're damn right. I'm in the gutter right now and all because of your politics. You can afford to speak nice and easy in your armchairs, while my husband has to do the dirty work and I the suffering."

"I find your attitude most peculiar."

"Do you really? I've found yours peculiar since we were first at school and your mother seems to agree with me."

"How perceptive of both of you."

"Now, please go and leave me alone."

"You disgust me."

"Do I? Why don't you go and look after your neglected mother instead of worrying about me?"

"Come on, Andrew, I need that bath badly."

He turned away. Andrew had watched all this with distaste. He picked up the parcel and followed. Florence stood quivering, glaring at both. Abe suddenly became tense, all senses alert.

"Turn that thing on louder!" he commanded.

"Who d'you think you're speaking to?"

He strode over to the radio and turned the volume up.

They were in time to listen to the last part of an announcement.

". . . to maintain public order, I hereby declare that a state of emergency exists within the areas specified as from the 29th of March 1960."

There was a stunned silence. Florence sat down on the bed, a sneer on her face. Abe smiled cynically. Andrew was breathing rapidly, his nostrils quivering.

"So, it's come at last!" Abe said calmly.

"Christ!" was all Andrew could add.

"Well, now the fun begins."

"Let's get to Langa fast!"

"What!"

"We've got a job to do in a hurry!"

"You're crazy!"

"Come on. We've got to distribute the pamphlets."

"You're crazy as hell!"

"If you don't want to, I'll go alone."

"You're mad. First you make me come to Cape Town, then to meet this woman. Now, when a state of emergency is declared, you want to go to Langa."

"Are you coming?"

"Absolutely not!"

"Please, Abe!"

"You're sick, Andrew."

Abe looked at him and saw tears swimming in his eyes. He had never known Andrew like this before. There was a pale, unhealthy flush under his dark skin.

"Please, Abe."

"I think you're stark raving mad and it's the last time I ever do you a favour."

"Will you come?"

"I'll come."

12

Abe stepped down on the accelerator and the car sped along Vanguard Drive. Andrew maintained an intense silence. Abe looked at him once or twice, noticing his unhealthy flush and the drops of sweat standing thickly on his forehead.

"Stop here!" he shouted at Abe.

The Austin came to a screeching halt. Abe switched off the engine.

"Now that we've arrived what do we do?"

"Get through the fence. We only have this field to cross and we're in Langa."

"Then what?"

"We give out the pamphlets."

"You're crazy!"

"I promised Justin that I would help."

"Do you realize at all that a state of emergency has been declared?"

"I promised I'd help give these out. I must, now that Justin is in gaol."

Abe stared at him unbelievingly.

"You're sick, Andrew."

"Maybe I am."

"Physically and mentally."

"Are you coming or not?"

Andrew took the parcel and climbed out of the car. He struggled through the barb-wire fence, getting his coat torn in the process. Abe watched hesitantly for a moment, then followed slowly and reluctantly. Once on the other side of the fence, he paused and looked appealingly at Andrew.

"For God's sake let's go back, Andrew."

"I'm going on."

"But think of the risk you're taking."

"If you have no guts I'll do it alone."

Andrew went on, limping badly over the uneven ground, and stumbled over a tussock of grass. Abe ran to help him up. He staggered clumsily to his feet, his face screwed up with pain and dripping with sweat.

"You're a sick man, Andrew."

"I'm well enough to go on."

He hobbled on, clutching his parcel of pamphlets. Abe followed a little way behind, a worried look on his face.

"For goodness' sake, let's go back while there's still time."

But Andrew wasn't hearing or seeing him any longer. He was stumbling on, oblivious of his surroundings, obsessed with the necessity of continuing. Driven by a stubborn intensity. Justin wanted him to do it. Justin was in gaol. The parcel was becoming undone and a few pamphlets floated to the ground. Abe picked them up and was forced to run in order to keep up with the figure limping ahead.

They started passing small, sub-economic houses standing in sandy, wind-blown gardens. Women and children came to their gates to witness the unusual spectacle. Andrew finally stopped outside a small grocery shop in Mendi Avenue. He breathed heavily and sweat was pouring down his face. Then he began fumbling about in the parcel and handing out leaflets. Those who had taken part in the Cape Town demonstration were now returning and a crowd started to collect. Andrew gave out pamphlet after pamphlet to everyone he could reach, groping in the brown-paper parcel for more. Abe stood a distance away, a contemptuous, though nervous, look on his face. The crowd was by now packed closely around Andrew.

"Why are you giving these out?" asked a young African, obviously suspicious of his motive.

"The strike must go on. Everyone must hold out. Right and victory are on our side!"

"Are you on strike?"

"I am not at my job. Come, all of you, take a pamphlet!"

"Are you a supporter of the P.A.C.?"

"That's not important. Please, all of you. We must hold out. We cannot lose."

"Do you support the A.N.C.?"

"That's not relevant either. Come on, people, take one of these pamphlets. I have come to pledge solidarity with you. Your cause is our cause!"

"Why are the Coloureds not on strike?"

"I am not going to defend anybody. I identify myself with you because I am one of you. Come on, everybody! Please take a pamphlet each!"

The crowd stared suspiciously at the intense young man, his bloodshot eyes and the sweat pouring down his cheeks. Andrew continued to address and harangue the crowd of sullen men in a high-pitched voice.

"Police!" the warning sounded.

A patrol van with wire-enmeshed headlamps snailed its way through the mass. Abe started shivering involuntarily. Two steel-helmeted policemen jumped out of the back and grabbed hold of Andrew, twisting his arms behind his back.

"What the hell are you doing?" a sergeant demanded. Andrew winced with pain. The crowd watched hostilely.

"Where's your permit to be here?"

Andrew started coughing helplessly, his face contorted with pain.

"Throw him in, we'll deal with him, the bloody agitator!"

Andrew tried to speak as they forced him round to the rear. The crowd murmured threateningly. He struggled to loosen his arms, kicking his legs impotently. Abe watched with horror and disbelief, then suddenly he was galvanized into action.

"Let him go, you bastards!" he shouted as he rushed the police. In a moment he was flat on his back with a heavy boot on his chest. The first stone smashed against the van door. The police swung around to face the mob, at the same time drawing their revolvers. The crowd retreated crushing those behind them. A second stone caught a constable on the cheek, drawing blood.

"Get back or we shoot!"

A spark ran through the crowd.

"Throw them both in!" commanded the sergeant, his face white with fear.

Then the situation exploded. It happened so quickly that the police were caught off their guard. Like an enraged beast the crowd charged. Fists, arms, sticks whirling and lashing out. Feet trampling. Bodies falling over one another. Hands grasping frantically and blows raining down. A crazy vortex of limbs and weapons. Struggling bodies and heaving torsos. With a splintering crash the patrol van was overturned. Pistol shots rang through the air. The three policemen retreated into the shop shooting over the heads of the crowds. Boys shinned up poles to cut telephone wires. The police van was a blazing inferno. There was a loud bang as the petrol tank exploded. Angry shouts and roars. Screams of terror and uncontrolled fury. Hundreds of feet trampling everything underfoot. Stones crashing into the window of the shop. Heavy breathing and running feet, then the shop also went up in flames.

Andrew felt himself being dragged and carried across the field. Willing hands helped him through the fence. Abe's face a misty haze. The last thing he remembered as he was pushed into the back of the car was seeing the black pall of smoke over the shop and the police van, and hearing the sharp whine of bullets whistling through the air. Then he fainted.

13

The first thing Andrew was aware of was the sound of music playing softly in the background. He tried to recognize the tune but had to give up. Sounded like Stravinsky or something. There was also a hushed conversation going on somewhere. His head throbbed dully and he found difficulty in focusing his eyes. He could make out vague patterns of light against the ceiling. He attempted to sit upright but a firm hand gently held him back on the couch. He could smell perfume faintly. Ruth. He made out her face, at first a white blur, then he saw the worried smile around the mouth.

"Ruth!"

"It's me, Andy, lie still."

"Where am I?"

He pulled himself upright with a jerk. Then the recollection of the riot came back to him with a rush. Abe and Altmann sat in deep chairs on either side of a fire burning in the grate.

"How are you feeling now, young man?" Altmann asked, looking towards him.

"Slightly groggy."

"Have a drink."

He poured a stiff brandy and came over to the couch. "This should help," he said, holding the glass to Andrew's lips.

He felt the brandy burning down his throat and a pleasant warmth creep over his stomach. He gasped for breath.

"I would like another please, a big one."

Altmann carefully measured out a second glass and gave it to him. Andrew gulped it down, screwing up his face as the brandy almost knocked his breath away. He sighed deeply.

"That was good, I feel better already. What time is it?"

"Ten o'clock," Ruth said.

"Have I been asleep that long?"

"You've been resting, Andy."

"I feel fine now."

"I am glad to hear it," Altmann said kindly.

"Lie back, Andy," Ruth urged.

"I'm all right." Andrew sat up and looked at Abe. "Thanks for getting me out of that mess, chum."

Abe continued to stare steadily into the fire without making any comment.

"Come to think of it I did act kind of silly."

"Don't bother about it now," Altmann suggested.

"Abe, please accept my apologies."

Abe turned around and looked at Andrew with absolute contempt and disgust. "Apologies! What good are your apologies now? You could have got both of us killed and I can't bear to think how many others might in fact be maimed or even dead at this moment as a result of your thoughtlessness and your . . . your sickly sentimentality."

"Please, Abe," Andrew pleaded, "don't look at it like that. I sincerely regret it, I assure you."

"Till the next time?"

"I don't think there'll be a next time."

"What a hell of a guarantee." Abe turned back and stared into the fire again. "It's time you learnt that sentimentality, particularly of your sickly brand, always has disastrous results."

Andrew was now on the defensive. "My sentimentality as you call it can be a considerable force. Look what it has done to rouse white Afrikanerdom."

"This situation calls for an objective assessment, not a puerile emotional reaction."

"There comes a point, Abe, when human nature can stand injustices no longer."

"Oh, I see. And then one gives out pamphlets in Langa and one causes a riot?" Abe turned to face him, his lips quivering with rage. "Are you stark, raving mad? Do you realize the enormity of your irresponsibility?"

"I fully appreciate the implications of what I did."

"And yet you did it?"

"In a way, yes. It was my way of registering my protest against Saracens, Sten guns, intimidation and injustices."

"For Chrissake, hundreds might be hurt, those police-men might be killed!"

"Wouldn't it be a sort of rough justice?"

"What?"

"Haven't they been asking for what's coming to them?"

"No, absolutely not! We're fighting injustice, not men in uniform!"

"Damn it all, Abe, stop being an idealist. You call me sickly, but look how sickly you're getting. Policemen are the instruments. You can't just separate them off from the policy."

"You sound just like Justin and that bunch. When will you people realize that you cannot fight hatred with more hatred?"

"With what do you fight it? Love? Do you lavish affection on those who oppress you? Get out of your ivory tower and fool's paradise."

Andrew found and lit a cigarette. Ruth stared be-wildered from the one to the other. Altmann stood look-ing into the fire.

"You cannot fight racialism with racialism."

"Granted."

"Our ideological weapons have to be superior. The only way of fighting racialism is with non-racialism. We've got to explore and then obliterate the myth of race. Look at the situation from a completely non-racial point of view. You can't condemn a man because his skin is black, or white, or brown. You cannot hate the white bus con-ductor or shop assistant just because his skin is different from yours. They are as much victims of the situation as we are."

"What an idealist you are, Abe. So we've got to learn to appreciate and understand racial domination."

"No, we don't have to learn to appreciate it, but we must learn to understand it. We can only oppose situa-tions which we understand, and we can only fight with superior ideological weapons. We must learn to under-stand Africans and Europeans. If we can't learn to look at all people just as human beings, truism as it may be, we have no moral justification for our stand. We've got to raise everyone to our level of understanding and never compromise at any other level."

"And how does one achieve that?"

"Achieve what?" Abe asked.

"Raising people to our level of understanding?"

"Not by shabby exhibitionism. By opposing and hammering at all forms of discrimination and injustice within the limits of our abilities."

"Individually or in organizations?"

"Both."

"You haven't been too happy about aligning yourself with organizations."

"No, I haven't, because I have found most organizations riddled with racialism. For God's sake I am not a non-European or a Coloured man. I am a South African. Besides, organizations alone cannot bring thousands of men and women together to defy the authority of the state, backed as it is by lethal weapons. There has to be a more compelling motive. And the way of deciding whether a Government policy is right or wrong is to analyse the principles on which it is founded and to test its results. Legalized separatism cannot be right because it denies links which do exist in our society and the result, as we have seen, is Sharpevilles and Langas. Agitators could do nothing with a contented and thriving population."

Abe got up and poured himself a drink. Andrew watched him cynically.

"So, do we hurl back the Saracens with philosophical bomb-shells and silence the Sten guns with dialectical mortars?"

"You people are always denigrating the fight on the level of ideas, but there has to be a moral justification for what we are doing or the battle is lost before we have even started."

"Is opposition to injustice immoral and without justification?"

"It depends on the kind of opposition. What I'm saying is: don't denigrate the power of ideas. It's at that level that we are superior. They can't gaol an idea. They can't ban an idea for five years. They can't silence an idea with Saracens and tanks."

"How many oppressed people in South Africa are perceptive enough to appreciate your argument? Do you really think that they could march from the locations to Cape Town fortified by the ideals of non-racialism?"

"Yes. If they march on Cape Town as black men in

order to oppose whites, their cause is lost. But if they march for the emancipation of all South Africans, they must win in the end. We know that white racialism is doomed, but so is the black racialist. Discrimination in this country is not based, as it is claimed, on the backwardness or lack of civilization or incompetence of the people discriminated against. It is based on race and race alone. Therefore we've got to fight racialism."

"You have come a long way from your old class theories."

"Have I? I still think that we are living in a class society, but it is complicated by this artificial caste structure. We have to get rid of legalized prejudice before we can see class issues more clearly."

"Don't you think that Justin and Braam are sincere?"

"Of course I think they are, but sincerity is not enough. The racialist who is prepared to defend his privileged position with his life is probably sincere. Our fight has to be more than sincere, it has to be right."

"And from where do we fight? From the sanctuary of our armchairs or the security of Basutoland?"

"I thought you would ask that in the end. I wish you would look at our position a bit more sensibly. A state of emergency has been declared and the police are after us. What purpose do we serve by staying here? We can't do anything, but there are plenty of people who can and do make valuable contributions, while we either go on aimlessly dodging the police or give ourselves up and are detained indefinitely. I just refuse to be a political masochist. I have no wish to rot away in gaol unless there's some sense in it. The logical thing is to get away to Basutoland. From there we could go to Europe and spend our time more profitably doing post-graduate work at some university or other. We can't achieve anything at all by staying here. Call it running away if you want to."

"You know, Abe, all my life I've been running away. I ran away from District Six. I ran away the night my mother died. I ran away from Miriam's place. I've been running away from the Special Branch. Now I'm hiding in Lotus River, like any common criminal. Maybe I've been running away from myself. But that's all over now. I am determined to stay. And I don't know why you had to deliver a sermon on non-racialism to me. I agree and always have with most of the things you say. But I still retain my right not to give up the fight against every form of racialism and therefore I shall remain here, not run away to Basutoland or Europe. I shall fight with all the others whenever and wherever I can identify myself with them. If there is another march on Cape Town I shall be in it. I want to live my own life. I have reached the stage where I am prepared to ignore any legislation that denies me the right to go where I please, to love the girl I love and to think the things I think."

"You can't ignore unjust legislation, Andrew. You've got to recognize and oppose it."

"From the safety of Basutoland?"

"Yes, if there's nothing we can do here. I know perfectly well that if I stay here I'll only be a danger to other people."

"You're more right than you think. It's useless, Abe. You go to Basutoland and I'll stay here. If they get me it's just unfortunate."

"But you're stark raving mad," Abe said again, his face contorted with anger.

"Am I really? I suppose thousands of people were mad to go to gaol during the Defiance Campaign. Thousands are mad for being in gaol because they destroyed their passes. Justin must be stark raving mad. Well, so am I. Let them get me if they want to."

Abe winced. Andrew got up and searched for his jacket which he found on a chair.

"What the hell do you think you're doing?"

"Who, me? Oh, I'm going to Ruth's flat to listen to Rachmaninov."

"Stop putting on a cheap bloody act."

"But I like music."

Abe stared hostilely at Andrew who met his glance coolly.

"Coming, Ruth?"

She looked miserably at Andrew, undecided what to do.

"I'm longing to hear the third movement."

Mrs. Altmann came in with a jug of coffee on a tray and stood uncertainly in the middle of the room.

"Andy, please, you're not well."

"I won't have any coffee, thanks, Mrs. Altmann, but another brandy would be extremely welcome."

Altmann carefully poured him one. Andrew drank it all in one go, smacking his lips afterwards.

"Well, sir, I must thank you and your wife for your kind hospitality, but I'm afraid I must be going. Coming Ruth?"

She stood up hesitantly and looked at Abe for a brief second. There was no response from him.

"Please, Andy."

"We need some music badly."

"What about your car, Abe?"

"I'll come along to pick it up. I'll be back tonight, Mr. Altmann, after I've said good-bye to my mother. I'll drop in just to pick up my things."

"You're all very welcome to come whenever you wish," Altmann said, smiling as he stared at Abe and Andrew.

"Well then, let's get a move on," said Andrew in a decisive tone.

"Won't they be staying over?" Mrs. Altmann asked her husband.

"I don't think so," Andrew replied. "Good-bye and thanks again for everything."

He walked out stiffly, Ruth following. Abe bit his lip and clenched his fists till the nails bit into the palms. Then he followed the other two through the door without saying a word.

14

Their drive back was a frightening one. Ruth drove, trying to concentrate on the road ahead. She could feel tears running down her cheeks. She didn't doubt her love for Andrew for one moment, but she sometimes found him strange and enigmatic. Liable to do unpredictable things. Abe sat next to her, frigid and silent, staring straight ahead of him. Only Andrew seemed completely relaxed at the back. He had made attempts at conversation, but having received no replies he had given up and eased himself against the seat. They drove along Ottery Road in an attempt to avoid the road-block on Prince George Drive. After a long and frustrating journey, Ruth at last pulled up in Milner Road.

"Well," said Andrew, forcing a smile, "I think we separate here. When do you leave, Abe?"

Abe sat immobile, not a muscle moving.

"I hope we're not going to part like this."

Abe turned around slowly and looked Andrew straight in the eye.

"My plans are quite simple. I shall go home to see my mother because I don't know whether I shall ever see her again. Then I'll pick up my things at Altmann's and drive north throughout the night. . . . Please, Andrew, there is still time. It's not too late. Come with me."

Andrew paused for a moment. He looked at Abe hesitantly, then he said, "Thanks very much, Abe, I appreciate your offer, but I much prefer to listen to music."

"You're a bloody fool!" said Abe, measuring his words. "You're a bigger bloody fool than I ever thought."

"Maybe you're right."

"Don't you realize that they'll watch this place day and night?"

"They're welcome to come whenever they like. I'm quite prepared for the worst they can do."

"And if they connect you with this Langa riot?"

"If they ask me about it I'll tell them what I did and why."

"Andrew, look, we've been friends from schooldays, but I just cannot go along with something which I consider suicidal. I'm afraid we'll have to make a clean break."

"I'm sorry."

"Believe me, so am I."

Abe got out of the car. Andrew and Ruth followed.

"Good-bye, Abe," Ruth said softly, "and best of luck."

"Good-bye, Ruth, and best of luck to you also. You'll need it."

Then he turned to Andrew and they looked at each other for a long time. At last Andrew shoved out his hand. Abe stood uncertainly in the road. Then he put out his hand as well.

"Good-bye, Abe."

"Good-bye, Andrew."

Abe walked quickly to his car. Andrew and Ruth watched him as he switched on the engine and drove off towards Mowbray.

"Well, that's it," Andrew said at last. "Let's get to the flat."

Ruth tried to help him up the stairs but he refused assistance, limping painfully and clutching at the banister. She fumbled for her key in her handbag and unlocked the door. Then she switched on the light and the two stood self-consciously together in the room. Ruth smiled nervously at him, then Andrew started to open the French windows.